Rush

NEW YORK TIMES BESTSELLING AUTHOR

DEBORAH BLADON

FIRST ORIGINAL EDITION, JULY 2020

ISBN: 9798608777264
eBook ISBN: 9781926440590

Book & cover design by Wolf & Eagle Media

www.deborahbladon.com

Also by Deborah Bladon

Chapter 1

Case

What was I thinking?

My flight landed less than an hour ago, and I'm already itching to get the hell out of here.

Coming back to Manhattan was never part of my plan, even though I still have ties here. The unit I own in this building is one of them.

It's a two-bedroom apartment on Madison Avenue.

I bought it seven years ago when I was a twenty-two-year-old kid with more money than wisdom. Three months after I moved in, I fucked off to California and never looked back.

"Mr. Abbott, is that you?"

I turn to the left to see one of the doormen headed my way.

Lester. I remember him from back in the day before gray hair was poking out from under the hat on his head.

He introduced me to the best vodka money can buy and expensive cigars.

I gave up both when I moved across the country.

Lester stops just short of me. "Nice suit, sir. Very nice suit."

I'm learning to appreciate luxury more, including the meticulous care that goes into a custom-tailored suit. I'm the CEO of one of the biggest mobile gaming app companies on the planet, so I need to look the part.

I pull off the disheveled college kid look that other tech giants go for, but I take it up a notch when I know a camera is on me.

I took off from LAX earlier today under the watchful eye of the paparazzi. They weren't hanging out at departures trying to grab a photo of me, but the ones they did capture will pad their bank accounts for a month or two.

My claim to unwanted fame is that I landed on this year's list of the nation's wealthiest thirty under thirty.

Unfortunately, that comes with the bonus of losing the ability to trust anyone I haven't known since my lean years.

That's a lesson I've learned through trial and error.

"You're looking good." I pat Lester on the shoulder. "How's life been treating you?"

My gaze wanders the lobby. Little has changed since I packed up the bare essentials one Monday morning and left New York City behind.

I thought about selling the apartment back then, but my best friend, Drake Owens, offered me a deal I couldn't refuse.

He gave up a percentage of his yearly salary as the head of the east coast office of Cabbott Mobile in exchange for living in the apartment for free.

Drake is a good man. He's always had my back in business and life. It's my turn to lend him a helping hand.

"I can't complain." Lester rubs his glove covered thumb and index finger together. "Retirement is on the horizon, sir. I can almost taste it."

I have no fucking clue if the hand movement is a signal for me to tip him, but I'll oblige. He deserves it.

I didn't realize how much he did for me when I came into a small fortune virtually overnight. Lester watched over me when I needed it the most.

I fish in the inner pocket of my suit jacket for the five one hundred dollar bills that are always there.

I place them in his palm with a grin. "Get yourself a cigar tonight, Lester."

Closing his hand around the money, he nods. "Thank you, sir. I'll do just that. Do you have more bags in the car?"

Gripping the handle of my leather laptop bag, I glance down at the rolling suitcase at my side. "This is it. I plan on heading home within the week."

His blue eyes skim my face. "This used to be home."

"Now it's not," I say matter-of-factly as both of our gazes catch on a deliveryman waving his arm in the air near the double glass doors that lead into the lobby. "It looks like someone needs you more than I do, Lester."

"I hope you and your friend enjoy your time in the city, sir." Glancing over my shoulder, he tips the brim of his hat with his fingertip before he takes off.

I look behind me to find a pretty blonde on the approach with her eyes glued to me.

I can see why Lester might have mistaken her for a companion of mine, but I travel light in every possible way.

Just as the blonde closes in on me, I sidestep her. "Excuse me."

A night with her could have been fun, but I'm not here for a good time. I have work to do so I can get the hell out of this city as soon as possible.

***

High-pitched singing, combined with the muffled sound of running water, hits me when I unlock the door to my apartment.

I don't have a chance to process that before my gaze lands on a multi-colored laptop bag and a matching suitcase in the middle of my living room floor.

It's opened to reveal what looks like women's clothing.

That matches up with the voice streaming down the hallway.

"What the hell, Drake?" I seethe as I fish in the front pocket of my pants for my phone.

I pull up his number so I can give him shit about whoever the fuck is in my apartment.

We touched base this morning. He was about to board a flight headed to greener pastures. He's eloping with the love of his life.

If his bride-to-be is with him, who the hell is singing their heart out in my shower?

The call goes straight to voicemail. Cursing, I hang up and try again. His voicemail picks up for a second time. I leave a message that's simple and to the point.

"Call me back, now, Drake, or you're fired."

He told me he stopped juggling multiple women six months ago, but if that were the case, I wouldn't be listening to someone trying to hit the high notes of a song I've never heard before.

Or she's butchering it so badly that I don't recognize it.

I don't give a fuck that she can't sing on key. I'm pissed that she's made herself at home in my apartment.

This is classic Drake. We shared a rental house in Rhode Island when we were in college. He used to offer a key to our place and his bed to any woman he fucked who needed a place to crash for a few days whenever he flew back home to Seattle to visit his folks.

I shrug out of my suit jacket, roll up the sleeves of my button-down shirt, and head down the hallway with my phone in hand.

I don't give a shit if the woman in the shower is important to Drake or not. He's getting married. His fiancée will surely appreciate what I'm about to do.

The NYPD can take care of this woman since she's trespassing on private property that belongs to me.

Chapter 2

Emma

There's nothing like a hot shower to wash away a full day of travel. I had a missed connection and spent the last part of my cross-country journey sitting next to a toddler with a queasy stomach.

As soon as I got to my brother's apartment in Manhattan, I grabbed a change of clothes out of my suitcase and came into the bathroom.

Excess doesn't even begin to describe this place.

Drake has lived here for years. I've visited him twice before, but I'll never get used to how breathtaking his apartment is.

Coming here is like staying in a five-star hotel.

It's a perfect temporary escape since my life turned upside down. A few days away from Seattle will give me the clarity I need before I head home to face my new reality.

A loud rap on the bathroom door startles me enough that the bottle of body wash in my hand hits the stone shower floor with a thud.

Dammit.

Drake shouldn't be home from work yet. I thought I had time to get ready and order his favorite pizza before he arrived.

He has no idea that I'm in New York. The last time I visited, he gave me a set of keys so I could come and go as I pleased while he was at work. When I was leaving to fly back home, he insisted I keep the keys in case I ever wanted a place to hide out for a few days. I laughed it off at the time, but now I'm doing just that.

He knocks again, so I turn off the water and grab one of the fluffy white towels hanging on the heated towel bar.

Wrapping it around me, I hold it in place while my shoulder-length brown hair drips down my back.

"Surprise!" I call out when I hear him knock again. "Guess who came to visit you?"

The door flies open.

My jaw drops.

The man standing in the doorway is definitely not Drake.

"Who are you?" I screech while I search the granite countertop for anything I can use to defend myself.

My fingers curl around the handle of my hairbrush.

"Who the fuck are you?" The man barks at me. "What the hell are you doing in my apartment?"

I wave the hairbrush in the air toward him. "Your apartment? This is not your apartment."

The stranger rakes me from head-to-toe. "It sure as hell is. I'm calling the police."

"Do it," I challenge. "They'll arrest you for breaking and entering. My brother owns this apartment."

My words come out in a breathless rush because my heart is beating so hard in my chest that I'm sure it's about to break free.

His gaze drops to his phone before it levels on my face. "Your brother? Who is your brother?"

"Drake Owens," I say without thinking.

Why did I give up that information so fast?

"He'll be home from work any minute, and you're no match for him," I continue stringing random words together that make sense in my head.

This man is taller than Drake and more muscular. I doubt if Drake could win an arm wrestle against this guy.

"You're Drake's sister?" His green eyes narrow. "I'm his boss; his best friend."

My hand tightens on the towel. "You're Case Abbott?"

He turns his back to me. "Jesus, yes. I'm him. I wouldn't have barged in if I knew it was you. I'm sorry, Whitney."

Ouch.

Do I look eighteen to him?

Should I take it as a compliment that he mistook me for my younger sister?

"I'm Emma." I sigh. "Drake's other sister."

Raking a hand through his brown hair, he repeats my name. "Emma. You're Emma."

I nod even though he can't see me. "I'm here to surprise Drake for his birthday."

Taking a step forward, Case walks out of the bathroom before he turns to face me again. "I've got my own surprise to spring on your brother."

What does that mean? As tempted as I am to ask, I don't because I'm feeling way too exposed to continue this conversation. "I should get dressed."

"Do that, and then we need to talk."

With that, he closes the door behind him.

What the hell just happened, and more importantly, how did I not realize that my brother's best friend is drop-dead gorgeous?

***

By the time I've run the brush through my hair and gotten myself dressed in the jeans and black sweater I brought into the bathroom with me, I've tried to call Drake seven times.

Seven times.

He didn't answer.

I left six panicked messages asking where he is.

Case said that he has a surprise for Drake. I'm terrified that I might have cost my brother his job. It's clear that he doesn't own this apartment even though he told me he did. He told Whitney and our parents the same thing. We were all thrilled that he was successful enough to afford a place like this.

Is Case Abbott the type of man who would fire his best friend over a little white lie? Or a big lie about a very expensive piece of property?

I already know the answer to that. Drake has called me a few times over the past two years complaining about Case firing people. Some of those ex-employees had been with Cabbott Mobile from the beginning.

Since my makeup bag is in my suitcase, I have no choice but to leave the bathroom barefaced.

Case already thinks I look like a college freshman, so what do I have to lose?

Sucking in a deep breath, I steel myself so I can fight for Drake's job. I owe him that after everything he's ever done for me.

I swing open the bathroom door and head out to face the man who holds my brother's future in the palm of his hand.

Chapter 3

Case

Emma Owens.

I have no fucking idea what she's doing here. She seems to be under the impression that Drake is about to walk through the door.

My door.

I can't say I'm surprised that he passed this place off as his own. Impressing his family was always important to Drake. He told me how thrilled his parents were when he was accepted into the computer science program at Brown University.

That's where we met.

I was already on the path to my future. I was programming anything I could think of that would garner me a shot at my own company straight out of the gate after graduation.

Drake's goal was to land an entry-level position with one of the corporations based in Silicon Valley.

That changed when I sold my first company when I was twenty-one. It was a payment app that's since been buried by more streamline innovations. The money I made on that deal was enough to propel me forward.

I brought Drake on board my newly formed company because he wanted a job, and I needed his skills. Cabbott Mobile was launched, and we've never looked back.

I glance down at Emma's suitcase.

I want that out of sight within the hour because I'm expecting someone. I need Drake's sister out of here for that very same reason.

The sound of her clearing her throat behind me turns me around.

I mistook her for her younger sister earlier, but now that I'm getting a better look, I can see that she's not Whitney.

The picture that Drake sent me months ago that was taken at a party for his parents' anniversary didn't include Emma. Come to think of it, I've never seen an image of her.

She stands at least a foot shorter than me. My guess is around five foot two.

Her dark brown hair is damp. The ends are curling around her shoulders. Her thickly lashed brown eyes are focused on my face. A sprinkle of freckles dots her nose and cheeks.

She's stunning.

"I tried to call Drake, but he's not answering." She steps closer to me on bare feet. "Do you know if he's in a meeting? It's not like him to ignore my calls."

How the hell am I supposed to answer that?

Drake didn't hesitate when he told me that he was taking some time off so he could elope. I assumed everyone in his inner circle knew, but maybe that's a smaller group than I realized.

Rubbing my jaw, I answer truthfully. "He's out of town."

"You're kidding." The corners of her lips fall into a frown.

Shaking my head, I sigh. "I'm not. He left early this morning."

"No." She reaches to pinch the bridge of her nose. "This can't be happening. I came from Seattle for his birthday. Is he coming back soon? Please tell me it's just a day trip, and he'll be back tonight."

"He'll be gone at least a week." It's an estimate since Drake left his return date open-ended.

His last vacation was over a year ago, so I wouldn't be surprised if he stretches this trip out to a couple of weeks or more.

"Dammit," she says under her breath. "This can't be happening."

Since I'm already the bearer of bad news, I stay on that track. She may be Drake's sister, but I'm in Manhattan for a reason. I'm not about to sideline my plans tonight for anyone, not even a member of my best friend's family.

"Listen, Emma." I take a step toward her, jerking my thumb at the open suitcase on the floor. "I had no idea you'd be here. I'm only in town for a few days, and I have plans tonight."

Her gaze darts to the suitcase. "I'll put that in the guest room. I can hang out by myself tonight. Please don't think you have to stay in because of me."

Fuck.

I need her and her stuff out of here now.

Brushing past me, she drops to her knees to zip up the suitcase. "I should have called Drake to tell him I was coming. Surprises never work out for me."

I can't tell if the words she's muttering are meant for my ears or not.

It doesn't matter. She's not hanging out in my apartment tonight. "The woman I'm meeting is coming here."

Rising to her feet, she looks over at me. "I shouldn't be here. I need to go."

I stare at her. She's Drake's sister. He'd want me to do the right thing, but I already believe that I am. I'm in New York so I can do what's best for him. I didn't count on his sister showing up to throw a wrench in my plans.

"I left a few things in the bathroom." She glances toward the hallway. "I'll grab them and get out of your way."

It doesn't solve all of my problems, but at least one will be scratched off the list when she leaves.

Watching her walk away, I think about how often Drake has gone to bat for me. He may give me shit when he realizes that I tossed his sister out onto the street, but he'll forgive me.

I'm doing everything in my power to give him a wedding gift he'll never forget. If his sister is inconvenienced because of that, so be it.

Disappointment is a part of life.

Chapter 4

Emma

Case Abbott is almost too good-looking.

His shoulders are broad, his chest is wide, and his face is utter perfection.

A sharp jawline combined with full lips and piercing green eyes hit every mark for me.

The skin on his forearms and face is tanned. His hair is a blend of medium brown and what looks like sun-kissed streaks.

Drake once mentioned that his boss likes to surf. It's impossible not to imagine Case shirtless standing on the beach before he hits the waves.

I shake my head.

What am I doing?

Why am I daydreaming about my brother's boss when he just kicked me to the curb?

I have to figure out where to go.

Home. I need to go back to Seattle as soon as possible even though that's the last place I want to be right now.

I scroll through the emails on my phone as I walk down the hallway toward the washroom.

I haven't even been in New York City for a day. I don't know what the airline's policy is about the exchange of return tickets, but they will be my first call.

With any luck, I'll be on a flight back to Seattle tonight. If that can't happen, I'll have to find a cheap hotel to stay at until my travel plans can be altered.

Clicking the phone number link in the reservation email from the airline, I listen while it rings.

I press my way through their automated menu until I'm on hold waiting for an agent.

"We value your business. Please note that your current wait time is approximately…"

I hold my breath, hoping by some miracle, I'll be talking to a customer service agent in the next twenty seconds.

"Fifty-two minutes."

"Dammit." I end the call. "I'll try changing it online."

Scouring the email for a link to take me to their website, my gaze lands on the fine print.

Squinting, I read it aloud. "No ticket changes and no refunds permitted."

This is what I get for buying a discount seat at the last minute. I vaguely recall a warning popping up on my laptop screen about the ticket being non-refundable and changes not allowed, but I quickly skipped reading that in full so I could grab the low price seat.

I plugged in my credit card number, hit the purchase now button, and breathed a heavy sigh of relief.

That was less than two days ago.

I walk into the bathroom and grab my hairbrush and the clothes I was wearing when I arrived. A glance in the mirror brings a scowl to my face.

I'm tired, I'm frustrated, and most of all, I'm pissed at myself for thinking it was a great idea to surprise Drake. My brother is never far from New York City. The last time he took a real vacation was when he surprised our family with a trip to Hawaii. He came to Seattle months ago for our parents' wedding anniversary, but he spent more than half of his time on the phone dealing with work issues. He was back on a plane to New York less than twenty-four hours after he landed in Washington State.

"I called Drake's driver. He'll meet you downstairs. He can take you anywhere you want."

The sound of Case's voice turns me toward the doorway.

"Can he take me to wherever Drake is?" I ask with a half-smile.

He shakes his head. "That's the one place he can't take you. Are you going to crash with a friend? Or do you need him to drop you off at a hotel?"

He can't get rid of me fast enough.

His date must be due to arrive at any minute.

I'd say she's lucky, but he's not exactly the nicest guy I've ever met.

Not that I'd go for another *nice* guy after the hell I went through with the last one.

"My brother is the only person I know in New York." I breeze past him into the hallway. "I was going to fly home, but my ticket is locked in, so I'll find a hotel for the night. When I wake up tomorrow, I'll price out return flights to Seattle. I'm hoping that I can find a deal on a seat back home. If I can't, I'll be spending the week in Manhattan."

At this point, I'm thinking out loud, so I keep going. "I should download one of those travel apps. They're always advertising that they can find the cheapest hotel rates."

I can hear the sound of Case's shoes on the floor as he follows me into the main living area.

I unzip my suitcase far enough to stuff my hairbrush and clothes inside of it. "One of them had a commercial during the Super Bowl last year. They have that incredibly annoying jingle, and now they're advertising everywhere on social media. Everywhere. It's overkill. I'm crossing that app off my list right now."

"You're talking about Duotrip."

I spin around to face him. "That's it. The name isn't great either."

His arms cross his chest. "Your brother would disagree with you."

I drop my hands to my hips because I think I know Drake better than this guy ever will. They may be best friends, but I share a close bond with my brother. We're a lot alike.

"Drake would hate the name," I quip.

A wolfish smile settles on Case's lips. Dimples. The man has dimples.

How is he real?

I glance down at the floor because a smile like that is contagious, and I sense we're in the middle of an argument about my brother that I want to win.

I want at least one thing to go my way today.

"He named it."

My head pops up. "What?"

"He named it." He steps closer to me. "He developed it. He's the last one to approve all marketing for it, so I'll be sure to tell him that you think the commercial was shit."

I raise a hand to stop him from talking. "Drake named it?"

"He stuck the word trip after his initials. D.U.O. Drake Ulysses Owens. The result of that is Duotrip."

Speechless, I stare at him.

"Did I love the name when he brought it to me? No, but I gave him carte blanche on the project, so I let him take it to market," he says with a sly grin. "It's killing it, Emma. You should be proud of your brother."

I exhale, trying to steady myself. "I thought Cabbott Mobile only developed games."

"That's how we started." He nods. "We've branched out the last couple of years. I'm surprised that Drake didn't mention Duotrip to you. He tells anyone who will listen about it."

I'm just as surprised that my brother didn't mention it to me. I had no idea. We used to tell each other everything.

Why do I suddenly feel so far away from Drake?

Tears threaten my eyes as I glance down at my phone. "I'll download it and find a hotel unless you have one to recommend."

When I look up, Case's gaze is locked on my face. Rubbing his jaw, he tilts his head as he studies me. "Fuck it. Stay here. Drake would want it that way."

Relief washes over me. The thought of being thrust into the clutches of a city I'm unfamiliar with is overwhelming. At least now, I can stay here until I sort out a flight home.

"Are you sure?" I ask, even though I don't want to give him an out to change his mind. He may be a stranger, but I feel safe here.

"I'm sure, but there's one condition." His gaze drops to my laptop bag and suitcase.

"I'll put all of that in the guestroom," I say hurriedly. "I'll stay out of your way. You won't even know I'm here."

"I need you to not be here five minutes from now. You can grab a drink. There's a pub across the street. Eager Pour is the name of it."

His date. I almost forgot that a woman is meeting him here. I like his suggestion. I can use a cocktail after the day I've had. I deserve the treat.

"Drake took me to a pub across the street called Durie's the last time I was here." I shrug. "Could that be the same place you're thinking of?"

"Shit. Maybe the bar changed hands since I left the city." He slides his thumb across the screen of his phone. "Give me your number. I'll text you when I'm done. She'll be in and out of here in fifteen minutes."

Fifteen minutes?

I think I found Case Abbott's one flaw. He's a rushed lover.

I no longer consider the woman meeting him lucky at all.

After calling out my phone number to him, I grab my laptop bag and the handle of my suitcase. I turn to him because I want him to know I'm grateful. "Thank you, Mr. Abbott."

I have no idea what to call him. He may be my brother's best friend, but he's his boss too. I've learned in life that you should always show respect to the people who help you.

"Case," he corrects me. "Call me, Case."

I grin because that contagious smile of his is on full display again.

A tap of his finger on the face of his watch breaks the spell. "It's time to get moving, Emma. My guest will be here in ten minutes."

I roll my suitcase over the floor as I walk toward the guestroom that I've stayed in before. This isn't how I thought today would play out, but I have a bed to sleep in tonight. For now, that's all that matters.

Chapter 5

Emma

I snuck into the washroom at Durie's before I took a seat at a table in the corner.

As I was rushing out of Case's apartment, I tossed my makeup bag into a clutch that I packed in my suitcase. With the addition of a couple of hair elastics, my wallet, and the keys that Drake gave me, I was set.

I applied a touch of makeup before I twisted my hair into a messy bun. The lighting in the bar's washroom wasn't ideal, but I look presentable.

I've already been mistaken for an eighteen-year-old once tonight. I don't want a repeat with the server.

I grin at her as she approaches me.

"What can I get for you?" she asks with a bright smile.

I go for a repeat of what I had the night Drake brought me here. "A lemon drop martini, please."

"My favorite." Her blue eyes widen. "You have excellent taste, Emma."

Furrowing my brow, I lean back in my seat. I haven't handed over my credit card yet, so how does she know my name?

Smiling, she rests a hand on my tense shoulder. "You're Emma, aren't you? Drake Owens is your brother?"

Stuck on a stalled breath, I nod. "I am."

"We met when you were here with him last year." Her hand drops to her side. "He talks about you sometimes when he stops in for a beer."

I study her face. Her eyes are blue. Her hair is a dark shade of blonde. She's pretty. She's exactly my brother's type.

"I'm Kendall, by the way."

"It's good to meet you again," I say with a soft laugh. "Does my brother come in often?"

I'm hoping small talk will bury the subject of our first meeting. I rarely forget a face. It's part of my job to match faces with names.

"When he wants a beer, he shows up." She shrugs. "I have a feeling that once he gets back from his trip, he won't be popping in as often."

Even this woman knew that Drake was headed out of New York City.

Maybe she can fill in the gaps that Case was unwilling or unable to.

Just as I'm about to interrogate her, a man at the next table calls out her name and what sounds like a complicated drink order.

"I'll grab your martini." She slaps a dark blue cocktail napkin on the table in front of me. "I'll put it on Drake's tab."

"That's not necessary." I reach for my clutch. "I can pay for my drink."

With a shake of her head, she huffs out a laugh. "Not according to your brother. All friends and family of Drake Owens drink on his dime. Those are his exact words."

That sounds like Drake. He's generous to a fault.

"I'll be right back." She turns to walk away. "Oh, and can you do me a favor?"

I sense that she's about to ask me to put in a good word for her with my brother. He's good-looking and fun. It wouldn't be the first time someone asked me to set them up with him. One of my friends back in Seattle wanted a dinner date with Drake when she visited Manhattan last year. I asked him if he'd indulge her request, but he shot it down.

I nod even though I know that Drake would have already asked her out if he was interested.

"When you talk to Drake, can you offer my congratulations?"

Before I can ask what for, Kendall blurts out the answer. "I admit I never thought he was the marrying type, but he proved all of us doubters wrong with this elopement."

Confused, I stare at her.

"I may feel a little envy about the whole thing. I mean, who wouldn't? What's more romantic than getting married in a castle in Ireland?"

I don't respond to her question as she walks away. I don't try to talk at all.

I'm speechless.

***

Three martinis later, I wonder if I'll be able to get out of the chair I've been sitting in for the last two-and-a-half hours.

I've spent all of this time thinking about my brother and his wedding.

His wedding.

Drake is getting married, and I had no idea. My parents didn't either. I know that because I called them mid-way through my first martini to tell them that I'd arrived in Manhattan safe and sound.

They didn't ask for an update, but I wanted to hear their voices. My mom talked about the pot roast she's planning to cook for dinner tomorrow. My dad was focused on one of the used cars he sold today.

It was obvious that they didn't know anything about Drake flying to Ireland to marry a mystery woman.

I had no idea that he had a girlfriend and the next time I see him, he'll have a wife.

Hanging my head, I shut my eyes.

There's nothing I want more than for the people I care about to be happy. I'm thrilled that Drake found someone he loves enough to marry, but the sting of disappointment I feel is undeniable.

I always thought we'd be there for each other on the monumental days of our lives.

"Did you give me a fake number?"

I glance up at the sound of that voice because I recognize it. I may have only heard it briefly, but the tone has a rough edge that is unmistakable.

"Case?"

"Emma." He gives me a curt nod. "I've sent you a few text messages."

I shrug. "I haven't checked my phone."

It's the truth. After I talked to my parents, I silenced my phone and shoved it into my clutch. I didn't expect Drake to get in touch, but I didn't want to risk answering his call in the mood I'm in.

I need time to process everything that's happened today before I talk to my brother.

Glancing around the almost empty bar, Case crosses his arms. "How many of those have you had?"

How is that his concern? He's the one who sent me here so he could get down to business. That would be the business of quickies.

It's a shame.

If he took his time, he might not look so wound up.

His jaw is clenched, and his brow is furrowed. He seems tenser than when I left his apartment.

"A couple," I answer semi-honestly. I haven't finished the third martini, so technically I've had two-and-a-half.

"It's time to call it a night." He slides a credit card out of his pocket and waves it at Kendall.

"Put that away," I say with a shake of my head. "My brother paid for my drinks."

His hand drops. "Your brother?"

"You know him." I laugh softly. "Brown hair, glasses, and the world's best secret-keeper."

Expecting at least a smile from him, I scrunch my nose as he stares at me.

"Speaking of secrets, earlier you said you have a surprise for Drake. What is it?" I ask to lighten the mood. "I promise I won't say a word to him."

His expression doesn't change at all. "Let's get you upstairs, Emma."

I swallow the rest of the martini because why would I waste a perfectly made drink? Pushing back from the table, I level my gaze on Case. "Fine. Don't tell me about the surprise, but can you at least tell me if you knew he was getting married?"

Reaching for my arm, he exhales. "Who told you?"

26

"She did." I point to where Kendall is standing next to a customer. "She knew. Don't tell me that you didn't know."

He wraps his fingers around my forearm. "Drake would kill me if he knew I let you get drunk your first night in the city."

"I'm not drunk." I let out a stuttered laugh. "You think I'm drunk?"

I might be drunk. I'm probably drunk. I haven't eaten anything since I left Seattle this morning, so yes, I am officially drunk.

"Come with me, Emma." He tugs on my arm. "I'll get you to bed."

I don't argue because sleep sounds good. Tomorrow everything will be better.

Chapter 6

Case

I live on the beach in California. When I step outside every morning, I'm met with a sense of peace that I've never been able to find anywhere else.

New York is in your face from the moment you wake up. My apartment sits twelve floors above the ground, but I could still hear the heartbeat of this city as I tried to fall asleep last night.

Honking horns.

Patience doesn't exist on the streets of Manhattan. Everyone is in a rush to get from point A to point B.

I can't condemn any of them. Once I get to my office in San Francisco, I'm full steam ahead. I put in twelve to fifteen hours, six days a week.

I save one day a week to recharge. Most of the time, that's spent on a surfboard in the ocean if the waves are just right.

Mere days from now I'll be back where I belong.

I glance over at the closed door of the guestroom.

Drake's sister was numbing her pain when I sought her out at the bar last night. I'd sent her three text messages telling her that the coast was clear. I got nothing in response. I ignored the pull to look for her at first.

Once I started thinking about the consequences I'd face if she got herself into trouble, I took the elevator down to the ground floor with the hope that she was still in the bar.

She was. Emma was alone, drinking in a corner.

I don't know where her relationship with Drake stands. He rarely mentions her. I can't recall how old she is or what she does to earn a living.

The only thing I'm certain about is that she was blindsided by the news that her brother is getting married.

I'm grateful that the server at the bar dropped the bombshell on her. I wasn't looking forward to that conversation.

Drake's family drama is his to sort out.

The sound of the doorknob of the guestroom rattling draws my attention to it. I've been parked in a chair for the last hour with my laptop. I woke up to a few dozen emails and just as many text messages from Cabbott employees here on the east coast.

I'm the go-to now that Drake is out of town.

Dealing with the host of issues that are popping up has kept my mind focused on work and not on how Emma looked last night.

Her cheeks were flushed pink when I found her at the bar. She had piled her thick dark hair up in a messy bun. There's no denying that she's beautiful.

I stand when the door to the guestroom opens. Emma walks out dressed in a pair of dark jeans and a light blue silk blouse.

Her lips part when she sees me.

"Good morning," I offer.

"Morning," she mutters. "I had one too many martinis last night."

I wondered if she'd bring it up. I hadn't planned on it. When I lived in this apartment, I was known to overindulge often, too often.

Before I can change the subject, Emma carries on. "I don't usually do that. I can't. Or I haven't been able to, but I guess now I can do whatever I want, whenever I want."

That's a hell of a lot to unpack this early in the morning.

I skate past whatever she just said and focus on what I need from her. "What are your plans for the day?"

She gazes around my apartment as if inspiration is going to hit her. "I'm going to see about a flight home."

That works for me.

"What about you?" she asks.

The question perks my brow, but I ignore it in favor of my agenda. "I need you to hang out somewhere else until at least five."

"I can't come back until five?" She studies me.

I toss her a curt nod. "At least until then. It could be as late as seven. I'll let you know if five doesn't work, so you may want to pay attention to your phone today."

She pushes her hair back over her shoulders. "I guess I can find a coffee shop. Maybe I can go to one of the museums for a few hours."

That's the spirit.

I keep that comment to myself. "I'm leaving for the office. I'll see you out."

Her arms cross her chest just under her breasts. My eyes level on them because I'm not dead. She's a beautiful woman with a killer body.

The thoughts running through my head should land me a special place in hell.

I can't think about Emma's tits or how her slender waist flows down to curvy hips.

"Can you give me a minute to get my stuff together?" She tilts her head. "I won't be long."

A cleaning crew is due to arrive in a half-hour, so I can spare Emma a minute or two.

"Of course."

"Thank you." She smiles before she sets off toward the guestroom. I watch her walk away. I've never noticed the fit of jeans on a woman before, but Emma's hug her heart-shaped ass perfectly.

My body reacts to that.

I look down at the floor because Drake would wring my neck if he knew that my dick is infatuated with his sister.

Emma Owens is off-limits. There's no way in hell I can go anywhere near her.

Chapter 7

Emma

The last time I was in Manhattan, my brother set aside a few hours each day to spend with me. We had lunch together at his favorite diner one afternoon and wandered around the Museum of Modern Art another day.

I jammed everything we did during that trip into today.

My first stop was a coffee shop down the street from Case's apartment. I logged onto their Wi-Fi and spent over an hour waiting to connect to an online agent from the airline so I could plead my case to have my return date changed.

I was denied.

The agent I was chatting with suggested I purchase a one-way ticket back home, but the cost is steep.

Wasting money to get back to Seattle a few days early is foolish. I don't need anyone to give me that lecture.

Once I finished at the coffee shop, I went to Central Park and people watched. Then I took a walk down Fifth Avenue to window shop. My next stop was the diner, followed by two hours at the museum.

My heels are blistered. I'm exhausted, and it's still not five o'clock.

I'm standing at the entrance to Case's apartment building, wondering if I should risk sneaking upstairs. I haven't heard from him all day, so I'm hoping that the plan hasn't changed and soon I'll be inside with my shoes off.

I pat the keys that are in the pocket of my short black trench coat.

Glancing down at my phone, I check the time.

In thirty minutes it will officially be go time. Since Case is doing me a huge favor by letting me stay at his place, I decide to settle in the lobby until the clock strikes five.

I nod at the doorman as he swings the door open when I approach.

"Good afternoon, Miss," he says the same line he always does when he greets me.

Drake introduced us to each other last year, but I can't imagine how many faces this man sees in a day.

I'm not surprised that mine got lost among them.

"Hi, Lester." Stepping into the lobby, I smile at him. "How are you today?"

"I don't have a single complaint." He tips the brim of his hat. "Are you enjoying our fair city?"

Enjoying isn't a word I'd use. Tolerating fits the bill.

Back home in Seattle, I live in a condo on a quiet street. A park borders the back of the property.

It's heaven in a small corner of Washington State.

Not wanting to steal Lester's smile, I sidestep the question with one of my own. "Have you seen Case Abbott today?"

It never hurts to be prepared. I don't know if Case will be in his apartment when I go up. Not that I would mind if he were.

I could use the company after spending the day alone.

Lester's smile widens. "It just so happens that Mr. Abbott and I had a discussion about you earlier."

Does Lester know that I was wrapped in a towel and brandishing a hairbrush when I met Case?

I doubt if Case even remembers what I looked like wet and trembling in fear.

Trying not to seem panicked, I paste on a forced grin. "What did he tell you about me?"

"I made an incorrect assumption when you first arrived, Miss Owens."

My brows pop when I hear him say my name.

"I thought you were here as a guest of Mr. Abbott, but your brother is Mr. Owens." He shakes his head. "We've met before, haven't we?"

I nod. "Last year."

"Please forgive me for that oversight." He smiles regretfully.

"There's nothing to forgive, Lester."

"Circling back to your initial question, I did see Mr. Abbott a second time today." Strategically holding out his hand, he rubs his index finger and thumb together.

Is he silently asking me to pay him for information about Case?

I have seen Drake slip the doormen some money when I've visited in the past, so maybe I need to follow that lead. Lester did hold the door open for me.

I fish in the pocket of my jacket. I pull out the five dollar bill I tucked in there earlier and hand it to Lester.

I have no idea if that's enough to buy me insight into Case's movements.

Lester closes his hand around the money before he clears his throat. "Mr. Abbott left fifteen minutes ago with the same lovely young woman who visited him last night. While I was arranging for the car to pick them up, I did overhear Mr. Abbott making a dinner reservation for two at Nova for seven o'clock this evening."

Nova.

It's one of the most expensive restaurants in the city.

"He let me know that he'd see me tomorrow, so I don't expect him back before my shift ends."

Unexpected disappointment nags at me. I shouldn't care that Case won't be home tonight or that he's having dinner at a fancy-as-fuck place with a woman.

After a soak in the bathtub and some take-out, I'll get a good night's sleep before I decide how I'll fill my time tomorrow.

"You don't happen to have any pictures of your brother's wedding, do you?" Lester points at the phone in my hand. "I've been anxious to see him and Jane dressed to the nines."

Jane.

That has to be the name of my sister-in-law.

My gaze drops to the screen of my phone. I haven't reached out to Drake today. He hasn't tried to call or text me either.

"Not yet," I answer quietly. "When I do, I'll be sure to show you."

"Thank you, Miss Owens." He tips the brim of his hat again. "Shall I get the elevator for you now?"

There's no reason for me not to go up to Case's apartment. Shaking my head, I start the trek across the lobby to the bank of elevators. "I'll take care of it."

"Enjoy your evening," he says cheerfully.

I won't.

I'm in a city filled with millions of people, but I've never felt so alone.

Chapter 8

Case

I'm officially calling it a day.

It's not even nine p.m., and I'm done. Jet lag is still right on my tail, kicking my ass.

I shove my key into the lock and turn the handle on my apartment door.

Silence greets me.

I exhale because I'm relieved. I was half-expecting Emma Owens to be planted on the couch in the living room watching the huge television her brother bought.

Drake's a hardcore fan of any and every sport in existence. He can rattle off the stats of every player on any of the teams that are based in New York City.

I admire his commitment to cheer on his heroes.

I don't have the time to devote to parking my ass anywhere for three hours straight unless I'm actively working.

Glancing to the left, I spot the touch screen on the wall that controls virtually everything in the apartment. There's another one in the hallway, and a third installed in the main bedroom. The system is the brainchild of Drake.

He had sent me mockups when it was in the development stage. I told him I didn't want to step into the already overcrowded space, but he was insistent on pursuing it as a personal passion project.

Scratching a brow, I study the screen.

Lights. I only want to turn on the goddamn lights in this room.

The panel is set on a timer, but there has to be a way to override that.

I punch one button, and loud classical music fills the room.

Fuck.

I tap that button to silence it before I push the button next to it.

The blinds that cover the massive windows overlooking Madison Ave open to reveal a breathtaking view of dusk settling over Manhattan.

I ignore that and yell at the damn thing, hoping that Drake followed through with his intention to integrate voice activation into the system. "Lights! Turn on the fucking lights!"

Warm light fills the space.

Shaking my head, I look around.

Everything is exactly as I left it a few hours ago when I headed to the Lower East Side. Cabbott Mobile's New York office is housed there.

I stopped in this morning to a lukewarm reception from the employees.

When I revisited this afternoon, it was a different story. I garnered a few smiles and greetings from the people who take home a paycheck signed by me.

I don't know what the hell I was expecting, but I spotted only two familiar faces as I toured the offices. Drake has followed my lead and cleared out the dead weight.

I keep the California office staffed with people who are not only talented but also ambitious. They need to prove daily that they deserve to work side-by-side with me.

I toss my keys and phone on a wooden table in the foyer. It's not a piece I purchased, but whoever bought it has good taste.

I strip off my suit jacket before I fold it over the back of the gray leather couch that's been here for as long as I can remember.

Nothing in this apartment resembles the house I live in back in California.

At one time, I thought I'd be happy calling this place home. Now, I feel like I've been dumped into the middle of someone else's life.

I have.

This is Drake's life, although that's about to change.

His marriage is the first step toward the future he's always wanted.

I'm doing what I can to keep him moving in that direction.

I make quick work of the buttons on my shirt before I slide it off and toss it onto the jacket.

My belt is next. With a tug, it's free and on the couch too.

Just as my hands drop to the zipper of my pants, I hear movement at the door of my apartment.

For fuck's sake.

I assumed Emma was somewhere in Manhattan living it up.

I didn't expect her back here yet.

I spin around as the door flies open and she walks in. White shorts and a black T-shirt cover her body. Her hair is tied up into a lopsided ponytail.

Her eyes widen as her gaze flits over my naked chest.

Seeing her reaction to finding me shirtless is enough to jerk my cock to life, but that's short-lived once I get a glimpse of the person on her heel.

"Cason fucking Abbott," he blurts out. "I heard you were back in town, you son-of-a-bitch."

Crossing my arms over my chest, I toss him a nod. "Do I know you?"

Panic flits across Emma's expression. Stepping forward, she stares at me. "He said his name is Gavin Fuller. He told me he's your cousin."

Her eyes don't leave mine even though Gavin is rounding her on his approach to me.

"I wouldn't have let him come up with me if I didn't believe his story," Emma says in a rush. "You don't look alike, so I was skeptical, but I don't look like my cousins. Most of them have blonde hair. My parents both have blonde hair, but my mom isn't a natural blonde if you know what I mean."

Why the fuck do I like that rambling thing she does?

She carries on at a breathless pace. "His hair is black, and your hair is brown, but you both have green eyes, so I thought that was a family trait. Is it?"

Gavin stops in front of me. "Tell her I'm your cousin."

I look him over. When I left New York, he was working his way through medical school. Now he's an E.R. doctor who is too busy to return my calls.

I raise a hand and pat him on the cheek. "Look at you all grown up."

With a swat of his hand against mine, he laughs. "Look at you. Still shirtless, I see. This is New York, Case, not California. If you want to be taken seriously here, put on a suit."

Inching closer to us, Emma catches my eye. "So you do know each other?"

Before I have a chance to respond to that, she continues. "He was talking to Lester in the lobby when I came back from the bodega. I went to get some bubble bath, but they were out."

"Tough luck," Gavin offers with a glance at her.

Emma shrugs. "It wasn't meant to be. Anyways, Lester called me over and mentioned that I was staying with you. So Gavin asked if he could come up, but I explained that you were having dinner with a woman at Nova at seven. Then Lester said your date must have been canceled because you just got home, so I thought, why not surprise you by bringing your cousin up here to see you?"

Gavin looks over his shoulder at Emma before his gaze focuses back on me. "What she said."

I'd forgotten how Lester hovers so he can overhear everything that happens in the lobby. He must have been listening when I was making a reservation for two. Lester didn't realize that the head chef at Nova owed me a favor. A happily married couple is enjoying a well-deserved gourmet meal on the house tonight.

Reaching for my shirt, I slip it on. "Have you eaten dinner yet?"

"No," Emma answers before Gavin can get his mouth open.

Fuck.

The question was directed at my cousin, not Drake's sister.

Gavin turns around to face Emma. "Do you like pasta?"

"Who doesn't?" she asks with a smile.

Jerking a thumb over his shoulder toward me, Gavin huffs out a laugh. "Cason."

Shaking my head, I button my shirt. "Fuck you, Fuller. You're thinking of Calvetti's, aren't you?"

That turns him back to face me. "I know from experience that you won't find authentic Italian food like that on the west coast."

I'd argue the point, but I see no need. If I've missed anything about this city, it's the food at Calvetti's.

Grabbing my suit jacket, I point at the door. "Let's go."

"Can I get a minute to change my clothes?" Emma asks hopefully.

"Take all the time you need," Gavin replies. "Case and I have some catching up to do."

"I'll be quick," she says before she crosses the room toward the hallway.

Gavin's gaze follows her every move, so I poke him in the chest.

"What the fuck?" He takes a step back. "Who is she, and more importantly, why the hell is she living here?"

"She's not," I answer as I slide my jacket back on. "She's Drake's sister."

His brows perk. "That's Whitney?"

"Emma," I correct him.

He takes a second to register that. "That's Emma Owens? What's going on between you two?"

"What the hell do you think?" I shoot back.

"I think she's your best friend's sister so you're behaving yourself." He tugs on the lapels of my jacket to straighten it. "So, what's she doing here with you?"

"Bad timing," I answer smoothly. "She came to New York to surprise Drake."

Furrowing his brow, his gaze darts to the hallway and the closed guestroom door. "Why would she come here when he's taken off to get hitched?"

"She didn't know."

"She didn't know?" he repeats. "All of Manhattan knew. You knew. How the fuck did she not know?"

It's a question that I don't have an answer to. I won't have an answer until Drake gets in touch, and I have no idea when that will be.

Chapter 9

Emma

Glancing at my reflection in the mirror, I smile. I look nice. I traded the white shorts for skinny black jeans and slipped a pink blazer over my T-shirt. With the addition of two silver necklaces and a brush of my hair, I look good.

It's not Manhattan chic, but it will have to do.

Sliding on the only pair of heels I brought with me, I spin in a circle.

This is the first time I've gone out to dinner in New York with anyone but Drake.

I never expected that I'd be heading to a restaurant with Case and his cousin, but I'm up for any adventure that falls in my path.

Two good-looking, well-dressed men and a glass of red wine is the perfect end to this day.

Cracking open the guestroom door an inch, I freeze when my phone buzzes in my purse.

Anxiety crawls up my spine. I've been dodging text messages all day from my sister. Whitney wants to know how Drake is since he hasn't answered any of her calls for the past two days.

It's not my place to tell her that he's in Ireland celebrating his nuptials.

I fish in my bag for my phone and glance at the screen.

My heart rate kicks up.

For the first time today, the incoming text isn't from Whitney. It's from my other sibling.

Drake: *Hey Em! You're in NYC? WTF? We need to talk. Are you free in 10 minutes?*

Part of me wants to ignore his text.

It's well after midnight in Ireland. He might go to sleep soon, which means I could push back this conversation until tomorrow. That would give me time to calm down so I don't say anything I'll regret to my brother.

He chose to get married without telling me. He must have had his reasons, so I need to hear him out.

I will hear him out. Tonight.

I shoot him back a quick message.

Emma: *I'm free.*

Clutching my phone in my palm, I open the door to find Case and Gavin standing at the entrance to the hallway.

"Are you ready?" Gavin asks with a smile.

The dimples must be a family trait. He's just as good-looking as his cousin, but I don't feel something deep inside of me light up when I look at Gavin.

It's there the moment my gaze shifts to Case.

"My plans have changed." I glance down at my phone. "I'm expecting an important call. I don't want to miss it."

"Maybe another time?"

I look up when Gavin asks the question. "Maybe."

"We'll get out of here and give you some privacy, Emma." Case turns to his cousin. "Let's go."

Gavin stays in place even though Case has started walking to the door. "It was good to meet you, Emma. I'm sure I'll see you around again."

I offer him a grin in response before I head back into the guestroom, shutting the door behind me.

***

"Are you good, Em?"

It's how my brother starts every conversation we have. I almost always respond in the same way; I lay out everything that's wrong in my life and then wait for him to offer advice for me to fix things.

I don't travel that route tonight because this conversation isn't about what's going on with me. It's about the major life decision that Drake has made.

"I'm fine," I answer.

I sit on the edge of the bed. My hands are trembling. Since I heard the apartment door shut behind Case and Gavin, I put the call on speaker.

"How are you?" I ask him, hoping that it will lead to a confession.

"Happier than I've ever been." His voice is joyful. I can hear the emotion in every word. "I'm so fucking happy right now."

Tears form in my eyes.

"Tell me why," I whisper.

I don't know if Case gave Drake a heads-up that I know about his elopement, but I want to give my brother the chance to tell me in his own words. I need that. I sense he does do.

"I'm getting married, Em." His voice quakes. "Can you believe I'm getting married?"

I thought he was married by now.

"You're getting married?" I manage to ask.

"I can't believe it either." He laughs softly. "I thought you'd tie the knot before me."

Until recently, I thought that too.

Keeping those words to myself, I drop my head and stay silent.

I hear movement on his end and what sounds like a door shutting.

"I feel like I'm the luckiest guy in the world," he goes on, his voice lowered. "She thinks we're on a trip for my birthday, but I planned her dream wedding. She has always wanted to get married in a castle in Ireland, so I'm doing that for her. It's just the two of us, but I'm going to throw the party to end all parties back in New York when things settle."

I cross my legs at the ankle. "She doesn't know that she's getting married?"

"She has no fucking clue." He exhales. "She pinned her dream dress to a board on Pinterest, so I tracked that down in her size. I arranged for a bouquet of her favorite flowers. I booked the castle. Ordered a three-tier chocolate cake and a string quartet. I did it all to surprise her."

If his bride-to-be doesn't even know she's getting married, how can I be angry with him for not telling me?

This might be the most romantic thing I've ever heard.

"Her name is Jane, Em." There's an unmistakable crack in his voice when he says her name. "You're going to love her."

If he does, I know I will.

I'm gaining another sister.

"Can I count on you to keep this between us?" he asks hopefully. "I want to tell mom and dad once I'm a married man, so give me a few days."

His birthday is in a few days. "Are you getting married on your birthday?"

"That's the plan." He chuckles. "I can't think of a better birthday gift than a lifetime with Jane."

"I won't say a thing to mom or dad or *Whitney*," I stress our sister's name. "You should at least text her, so she knows you're alive, Drake."

"I'll do that first thing in the morning." He takes an audible breath. "I feel like shit knowing you're in the city without me there. I swear I'll make it up to you soon. I promise."

Drake has never broken a promise to me, but he doesn't owe me a thing. I'm the one who showed up in New York without warning. "Please don't feel badly."

"I need to end this now, Em. If Jane wakes up, she'll come looking for me."

As much as I want to keep him on the line, I know I can't. "I'm glad we got to talk, Drake."

"Me too, Em. I love you."

"I love you too," I whisper before he ends the call.

Chapter 10

Case

After having dinner with Gavin, I planned on taking a shower and heading to bed.

That didn't happen.

I'm sitting on a stool at the bar in Durie's, watching a guy in a green sweater hit on Emma Owens.

After catching a glimpse of her through the window on my way home, I stepped inside.

That's when the blond guy made his move.

He sat down at her table with a martini in one hand and a bottle of beer in the other.

She smiled at him. He took it as an invitation, and they've been talking for the past twenty minutes. I've spent the bulk of that time reading over the text message exchange I had with Drake earlier.

He wants me to keep Emma in New York until he lands back at LaGuardia. I don't know the woman's schedule or when she's planning on flying back to Seattle, but he made it clear that he wants her here when he steps back on American soil as a married man.

I'll relay the message, but ultimately she'll make that decision on her own.

I have no intention of sticking around Manhattan that long. I want out as soon as possible.

"Can I get you another soda water?"

I glance at the server who brought the glass in front of me. The last time I sat at this bar for a drink, everyone who worked here was an army vet. I used to drop in a few times a week when the awning out front displayed the name Eager Pour. Back then, the owner was willing to listen to my bullshit before she'd cut me off after my second drink and send me home.

"I'm good," I answer curtly.

"You're Case, right?" She leans her elbow on the bar next to me. "Drake has told me so much about you that I feel like I already know you."

I can tell when a woman is flirting, but that's not what's happening here.

I recognized her name when she first introduced herself after I walked in tonight. She has to be the same Kendall who had a one-night stand with my best friend last summer.

I huff out a laugh. "Did he?"

"He showed me a picture of the two of you from your college days." She lets out a soft giggle. "You haven't changed as much as he has."

That's an understatement.

Drake didn't visit a barber for years. He's as clean cut as they come now. It's a far cry from the longhaired, bearded guy I said goodbye to when I left New York.

He's sought refuge at my home in California a few times over the years. We talk daily, but our face-to-face time is rare.

"Why don't you join Emma?" She questions with a grin. "I'm sure she'd appreciate the distraction."

Reading between the lines, I pop an eyebrow. "Do you know the guy with her?"

She nods. "Ned. He's a regular. When he spots a pretty new face in here, he always buys them a drink."

If I didn't know Emma, I'd buy her a drink too so I can't fault the guy for that.

"He's harmless," she goes on. "I've never seen him seal the deal. He always walks out of here alone."

That should be my cue to call it a night and head back to my apartment, but I stay planted on the stool.

I have a clear view of Emma's face. She's a beautiful woman with a smile that could stop any man in his tracks. I see no harm in watching her from a distance for a few more minutes.

Kendall glances at the phone in my hand. "Have you heard from Drake since he left?"

I won't betray my closest friend to appease the curiosity of one of his ex-lovers. If he wants Kendall to know the details of his wedding, he'll fill her in.

Downing the rest of the water in my glass, I lightly tap it on the top of the bar. "I'll get another one of these."

Disappointment draws her shoulders forward once she realizes I ignored her question. "Are you sure you don't want something stronger?"

"Water is fine." I glance past her to catch Emma laughing at something Ned said.

Envy isn't something I feel often, but it's there now.

That guy is no one to Drake. He can make Emma laugh. He can kiss her, hell he can fuck her without having to worry about the consequences.

She's off-limits because of my friendship with her brother. I've always craved what I can't have and what I shouldn't touch.

"Kendall," I call out her name as she steps away. "I'll take a double scotch neat."

"Do you have a preference for…"

"I don't," I interrupt her. "The label on the bottle doesn't matter. You choose."

With a nod of her head, she smiles. "I'll be right back with your drink."

I need it if I'm going to spend the next few days sleeping in the same apartment as my best friend's sister.

Chapter 11

Emma

Case isn't nearly as stealthy as he thinks he is.

I saw him walk into the pub and sit down at the bar. It took everything inside of me not to stare at him. I caught glimpses of him out of the corner of my eye as he talked to Kendall.

Jealousy tugged at me when I saw him lean closer to her.

I should have spent my time talking to the man who bought me a drink, but I struggled to focus on him.

I could feel Case's gaze on me when I did look at Ned, the stockbroker who thought it was impressive to tell me about the summerhouse he's planning on buying.

Ned's good-looking and charming. He might be fun to hang out with, but after I sipped my martini, I thanked him for the drink and pushed back from the table to leave.

That was when I noticed Case dropping a few bills on the top of the bar before he rushed out of the pub.

I'm back in his apartment now.

I can see a sliver of light creeping out from under the closed door of his bedroom.

I shouldn't feel as disappointed as I do. I wasn't expecting more than a few words exchanged between us before I called it a night, but that's not going to happen.

In his eyes, I'm nothing more than Drake's younger sister.

Letting out a heavy breath, I step out of my heels. Feeling my phone vibrate in my clutch, I fish it out.

I smile at the text message on the screen from my best friend.

Sandy: *Are you living it up right now?*

I click the phone icon under her name.

She answers immediately. "I take it that the answer to my question is *no*. Why aren't you spending the night with some sexy Manhattan millionaire?"

I laugh. "Technically, I guess I am."

"What?" She shrieks out the word. "Why are you talking to me? Get back to it. Make me proud."

Shaking my head, I glance at Case's bedroom door. "I'm staying with Drake's best friend until I come home."

"Why? You went to New York to see your brother. Why aren't you staying with him?"

I'll tell Sandy everything when I'm back in Seattle. We've been sharing all our ups and downs since we met in middle school. Getting into the details about my brother's major life change isn't something I want to do over the phone.

"He had a trip planned that I didn't know about," I offer to appease her curiosity.

"So, you're staying with his friend?" She sighs. "What's he like?"

"Case is nothing like Drake," I say quietly.

"I want more than his name, Em. Is he hot?"

"Very," I confess. "Tall, gorgeous, think surfer type with a corporate vibe."

"Send me a pic," she whines.

"I can't take a picture of him." I laugh softly. "Do you expect me to ask him to pose for it? How creepy would that be?"

"That's not creepy. It would be creepy if you asked him to get naked first."

I drop my gaze to the floor. "If I had a naked picture of Case, I sure as hell wouldn't be sharing it with anyone."

'That's reassuring."

The sound of Case's voice behind me almost drops the phone from my grasp.

"I need to go," I mumble to Sandy before I end the call.

My face heats red as I turn to face him.

The clothes he was wearing at the bar are gone. He's dressed in faded jeans and a black T-shirt.

I look down out of a desperate need to catch my breath. "It's not how it sounded."

He takes a step closer to where I'm standing. "Unless you know another man named Case, it sounded like you'd protect my privacy if you ever happened to get your hands on a picture of me in the raw."

I raise my chin so I can look him in the eye, but my gaze sticks on his biceps, and the way the material of his shirt is stretched taut across his chest.

Dammit, he's a perfect twelve on a scale of one-to-ten.

"Just so you know." His arms cross over that muscular chest of his. "I'd do the same for you, Emma."

A shiver runs down my spine when he rakes me from head-to-toe.

Should I thank him for that, or should I try to explain myself?

Before I have a chance to do either, his phone starts ringing. Tugging it out of the back pocket of his jeans, he silences it after glancing at the screen. "This is important. I need to go."

"See you later," I say as I watch him head out of the apartment before the door shuts behind him with a loud thud.

Chapter 12

Case

I heave out a sigh as I come down from the high of a much-needed orgasm.

Resting my forehead against the wall of the shower, I close my eyes to ward off the images that have owned my thoughts since I woke up.

The moment I joked with Emma about a nude picture of her, the wonder of what that might look like took over my life.

I left the apartment last night after our brief exchange because I craved fresh air.

I ended up on the sidewalk outside the building talking to my assistant in California. He ran through a litany of issues that he needed my help with, and then I blew him off.

I used the convenient excuse of jet lag to get me out of the conversation.

By the time I went back up to my apartment, Emma was in the guestroom, softly singing. I stood outside the door and listened. Every note was off-key, but I didn't find it irritating. It was charming in a way that makes no sense to me.

I tilt my head up to let the warm water slide over me. I need to get out of the shower and dry off since I have a meeting in less than an hour.

I bump my fist against the panel in front of me but miss the mark.

The water stops, but a sudden burst of steam envelops me.

This smart shower is another of Drake's not-so-brilliant ideas. When he had this prototype installed, he boasted that he could turn it on with an app on his phone.

I laughed because I never anticipated that I'd have to experience it in person. Slapping my hand against the panel again, the steam clears.

I'd use the other bathroom and its straightforward shower handle that controls flow and temperature, but that's reserved for my guest.

I grab a towel and dry myself.

A swipe of my hand across the steam-covered mirror reveals an unshaven face.

I haven't skipped a morning shave since I moved to California.

It's just one of the routines that keep my life in order.

I make a mental note to pick up a razor on my way to the office.

As soon as I've opened the door and taken a step into my bedroom, the sound of Emma singing hits me again.

It's the same song she was belting out last night, but this morning it's muffled by the sound of water running.

If I get my ass in gear, I might catch a glimpse of her crossing the hallway from the bathroom to the guestroom.

One step toward the door of my bedroom is as far as I get.

I look down at my body and the towel around my waist.

There's no masking the fact that I'm semi-hard.

Dragging a hand through my hair, I scold myself under my breath. "What the fuck are you doing? Get dressed now."

I drop the towel and head toward my suitcase while Emma eases into the chorus for a third time.

***

Thirty minutes later, Emma emerges from the guestroom, looking like she took two hours to get ready.

She paired dark jeans with a pink, short-sleeve sweater. The black boots on her feet match the leather bag slung over her shoulder.

As she nears me, she pushes a lock of her dark hair behind her ear, luring my eyes to her beautiful face.

I can't tell if the attraction I feel to her is based on the fact that she's off-limits or not. Either way, staring at her isn't the route I need to take here.

I drop my gaze to the screen of my phone. "Good morning, Emma."

"Morning," she chirps. "How are you?"

Does anyone ever ask that question expecting an answer other than *I'm fine,* or *I'm doing great*? I haven't been truthful in my response to it in years. I don't see a reason to change that up now. "I'm all right. You?"

"I'm fine." She bounces to her tiptoes. "Do I need to stay away until five again?"

There's no frustration in her tone. She's genuinely asking if I need her to get lost until late this afternoon. I appreciate her willingness to accommodate me even though she has no idea what I had going on yesterday.

I shoot her a glance. "No. You're free to come and go as you please today."

"That's good to know." She looks down at the watch on her wrist. "I think I'll explore the city for a few hours. I've only been to a handful of places with Drake. There's a lot more I want to see."

She's an untainted tourist. I may have left Manhattan years ago, but once you live here, the city becomes a part of you. I'm not a native New Yorker by anyone's standards. I'm just a guy who thought his dreams would come true on this island until his greatest nightmare became reality.

Since she brought up her brother, I relay the message he wanted me to deliver to her. "Drake got in touch with me last night. He wants you to hang around until he's back in town."

"He does?"

I nod. "I don't know what you're looking at in terms of time off from your job, but…"

"That's not an issue," she interrupts me.

Curiosity drives the next question out of me. "What do you do, Emma?"

She hesitates for a split second. "I'm a teacher."

It takes a certain degree of patience and compassion to devote your time to the education of others. I'm impressed.

"It's summer break so I have some time off before I go back to work." Her hand scrubs at her forehead. "I *will* be going back to work."

She spits out the word *will* like it's done her wrong. I don't ask what that's about because she's eyeing up the door of the apartment like she wants to break free.

Pushing back from the dining room table, I stand. Smoothing my hand over the front of my gray suit jacket, I toss her a glance. "I'm heading into the office."

"I'll see you later?"

It comes out as a question, so I answer honestly. "I should be back around six."

"I'll be here." She steps back when I approach her on my way to the door. "Have a good day, Case."

A good day would include me getting on a flight headed back to California. The sooner that happens, the better.

Chapter 13

Emma

Manhattan has endless hidden treasures.

I've spent almost thirty minutes on this block, admiring the art that covers the brick exterior of many of the businesses. None of it is extravagant and noticeable from the street, but I could see small, intricate paintings interwoven with romantic phrases once I got closer. The sun may have faded the colors, but their beauty is still undeniable.

They are random love letters written to people who may not even be alive anymore.

I snap a few pictures and save them to a folder on my phone. These creations are too unique to be forgotten after a stroll past them. They deserve to be appreciated over and over again. I'll print them and glue them in my scrapbook back at home.

The empty feeling in my stomach reminds me again that I haven't eaten anything yet today. I considered grabbing a hotdog from a street vendor, but then I remembered that Case's cousin said something about Calvetti's authentic Italian food. I looked up the address and made my way here before the neighborhood art sidetracked me.

I approach the glass door and yank it open to find the restaurant teeming with people.

The aromas wafting from the kitchen edge my hunger up a notch.

I'm famished.

"Welcome to Calvetti's." An older woman with a kind smile approaches me. "I'm Marti, and you're a beautiful girl."

Knowing that I'm sporting a huge grin, I dip my chin to hide it.

"That smile could light this city on its darkest nights." She reaches for my hand. "My grandson would be charmed by that smile."

"Your grandson?" I question with a lilt in my voice.

Her gaze drops to my left hand. "No ring. You're single?"

"Very," I answer with a grin.

"My grandson is as handsome as you are beautiful," she says with the slightest hint of an Italian accent in her voice. "He's a fireman. If you like heroes, I can give you his number."

"Grandma." A woman around my age makes her way closer to us. "Luke told you to stop trying to fix him up with every pretty girl who walks through the door."

Marti tosses her a look. "They'd make the perfect couple."

With a shake of her head and a laugh, the younger woman shifts her attention to me. "I'm Bella Calvetti. I take it you're trying to eat some lunch not looking for a life partner?"

I nod.

"A girl can have both." Marti shrugs her shoulders. "First, you'll have the spaghetti, then we'll talk more about Luke."

"She'll have whatever she orders from the menu, Grandma." Bella gestures toward an empty table. "Please, go ahead and have a seat."

I settle onto one of the wooden chairs next to a small circular table covered with a red and white checkered cloth. This might be the most memorable lunch I've ever had, and I haven't even taken a bite of the food yet.

I adjust my purse on my lap before dragging the chair closer to the table.

"I'm sorry about Marti." Bella hands me a menu. "She means well."

I glance up at her. She's pretty. Her long dark hair is the same shade as mine. Her blue-gray eyes pop as she looks down at me.

"I'm Emma," I offer even though she didn't ask. "And your grandma is very sweet."

"She's the best." She rests one hand on her hip. "Is this your first time at Calvetti's?"

I glance at the closed menu. "It is. What do you recommend?"

"One of everything." She rubs her small belly bump through the light blue dress she's wearing. "I'm eating for two so I stop in as often as I can for lunch. Marti feeds my little bundle of love and me very well. Today we had the ricotta and spinach stuffed shells."

The pear shaped diamond ring on her finger catches my eye.

It's no wonder she's practically beaming.

"Congratulations," I say, not sure if I'm commenting more on the baby or the ring. Maybe both.

"Thank you. I sometimes wonder how this is my life." She smiles softly. "I'll give you a few minutes to decide what you'd like."

I don't need it. "I'll have the stuffed shells."

She scoops the menu back into her hand. "Excellent choice, Emma."

Bella's right. I did make an excellent choice when I came here for lunch. This place is full of friendly faces and what I know will be to-die-for food.

***

"What do you think?" Bella plops herself onto the vacant chair at my table. "It's ridiculous how good it is, right?"

Swallowing the last bite of food, I nod. "So good."

It's not a lie. I don't indulge in pasta often, but this ranks at the top of the best I've ever had. I might have to sneak in another meal here before I go home.

"Your grandma is a fantastic cook."

Bella smiles. "She's the best cook and the best grandma."

I look over to where Marti is chatting with two women who just walked into the restaurant.

"She's probably trying to set them up with my cousins." Bella laughs. "I'm sorry if she seemed pushy about Luke. You two would make a great couple though."

I glance across the table to find her winking at me.

"I'm only visiting New York so I'll have to pass." I inch my eyebrows up. "I won't pass on dessert though. Do you have a recommendation for something sweet from the menu?"

Leaning forward, she rests both of her forearms on the table. "If you keep this between us, I'll let you in on a little secret about the best dessert in Manhattan."

I follow her lead and lower my voice. "Are you going to tell me that it's not at Calvetti's?"

"Don't get me wrong," she begins with a sigh. "Marti makes this honey ricotta cheesecake that I'd walk barefoot over rocks for, but…"

"But?" I interrupt with a soft laugh.

"If you love cupcakes as much as I do, Sweet Bluebells is the place to be."

"I probably love them more than you," I say. "I have two questions. Where's Sweet Bluebells, and do they make red velvet cupcakes with real cream cheese frosting?"

With a quick push back from the table, Bella is on her feet. "Not only are they made with real cream cheese frosting, but the crowning glory is a sprinkle of red, white, and pink candy hearts on top."

Sliding a few bills from my wallet, I drop them on the table before I stand too. "Point me in the right direction."

"Follow me, Emma." Bella turns toward the door. "I'm in the mood for one myself, so I'll show you the way."

Chapter 14

Emma

The dozens of treats on display inside Sweet Bluebells on the Upper West Side look decadent. I suddenly wonder if Case has ever been here. Does he have a sweet tooth?

Should I grab a few as a thank you gift since he's letting me stay at his place?

I shake away the thought because he doesn't seem like the cupcake type.

"Emma, did you hear me?" Bella elbows me in the side. "You're in a cupcake coma, and you haven't even taken a bite yet."

I tear my gaze away from the glass display case to glance at her. "How could I not be? This place is incredible."

"I agree." She flashes me a grin. "I'll introduce you to the cake artist behind these mini-masterpieces, and then we'll order."

I catch sight of a woman around my age approaching us. She's wearing a white T-shirt, faded jeans, and a light blue apron sporting the shop's name. Her blonde hair is styled into a tight, neat bun on the top of her head.

"Delaney," Bella calls to her. "Come meet my new friend."

I can't help but smile at the declaration. Bella and I chatted on the subway ride here. She was born and raised in New York City. Her best friend, Max, is in Boston for two months setting up a new location of his family's shoe store and she misses him like crazy. She was most excited to tell me that she's engaged to the love of her life, and according to Bella, a more perfect man doesn't exist. Although she's currently working as an executive assistant, she plans on leaving that job in a few months to help her fiancé launch the business they'll grow together.

When it was my turn to share, I told her about growing up in Seattle and my decision to pursue a teaching degree. I also slipped in the fact that I came to Manhattan to visit my brother who jetted off to get married right before I arrived.

As she listened to me talk about Drake's decision to elope in Ireland, Bella smiled and told me that sometimes she wishes she could run away with her fiancé to tie the knot.

I like her.

"Delaney Wilts, this is Emma…" Bella's voice trails. She looks to me for help.

"Owens," I add. "I'm Emma Owens."

I take Delaney's outstretched hand for a quick shake. Her blue eyes slide over my face. "It's great to meet you, Emma."

"Emma is visiting New York." Bella surveys the sugary treats in the display case. "I told her that she had to taste the best cupcakes in the state, so here we are."

Delaney beams. "Bella knows what she likes. We're grateful it's our cupcakes."

"I don't just come for the cupcakes." Bella glances at me. "Delaney is a gem. I come in so often that we've become friends."

Delaney giggles. "It's kind of impossible not to become Bella's friend. I've never met a kinder heart."

Bella wraps her arms around Delaney for a quick hug. "I'm extra hormonal, so don't make me cry."

"Fine." Delaney playfully swats her arm. "What can I get you two?"

Bella looks to me. "Emma wants a red velvet, and I'll take a vanilla with strawberry buttercream frosting."

I reach in my bag for my wallet until I feel Bella's hand on my arm.

When I glance at her, she's shaking her head. "I'm covering it today. Next time, you'll treat me."

I can't help but smile at the promise of more time spent with my new friend. "Deal."

***

Bella glances at her watch as we step out of Sweet Bluebells into the afternoon sun. "I need to get back to the office. This has been a blast, Emma."

It has been.

We ate our cupcakes and sipped lemonade. Delaney sat down with us briefly during her break. She's been working at the bakery with her aunt for years. Her love of all things cupcakes is apparent. When she told us about the new flavor combinations she's planning on introducing, I was in awe.

At home, a boxed cake mix is the foundation for any dessert I attempt to bake.

"I've had the best time," I say honestly. "Thank you for everything, Bella."

Before I can react, I'm drawn into a hug. "I got to see Marti, eat pasta, and meet you. It's been a great day so far."

I step back and smile.

"What are your plans now?" she asks as she looks over my shoulder. "If you're heading downtown, we can hop back on the subway together."

"I think I'll take a walk in Central Park, and I might try and find a bookstore. I have a lot of spare time right now and nothing to read."

"If you can hold off until tomorrow, I'll take you to the bookstore of my dreams." Her blue eyes brighten. "It's in Brooklyn. I've been going there since I was a kid."

Since my calendar is wide open, I nod. "I can hold off."

"We should exchange numbers." She palms her phone. "I promise I won't pass yours on to any of my single cousins unless you want me to."

"I live in Seattle, remember?" I ask teasingly. "I'm here for a brief visit. That's it. I'm not looking to find my soul mate in Manhattan."

"I wasn't looking for mine either and boom, there he was." She darts a hand into the air. "You never know when you're going to come face-to-face with the man who will own your heart."

"The chances of it happening during this trip are slim."

"There's just as much chance of it happening here as there are in Seattle." She gestures at my phone. "I'll give you my number. Text me tomorrow so we can set up a time to go to the bookstore."

I plug her number into my contact list as she recites it to me.

"My family has this habit of being too much at times." She holds back a smile. "If I'm doing that, tell me, but I know what it's like to miss your older brother. Mine has been living in Italy for a few months. He's coming back soon, but it's not the same as having him close."

"You're not too much," I reassure her with a squeeze of her hand. "I'm alone in New York for the most part. The only person I know is my brother's best friend. I'm staying with him."

Her eyes narrow. "What's he like?"

I shrug. "It's hard to tell. We've barely talked."

Leaning closer, she lowers her voice. "My brother's best friend is in love with my sister. She doesn't know it, but I see it whenever they're in the same room."

"Case barely knows I exist." I laugh. "I'm not even sure he likes me."

"You like him." Her eyebrows dance. "Your face lit up when you said his name."

"No, it didn't," I protest with a grin. "I don't know the man."

"Watch this." She takes a deep breath. "Barrett Adler."

"That's your fiancé," I say with conviction because of the dazzling smile she's sporting. Happiness radiates from her.

She circles her index finger in front of her face. "This is the face of a woman in love."

I mimic her movement in front of my face. "This is the face of a woman not in love."

"Yet," she says matter-of-factly. "I'll walk to the park with you, and then it's back to work for me."

Chapter 15

Case

Sitting in Drake's office is a glimpse into the mind of a genius.

I thought I knew where he was in terms of development and new product launches, but he's been hiding his best ideas in a blue file folder shoved under some books on a shelf in his office.

I wouldn't have given the shelf a second look except there's a framed picture of Emma on it.

It must have been taken when Drake surprised his family with a trip to Hawaii last year.

Drake's parents are both wearing white shirts and navy blue shorts. The hem of the long yellow sundress Whitney has on is kissing the sand on the beach. Drake is front and center in the picture decked out in red board shorts and a backward baseball cap.

A colorful beach towel is wrapped around Emma's waist, and a white string bikini top is covering her breasts.

Jesus.

With her brown hair flowing in the light breeze, she looks unbelievable.

She's beautiful.

I glance back at the image again, although there's no need. I took a snap of it with my phone yesterday.

Truthfully, I zoomed in on her before I took the picture.

I'll delete it at some point, but for now, it's saved not only to my memory but to a folder on my phone.

A knock on the doorframe draws my gaze up from the folder.

"Mr. Abbott?" Drake's assistant rakes a hand through his blond hair.

"What is it, Elias?"

Elias Svensson is a recruit that Drake brought on six months ago after his long-term assistant retired. I've known Elias for less than forty-eight hours, but I'm impressed by what I've seen so far.

"You mentioned that you wanted to know when Ms. Montgomery arrived." He jerks a thumb over his shoulder. "She's here."

I glance down at the desk. "Send her in."

"Will do, sir." He nods. "If I didn't mention it before, it's good to meet you."

He did mention it. *Twice.*

I looked over his resume. He's a twenty-four-year-old personal assistant who should be in our software development department. I have no idea why Drake gave him this position, but a few weeks from now, Elias will have a new job title and a bigger paycheck.

"You too," I toss back.

He inches forward. His gaze skates over the open file folder in front of me. "What do you have there?"

"The inner workings of Drake's brain."

He chuckles. "If you need anything, let me know."

"Will do." I point at the door. "Get Ms. Montgomery in here. I'm about to make her dreams come true."

***

In California, when I want to clear my mind, I pick up one of my surfboards.

The ocean has felt like home to me for years.

My mind can be thrumming with a dozen different ideas, but once I hit the waves, all I feel is tranquility.

Trying to find that in Manhattan is a fool's pursuit.

After I met with Blair Montgomery, she invited me to dinner at her apartment tonight. She wanted me to meet her husband and kids so they could thank me for the opportunity I just dropped into her lap.

I passed.

I expect great things from her, but friendship isn't one of them. She's a hard-working employee who deserves the chance I'm giving her.

She'll prove that I made the right choice. I have no doubt about that.

I step out of the building that is home to Cabbott Mobile's offices, button my suit jacket, and take a deep breath.

It's mid-afternoon.

The sun is bathing the island in heat today. A day like today brightens the spirit of the people who call this city home.

Summer has settled, bringing with it blue skies and warm breezes.

I'm not a New Yorker anymore.

I don't give a shit about the weather or what season it is.

I may be standing on a sidewalk outside the office of a multi-million-dollar company that I built from the ground up, but all I feel is regret.

My life was ruined in this city once.

I need to get the hell out of here and back to where I belong.

Chapter 16

Emma

I ready myself for the elevator doors to glide open on the floor that houses Case's apartment.

I stopped at a market a block over to pick up everything I need to make a salad for dinner. I bought enough for two with the hope that Case will have the time to eat with me.

I have all the essentials for a spinach, strawberry, feta cheese, and pecan salad. It screams California to me, so I'm hoping my temporary roommate will like it.

I take a step forward when the doors start to slide apart.

The sight in front of me stops me.

Case is standing close to a woman with black hair. Her hand is resting on his forearm as they stare into each other's eyes.

The instant they notice me, her hand falls to her side.

Awkward.

She turns toward me. Her blue eyes hone in on my face.

Tearing my gaze away from her, I look to Case.

He's wearing the same blue button-down shirt he had on this morning. An extra button is open at the collar. He switched out the gray suit pants he had on for faded jeans.

This casual, untucked look suits him well.

For half of a second, I consider retreating into the elevator and pressing the button to take me back to the lobby.

"Emma." Case clears his throat. "You're here."

"I'm here," I repeat in a hushed tone.

I might as well own that fact, so I step off the elevator. The doors glide shut behind me.

"I'm Maya Bishop." The pretty woman in the fitted red dress reaches a hand out to me.

Fumbling with my clutch and the paper grocery bag, I shuffle everything, so that I can shake her hand.

"Emma Owens," I offer.

Dropping my hand, she looks up at Case. "I'll be back at seven thirty."

I guess I'll be hanging out at Durie's again tonight.

Wanting an escape, I glance down at the grocery bag I'm holding. "I should put all of this away."

"It was good to meet you, Emma." Maya bats her long lashes.

"You too," I say before stepping around Case to head toward the door of his apartment.

"This afternoon went well." The gruff tone of Case's voice sends goose bumps scattering over my arms.

"I agree," Maya says. "Pam and Rod were the happiest I've ever seen them. I can't say I'm surprised. I knew once we took them into the bedroom that they'd walk out on cloud nine."

Wait. What?

I stumble forward, almost dropping the bag in my hand.

Timing is everything in life. If I had arrived back here earlier, I might have interrupted that foursome. I'm suddenly extra grateful that I met Bella today. She unwittingly kept me occupied long enough for Case to finish having fun.

Maya continues, "It felt a little rushed, but I know they left satisfied. That's all that matters. They'll be back."

Glancing over my shoulder, I catch Case looking in my direction. He shoots me one of his dimpled smiles.

The man has just as many secrets as Drake does. Maybe even more.

***

I shove everything in the grocery bag into the almost empty fridge. I'll make the salad at some point, but for now, I've completely lost my appetite.

It makes no sense that there's a sudden pit in my stomach.

I barely know Case. Why do I feel a knot of jealousy over the fact that he's had more sex in the past twenty-four hours than I've had in a year?

"Hey, Emma. Where are you?" Case calls out.

I step out of the kitchen and round the corner toward the foyer. I catch him shoving his hand into the front pocket of his jeans to grab his phone.

I liked the suit he was wearing this morning, but I love him dressed more casually.

What the hell is wrong with me?

I'm mentally rating his outfits. I need to get a grip and get him out of my mind.

He looks up from his phone's screen when I step closer to him. "We're going out for dinner."

That makes sense. I assume Maya and him worked up a substantial appetite this afternoon rolling in the hay with Rod and Pam. Can you safely roll with that many people on one bed, or will one tumble off the edge?

Would the other three people even notice if you did fall?

I have to stop with the wandering thoughts and focus.

"I hope you and Maya have a nice time." I paste an exaggerated grin on my mouth. "Will you be coming back here after dinner? Not that it's my business, but I know you'd like privacy. Or I assume you do, but maybe I'm wrong? What I'm trying to say is that I can hang out at Durie's if you need me to."

My eye twitches.

Please don't let him mistake that for a wink.

He narrows his gaze as he studies my face. "I'm not taking Maya to dinner. I'm taking you to dinner."

I close my eyes, not only to clear my mind because I'm sure I just mistakenly heard him say he's taking me to dinner but to stop the unrelenting twitch that has now migrated to my other eye.

"Maya is meeting someone here this evening, and she wants the place unoccupied, so that means we both need to clear out before she gets here," he clarifies.

I have a million questions related to that, but I just nod because where would I start?

"Aim to be ready at seven." He looks toward the main bedroom. "I need to hit the shower."

"I'll do the same."

"We'll keep it casual tonight." He glances at what I'm wearing. "Does sushi work for you?"

"Sure." I shrug, not wanting to admit that I've never tried it.

"Good. I'll see you in a couple of hours."

He disappears down the hallway, shutting his bedroom door behind him. I wait a beat before I head to the guest room.

I drop my purse on the bed, kick off my boots, and grab a pair of yoga shorts and a long T-shirt from my suitcase. It's enough to keep me covered when I cross the hall after my shower.

The moment I step into the main bathroom, I spot a gift bag on the counter. The logo for Matiz Cosmetics is printed on the side of the pale pink bag.

I've heard about their products. Almost everyone has, but I can't afford them on my teacher's salary.

I glance down at the simple white card next to the gift bag.

There are two words written in black ink.
Emma. Enjoy.

I pluck a few pieces of white tissue from the bag to find two bottles of bubble bath. One infused with lavender and the other a blend of citrus. Both bottles are square shaped and topped with silver lids. They look like they belong on a shelf on display.

I open one bottle and inhale the sweet fragrance. Closing my eyes, I savor the scent and the knowledge that Case got this just for me.

Chapter 17

Case

I tug a lightweight gray sweater over my head and take a step back. The full-length mirror Drake had installed in the walk-in closet is welcome. I don't put that much effort into my appearance, but I know I look all right tonight.

Dark jeans and black wingtip shoes are going to have to fit the bill of casual attire since I packed lightly for this trip.

Swiping a hand over my chin, I realize that I still haven't gotten around to cleaning it up. I make a mental note to take care of it tomorrow before my two-day-old scruff morphs into the beginnings of a beard.

I tuck my wallet into my back pocket and my keys in the front. With my phone in my hand, I head out into the main living area.

The instant I exit the bedroom, the fragrance of lavender envelops me.

Emma must have indulged in a bath after finding the gift bag I left her.

"Case." Her soft voice breaks through the silence.

Looking to the right, toward the open door of the guestroom, I'm gifted with the sight of Emma wearing a pair of black jeans and a ruby red sheer sleeveless blouse.

Her lips are tinted the same shade as her shirt.

I catch a glimpse of what looks like a red satin bra beneath the shirt before she slips into a black blazer.

Fuck.

With her hair in curls around her shoulders, she's a vision. She's tiny but curvy, and innocent with just a hint of sexy hidden beneath her jacket.

I hope to hell she loses the jacket at dinner.

"Do I look all right?" she asks with a tilt of her head.

I swallow back the urge to tell her what I really think. Instead, I settle on what Drake would want me to say to her. "You look great."

Understatement of the fucking year.

"You do too," she tosses back with a wink, or maybe that's a twitch.

Either way, she's still as off-limits as she was when I met her.

"I'm ready if you are." She tucks her clutch under her arm and starts toward me.

Frozen in place, I close my eyes as she breezes past. The scent of lavender, and something a little spicier wafts in the air.

Dammit, she even smells fantastic.

I have no idea how the hell I'm going to make it through dinner with this woman. I already need a cold shower, and we haven't even left the apartment.

***

"Thank you again for the bubble bath," she repeats the statement for the second time since we left for dinner. "It's so creamy. My skin is extra soft."

I swallow past the lump that's stuck in my throat.

It landed there when we hopped into the backseat of a black SUV driven by the man who chauffeurs Drake around town.

Emma dropped her ass into the middle of the seat, so I had no choice but to settle in next to her.

I watched her profile in silence as she chatted up the driver. I can't even recall the guy's name at this point. All I can remember about the ride is that Emma's tongue kept darting out to wet her bottom lip.

It happens again as she stands facing me.

I tear my gaze away from her heart-shaped mouth.

"It was kind of you to think of me," she says softly.

It was wrong of me to think of her naked in the bathtub. That's exactly what I did as I stood in front of the bubble bath display at Matiz Cosmetics. I smelled every scent until I decided on the two I purchased for her.

I took note when she announced to Gavin and me that the bodega had run out of bubble bath. It made sense to get it for her on my way back to my apartment this afternoon.

I knew she wanted it, so I made it happen. Whether that's because she's my best friend's sister is unclear to me at this point.

My attraction to her is blurring with my desire to do Drake a favor by making sure she has everything she needs during this trip.

Wanting to focus on something other than my imagined images of her naked body, I jerk a thumb to my right. "We're almost there. It's around this corner. You're about to experience the best sushi you've ever had."

I had the driver drop us a block over from our final destination because I couldn't listen to another second of him flirting with Emma. Greenwich Village is packed tonight, so the time saved with us walking the extra block as opposed to crawling along in traffic is a bonus.

Emma gives me a wary smile. "I can't wait."

Something tells me she can, but we're feet away from one of the best sushi experiences of my life, so I start toward the corner. "You don't have to. Let's go."

Chapter 18

Emma

Since I met Case, I've noticed that he has sad eyes. It's not that his eyes aren't beautiful because they are. They're a green shade that makes me think of summer days spent running barefoot through soft grass. They are intense in a comforting sense, but there's a level of sorrow that has settled within them.

I see it as he stares at the shoe store that now occupies the space where his favorite sushi restaurant used to be.

"It's gone," he mutters under his breath.

I'd offer my condolences, but we're in Manhattan. On this block alone, there are at least a half dozen restaurants open for business.

The plus is that not one of them is serving raw fish. I'm not opposed to trying new things, but since I'm not a fan of cooked fish, I'd prefer something that doesn't swim in the ocean to be my dinner tonight.

"This city has changed." He scrubs a hand over the back of his neck. "So much has changed."

Everything changes. I've learned that myself the past few weeks. Counting on anything to remain the same is foolish.

"Maybe they relocated to another part of the city," I say the words even though I hope like hell that the restaurant has shuttered its doors for good.

He glances at me. "Maybe."

Scrolling a thumb over his phone's screen, I wait impatiently with crossed fingers hoping that the restaurateur in question has decided to focus on another culinary specialty. Maybe he traded in his sushi rolling mat for a pizza oven.

"No luck." He pockets his phone and glances down the block. "I'm hungry. Are you okay with us eating something other than sushi tonight?"

"I'm totally okay with that," I say a little too enthusiastically.

He eyes me. "Why am I getting the feeling that you're not a fan of sushi?"

Drake once told me that Case values honesty more than anything else, so I travel that path. "Fish is my last resort meal."

Crossing his arms over his chest, he lifts a brow. "Your last resort meal?"

"If there was nothing other than fish to eat and I was starving…" I stress the last word with a pat of my hand on my stomach. "I'd eat fish."

"But you were willing to eat sushi tonight?"

"For you, I would," I blurt out without thinking.

His gaze lingers on my face. "What are you in the mood for, Emma?"

Sticking with the honesty policy, I point at a restaurant across the street. "Pizza."

His hands drop to his hips. "I'm in. Pizza and a bottle of red wine sounds like the perfect meal to me."

***

"If this pizza existed before I left Manhattan seven years ago, I was seriously missing out." Case swallows the last bite of food on the table.

After sharing a salad, we opted for a large simple pie with red sauce, shredded basil, and fresh mozzarella.

"It was delicious." I slip my coat off and rest it against the chair back. "I think I ate too much today."

Case's gaze flits over the front of my blouse. "You look flushed."

I always look that way when I drink wine.

The evidence of that is on my face now. It's probably there when I drink a martini too, but I feel it now. I push my hair back over my shoulder to try to cool down.

"I've been eating Italian all day." I laugh. "And cupcakes."

He takes a sip from his wine glass. "I need more details. Let's start with breakfast."

"That's a complicated subject." I avoid eye contact as I go on, "I'm a very picky eater when it comes to breakfast."

Studying me, he runs his index finger over his bottom lip. "Picky in what sense?"

In the sense that I eat the same thing for breakfast almost every morning.

My life changed when I stumbled on Bright Bagels. The Bright brothers run a food truck in Seattle. One Saturday morning when I was out for a walk, I spotted the truck and ordered a plain bagel. It was utter perfection.

"I eat a certain type of bagel with cream cheese, a side of fresh berries, and a coffee with one cream and one sugar."

"What type of bagel?" he asks with a curious lift of his brow. "Poppy seed?"

I make a face. "No."

He taps his index finger on his forehead. "Note taken that Emma Owens finds poppy seed bagels disgusting."

"My go-to is a plain bagel from the Bright Bagels food truck back home." I cross my arms over my chest. "They're next level."

"New York is full of great bagel shops," he says. "You'll find something close here."

"I haven't yet." I shake my head. "Drake and I did a bagel hunt during my last visit. We tried four different shops. Nothing compared to Bright Bagels."

His finger hits the center of his forehead again. "Emma Owens is a hard ass when it comes to breakfast."

I laugh. "Call it what you will."

"I always call it as I see it." A smile plays on his lips. "Tell me about lunch."

I lean back in my chair. "I had lunch at Calvetti's. Your cousin was right. It is the best pasta."

He slides his wine glass half of an inch to the left on the worn wooden table. "It's amazing, isn't it? Did you meet Marti?"

I stare at his hand. As delicately as he's cradling the stem of the glass, I can tell that his hands are strong. The skin is sun-kissed just like his chest. I wonder if all of him is.

Drawing in a breath, I smile. "I did meet Marti and her granddaughter."

"You got the full family treatment." He nods. "When you walk into Calvetti's, it's like walking into your grandma's kitchen."

That's exactly how I felt. It's a jewel nestled in the middle of a bustling city. It's much like the restaurant we're sitting in now.

"Bella, Marti's granddaughter, took me to a bakery for dessert after lunch."

"That's where the cupcakes happened?" He glances at an older man and woman being seated at the table next to us. "What was the name of the place?"

"Sweet Bluebells." I sigh. "The red velvet cupcake I had was incredible. I met the pastry chef. She's a master of her craft."

"If I liked cupcakes, I might be tempted to check it out."

I circle a finger over a small spot burned into the tabletop. "Trying one of their cupcakes might make you realize you like them."

"Cupcakes happen to be my last resort dessert."

I laugh under my breath. "What?"

His hand sweeps a path in the air over our table. "If you put a dozen desserts on this table, a cupcake would be the last I'd sample."

Smoothing a hand over the front of my blouse, I tilt my head. "You have no idea what you're missing out on, Case."

His gaze follows the path of my hand. "I can't argue with that."

Chapter 19

Emma

The ring of his phone took Case to his feet five minutes ago. He mumbled that it was Maya and that he had to take it.

I watched him talk as he stood near the entrance to the restaurant. He stepped aside when a man and his daughter came rushing in, soaked from the sudden short thunderstorm that bore down on the city.

I glance away, not wanting Case to think that I'm studying every move he makes, even though I am.

He has to be one of the most handsome men in Manhattan.

I reach for my phone to fill the gap until Case comes back. Opening my message app, I see a text from Sandy.

Sandy: *I picked up your mail. I can report nothing exciting arrived other than a coupon for a cut and color at the salon you swore you'd never go to again.*

Grinning, I type a response.

Emma: *Remember how short my bangs were after that? What was that nickname you gave me?*

Her reply is instant.

Sandy: *Baby bangs. Why don't I still call you that?*

I feather my fingertips over my forehead.

Emma: *Because I haven't had bangs in three years.*

I let out a giggle because I know Sandy has to be doing the same.

Sandy: *That's a technicality, baby bangs.*

"I take it you're not texting your brother."

I look up to find Case standing next to me, his gaze pinned to the screen of my phone.

I set it back on the table. "Why would you say that?"

He settles back into his chair. "You were having a good time."

I laugh that off. "I have a good time when I text Drake."

"You've been pissed with him," he accuses with a smile. "He ran off to get married without saying a word to you."

That stings because it's ground in truth. I skip around the subject of my brother because I don't want Case repeating anything to Drake that I say in spite. "I was texting a friend back home. She reminded me of the nickname she used to call me that I hated."

"Let me guess what that was."

My eyebrows dart up. How does he think he can guess something that personal? We barely know each other. "Guess."

"Freckles."

That lures my hand to my nose. I thought I put on enough foundation to cover my freckles. My mom may see them as adorable, but I'm not a toddler anymore. They were cute at one time. Now, they're a reminder of the bunch of bullies I went to middle school with.

Girls can be cruel to other girls. It's one of the reasons I became a teacher.

"No," I say quietly. "Not Freckles."

"You try to hide your freckles, but I like them."

I lock eyes with him. "You do?"

He studies me, tilting his head up slightly. "They're a unique part of you."

Running a finger over the bridge of my nose, I bite back a smile. "I guess they are."

"Was your nickname small fry or maybe shorty?"

Shaking my head, I finally grin. "I'm five foot two. That's not short."

His eyes widen. "Tell me the nickname, Emma."

I have no idea why this is important to him, but I oblige. "Baby bangs."

"I don't see it."

I laugh. "Thankfully."

We settle into a quiet moment with both of us sipping our wine. It's interrupted by the buzz of Case's phone.

His gaze drops to it momentarily. "It's your brother. He's wondering how you're doing, Freckles."

I cover my mouth with my hand but smile. "You didn't just call me that."

94

"Oh, I did." He punctuates his words with a swift nod. "And you liked it."

I ignore that because he's right. "Have you ever had a nickname?"

"Me?" He darts a finger into the middle of his chest. "What do you think?"

All I know is that Drake calls him Case. I've never heard him use a nickname for his best friend.

"You tell me," I challenge.

He looks me over. "I could say no."

"But that wouldn't be the honest answer, would it?" I bite my lip, studying his handsome face. "Everyone has at least one nickname in their lifetime whether they want to admit it or not."

That statement isn't based on any actual facts. I'm speaking from experience working with kids. Most, if not all, of the children I've come in contact with through work have had a nickname or two bestowed on them by their parents or a best friend.

"Is that so?" he asks, eyeing me as though he half-believes what I say. "I've had a few nicknames in my time. The first was my least favorite."

"You got that when you were a kid?"

"Yeah." He draws a finger over his bottom lip. "One of the twins who lived next door thought it would be fucking hilarious to call me Rabbit."

"Because?" My smile makes it obvious that I'm taking way too much pleasure in this.

"Before braces were slapped on these pearly whites, I had an overbite that was so severe that when someone told me to shut my mouth, I literally couldn't." He flashes me a glimpse of his perfectly straight, white teeth beneath a brilliant smile.

"So the boy next door called you Rabbit because…"

"It rhymes with Abbott and because I looked like a rabbit for a good year or two." His gaze drops to the table. "Frannie thought it was the funniest thing every time she called me that."

The twin was a girl.

"Did you have a nickname for Frannie?" I tuck a strand of hair behind my ear.

"No." He shakes his head. "She was just Frannie to me."

I run a fingernail over the rim of the wineglass in front of me. "You said that was your least favorite nickname, so what's your favorite?"

"Rush," he says without hesitation.

I blink twice. Sandy called one of her boyfriends in college Rush because he was a two-minute man in bed. She bestowed that name on him after they slept together. I'm the only person who heard her say it, but whenever we take a trip down memory lane, she brings him up.

There's no way Case earned that nickname for the same reason. Although, he did only need fifteen minutes with Maya the other night and today I overheard Maya say that their time with Pam and Rod in the bedroom was hurried.

"Why don't you seem surprised that's my nickname?" he questions with a raise of one brow.

I laugh off that comment a little too exuberantly. "My roommate in college had a boyfriend she nicknamed Rush. Who calls you that?"

Leaning back in his chair, he narrows his eyes. "Only one person does."

I might as well take this conversation to its destined end. "Is it Maya?"

He recoils back. "Maya? Why would she call me Rush?"

Dammit.

Since I don't want to answer that directly, I try a new approach. "Is it another woman?"

His brow furrows. "It's my grandfather."

"Oh," I start laughing. "I thought…well, I was wrong."

I pick up my glass and finish what's left of my wine. I look over to the bottle, but it's empty.

"Why did you think Maya or any woman would call me Rush?" His voice is gruff.

If I confess the truth, I may end up having to use the Duotrip app tonight to find a hotel room. If I lie, I may very well end up in the same spot.

Truth or lie. I weigh both as he stares at me.

"Why does your grandfather call you Rush?" I ask in a desperate last-ditch attempt to avoid the question.

"I'll tell you as soon as you answer my question."

I swear I spot a grin flash across his lips, but it disappears quickly.

Sucking in a deep breath, I fumble my way through the truth. "You didn't need much time with Maya the other night and then… today…well, today, there were four of you in the bed, and it sounded like it all happened pretty fast, so I thought…"

His laughter booms through the restaurant, drawing curious glances from the people around us. "Jesus, Emma. You thought I was a quick fuck?"

I shrug. "I overheard you talking to Maya. I just assumed…"

His brows arch. "You thought Pam and Rod were in my bed today?"

He laughs again. This time his hands dart to his face.

I watch as he clears tears away with a brush of his fingertips.

"I haven't laughed that hard in," he starts before he chuckles again. "Fuck, it's been years."

His big frame shakes as the laughter rolls through him. I sit silently watching as it slows, until he sucks in a deep breath, letting it out on a heavy exhale.

My gaze falls to the table. "I'm sorry."

"For making me laugh?" He swirls the wine left in his glass. "Or for assuming I'm a horrible fuck?"

I shrug. "Both."

He brings the glass to his mouth to swallow what's left. His tongue darts out to capture any droplets of liquid lingering on his bottom lip.

Lowering the glass, he looks at me. "Let me clear up any confusion. When I'm with a woman, I savor every moment. I take my time, and I guarantee that when we part, you'll be completely satisfied."

Freudian slip or not, I want confirmation of what I think I just heard. Before I can ask if he meant what he said, he clears his throat.

"She'll be completely satisfied," he corrects himself. "I meant *she* will be."

Chapter 20

Case

I change the subject after the slip of my tongue because I know damn well that my tongue or any other part of my body can't get near Drake's younger sister.

I wish I never met him.

"Why does your granddad call you Rush?" She asks with a wink of her eye.

I'm becoming more convinced that's a nervous twitch because I thought I saw her toss one in the direction of our server. The kid can't be older than twenty-one. Maybe I'm wrong, and Emma's interested in him, but I've noticed the way she's been watching me all night.

"My middle name is Rushton," I explain. "It was my grandmother's maiden name."

Her eyes widen. "That makes a lot more sense than what I thought."

It sure as hell does. I may have rushed in the sack when I was younger, but I've never been that fast. Nothing is more satisfying than knowing that you've given a woman a night to remember.

I take as much pride in that as I do anything else in my life.

I never want a woman to walk away from an encounter with me, wishing it hadn't happened.

"You said he's the only one who calls you that?" She tugs on the end of a strand of her hair. "No one else is allowed?"

"It's not that." I glance at the table. "My brother called me Rush for a time. That was years ago."

The server picks that moment to approach us to boast about the dessert menu. Emma scrunches her nose as she listens to him run on about the selection of gelato they offer as well as what sounds like cherry-topped cheesecake, although he gifts it with an Italian name.

"I had my fill of sugar today." She looks at me. "What about you?"

I'm tempted to order one of everything to keep us in these chairs for the next two hours, but I need to check in on Maya.

"I'm good, Freckles."

Her cheeks blush. "Okay, Rush."

I like it. I don't know why the hell I like hearing her call me that, but I could get used to it.

"Just the check, please." She moves to grab her purse. "Let me get my credit card."

"No damn way," I interject, reaching for my wallet when the server takes off. "Dinner is on me."

"That's not happening." She punctuates the words with a wave of her hand in the air. "This is partial payback for letting me crash at your apartment."

I doubt like hell I can change her mind about paying for the meal based on the look of determination in her deep brown eyes.

"Partial payback?" I chuckle. "What does that mean?"

She pushes her hair back over her shoulders, giving me an unobstructed view of her sheer blouse and the bra beneath is. "You know what it means."

I know I'm reading way too much into what's happening in front of me. I also know that my cock needs to calm the hell down.

"I owe you for letting me stay with you." She looks to where the server disappeared as she taps her credit card on the table. "If there's any way I can repay you, I want to."

Crawl into bed with me. Let me keep you there for days.

I swallow the words in favor of a decent response. "You don't have to repay me, Emma."

"I want to." She leans back in her chair.

My gaze falls to the front of her blouse and the peaks of her hardened nipples beneath the thin fabric of her bra.

If I thought I was fucked before tonight, I was an oblivious fool. I haven't had this much fun with a woman in a very long time. Now, I have to go back to my apartment and fall asleep knowing that she's in the room next to me.

***

"Maya is here?" Emma stops just short of the open doors of the elevator. "Maybe I should go across the street for a drink. I can hang out at Durie's until you two are done."

"Done?" I question with a quirk of one brow. "Done doing what exactly?"

"She's your girlfriend, right?" she asks nervously. "It's a long-distance thing, isn't it?"

I glance over to where Lester is standing. He's got one ear turned in our direction. For an older guy, his hearing is next level. I'd bet money on the fact that the man could hear a pin drop a block away.

I ignore that because I'm enjoying watching Emma try and piece together what's happening between Maya and me.

When I told her that Maya was waiting for me upstairs, the look on her face was one I won't soon forget. It was confusion mixed with curiosity. Since she's still sporting the same expression now, I gesture toward the elevator.

"I can't keep the elevator here forever, Emma." I nod my chin toward where my finger is pressed on the call button. "Get in, and let's get upstairs."

"I can go to my room," she mutters under her breath as she boards.

I follow right behind her. "Or you can hang out with Maya and me."

As the doors slide shut, she looks to me with a hint of panic in her eyes.

Emma Owens has no idea about the surprise that awaits her once we get upstairs.

Chapter 21

Emma

I'm two steps behind Case when he unlocks the apartment door, and we step into the foyer.

For a half-second I hope that Maya took the other elevator down on our way up. Maybe I won't have to bear witness to them exchanging knowing glances while I try to make small talk with the two of them.

I'm still hopeful that I can duck into the guest room in a few minutes.

"Case." I hear Maya's voice before I see her. "You're back."

With me in tow, I want to add, but I stay quiet as he drops his keys on the table of the foyer.

I spot her standing in the middle of the living room. She's wearing a blue dress that perfectly matches the color of her eyes.

Her black hair is sleekly styled.

There's nothing about her that doesn't scream confidence and success. The three simple silver bracelets she's wearing on her right wrist complement the silver watch on her left.

My gaze follows a path up her wrist to her hand and the pear-shaped sapphire ring on her finger. It's surrounded with small diamonds and nestled right next to it is a stunning band of larger diamonds.

She's married?

"Tonight was a success." She throws herself into Case's arms while I stand back watching. "It couldn't have gone better. Anton was floating on cloud nine when he left."

The pieces of this puzzle don't fit together.

Every time I turn around another person's name is tossed into the mix.

Maya takes a step back from Case. Her gaze floats past his shoulder to land squarely on my face. "Emma! I didn't see you there."

"Hi," I say with an awkward wave of my hand in the air. "It's good to see you again."

"You too." Her gaze darts from my face to Case's. "You look happy. Did you two have a good dinner?"

"Very good," he replies with a glance over his shoulder at me. "I told Emma about the nickname your sister gave me when we were kids."

I just fit two pieces of the puzzle together. Frannie and Maya are sisters.

"Rabbit?" Maya lets out a laugh. "Oh my god, Case. I remember that. Tilly was always telling her to knock it off."

"Tilly is Frannie's twin," Case offers with a curl of his finger luring me to approach them.

I do. I take a few tentative steps until I'm standing next to him.

"Case had this little issue with his teeth." Maya pulls her top teeth over her bottom lip. "It was hardly noticeable."

"Bullshit," Case fires back. "You don't think I heard you calling me Rabbit behind my back, Maya?"

Her hands drop to her hips. "Me? I would never have done that."

"You did do that." He taps the tip of her nose with his index finger.

I watch the movement. It's intimate in a way that speaks of a bond, but it's playful too. Maybe they aren't lovers. Did I read this wrong from the start?

Maya shrugs. "You've always been like a brother to us. Don't sisters tease their brothers?"

I definitely read this wrong.

"Julian's sister teases him all the time," she goes on with a glance at her left hand. "My husband loves it. I know you love it when I tease you too."

"Speaking of your husband," Case begins, stealing a glimpse at me. "How did you and Julian enjoy dinner at Nova the other night?"

"It was heaven." Her hand leaps to her chin. "The food was delicious. The wine was perfect. It was the romantic escape we needed."

"Good." He leans down to press a kiss to her forehead. "I knew Tyler would take the best care of you."

He's talking about Tyler Monroe. He's the owner and head chef of the restaurant. I know that because I saw him on a cooking segment on one of the late-night talk shows.

"Where did you two have dinner?" Maya turns her attention to me.

I don't know the name of the restaurant, so I stick with their primary offering. "We had pizza."

"Decent pizza for New York," Case interjects.

"So a good time was had by all?" Maya searches his face for something.

When Case sighs, I step in. "I had a good time."

"Case did too." She smiles at him. "I can tell."

I take that as a good sign. It's an even better sign that Maya appears happily married. I don't feel nearly as bad for semi-flirting with Case at dinner.

Maya looks to the watch on Case's wrist even though she's wearing one. "It's getting late. We need to talk. I have some news."

They need privacy, and I'm more than happy to give it to them.

"It was good to see you again, Maya." I smile at her before I look to Case. "I'll talk to you tomorrow?"

"Sure thing."

I turn and start toward the hallway, stopping when a small rectangular card on the floor catches my eye. I hear the sound of footsteps, and lowered voices as Case and Maya make their way to the foyer.

With a quick bend of my knees, I scoop the card into my palm.

Flipping it over, I read the first line etched in gold ink.

Maya Bishop. Licensed Real Estate Broker.

Chapter 22

Case

Glancing at my closed apartment door, I jab a finger into the elevator call button just as Maya pushes a finger into the middle of my chest. "You like her. You like Emma, don't you?"

"She's Drake sister," I remind her, and myself, if I'm honest.

"So?" She cocks her hip. "What does he have to do with this?"

I shake my head. "Everything."

Letting out a breath, she rolls her eyes. "In my opinion, this is none of his business."

"He's my best friend, Maya." I drag a hand through my hair. "She's off-limits."

"She's not," she stresses the words with a raise of her voice. "He doesn't get a say in what or who you want."

This is a conversation I don't want to have with her, so I change the subject. "What's the good news?"

"Pam and Rod are this close to placing an offer on the apartment." She holds her index finger and thumb an inch apart. "I can sense when an offer is imminent, and I think I'll have something concrete to put in front of you tomorrow."

I crack a smile. "No shit?"

"Anton was interested too." She brushes a hand over her shoulder. "With any luck, we'll have a bidding war on our hands."

That would be the brass ring. I'd settle for any decent offer at this point. I want the apartment out of my hands so Drake can start married life with his new bride in the place he belongs. I know what his dream future looks like, and I'm going to help him make it a reality.

That means the apartment has to sell, so he's free to pursue what he needs. He has lived here so I haven't had to come back to face this city, but all of that is changing now. New York is a part of my past, and it's time I left it there forever.

***

Thirty minutes later, I walk back into my apartment.

After I rode the elevator down to the lobby to see that Maya got safely to Drake's car and driver, I made a few calls.

Lester stood a few feet away, gathering details that he'll likely sell to anyone who will drop a dollar in his palm.

Thankfully, the calls didn't involve anything remotely sensitive personally or professionally.

I stop when I notice Emma sitting on the couch.

She's changed into black yoga shorts and a white tank top.

I don't know what the hell I did to deserve more time with her tonight, but I'll take it.

"Emma," I call to her as I drop my keys and phone on the foyer table. "I thought you turned in for the night."

She flicks a fingernail over a card in her hand. "Can we talk?"

Her tone gives nothing away. I don't know her well enough to read anything into it. If the expression on her face is a clue, this conversation is going to be a hell of a lot more serious than the one we had over dinner.

"Sure," I toss back, stalking toward her.

Whatever it is, I can handle it as long as she's not about to tell me she's as insanely attracted to me as I am to her.

If that's the case, I might have to bid farewell to my friendship with her brother.

I settle onto the leather. I give myself at least two feet from her so I can semi-focus on what she's about to say and not the fact that she's braless beneath the tank.

Whatever makeup was on her face earlier has been scrubbed clean.

She's so fucking beautiful.

"I found something on the floor," she confesses before I can say anything. "I don't understand it."

I glance down at the card in her hands. All I see is a blank white canvas. "What did you find?"

She flips it over and pushes it toward me. "Maya works in real estate. Is she selling this apartment? Does Drake know? I'm sure he would have told me if he's planning on moving, but maybe not given the fact that I had no idea he was getting married."

Her knees are bouncing and her hand is shaking. Realization hits me that words rush out of her at breakneck speed when she's anxious.

I take Maya's business card from her. This is the moment of truth.

"Drake doesn't have a clue." I lock eyes with Emma. "By the time he gets back to New York, I want this place sold."

Chapter 23

Emma

I thought Case was a decent guy, but this is proving that I'm a horrible judge of character.

How can he sell this apartment without telling Drake? Where is my brother supposed to live once he returns from his wedding?

It's not as though Drake will be homeless. He can afford to rent a nice apartment, but that's not the point.

It feels like Case is ripping the rug out from under Drake's feet. Technically, it's exquisite hardwood floors.

What a great way to start married life.

I inch back on the couch because I don't want to be too close to a man who would betray his best friend this way.

"That's unfair." I work to even my tone. "Drake would never do that to you."

I don't think he would. I have no scope of his friendship with Case. Maybe they pull these '*fuck-you*' moves on each other all the time.

It's impossibly hard for me to imagine my brother doing this to anyone though. Drake is a good man. He's always gone out of his way to help the people he cares about.

"I'm doing it for him, Emma." Case turns to face me directly. "I'm selling this place because it's time. It's time for Drake to move on."

Anger burns a path up my belly to my throat. I swallow hard, hoping to tame it so I don't say anything I'll regret. "Move on? What if he's not ready to move on or move out? Why wouldn't you talk to him about this before he left for Ireland?"

There's an undercurrent of something in his eyes. Maybe it's regret, or perhaps it's indignation that I'm questioning him on a decision that has nothing to do with me.

I don't care if it's not my place to have this discussion with him. I love my brother. I want what's best for him, and it's hard to understand how being kicked out of the home he's lived in for the past seven years without any warning benefits him.

He blows out a breath. "This was meant to be a surprise for Drake. It's part of my wedding gift for him."

A laugh bubbles inside of me. It's not based in joy. It's bitter. I don't let it escape. Instead, I slap my hand on the couch next to me, knowing that I'll likely be packing my suitcase headed for a hotel within the hour. "This is the surprise you mentioned? Tossing Drake out on his ass is definitely a wedding gift he'll never forget."

A ghost of a smile plays on Case's lips. "You love him a lot, don't you? You'd go to battle for him."

I have no idea why he finds that amusing, but I nod. "I'd do anything for him."

"Me too," he affirms with a heavy exhale. "Your brother's dream is to move to London with Jane, so I'm doing everything in my power to make that happen."

***

Drake is moving to London.

My mom and dad are going to retire in Florida in three months, and Whitney is headed to Ohio for college at the end of summer.

Everything's changing so fast. It's too fast.

It's been less than a week since my parents dropped their bombshell on me. I've known about Whitney's acceptance into Ohio State for months, but watching her gleefully start packing last week was a stark reminder that soon she won't call Seattle home.

"How long has Drake been thinking about moving to London?" I ask, rubbing both hands over my eyes.

"I'm not sure," Case confesses. "He didn't tell me he wanted to make the move."

My head darts up. "Who told you? Jane?"

"We've never met." He half-laughs. "Drake mentioned her a couple of months ago once things were serious between them."

Envy shoots through me knowing that Drake confided in Case.

I've shared a lot with my brother since he moved to the east coast. He did the same, although he was always so focused on work that almost everything he told me revolved around that.

"I first heard London mentioned last month during a phone call with our branding manager here in New York." He exhales slowly. "He told me that Drake was throwing out ideas about working remotely from London. He planned to be in the office here two weeks a month and then spend the other two with Jane in London."

"She lives there?"

He brushes a hand over his knee. "Her family does. They have a business that's ready to change hands to the next generation. Jane's the one to take that on."

"You never talked to Drake about any of this?" I sigh. "Why wouldn't he discuss this with you?"

His gaze floats around the apartment. "I believe he thought he'd be letting me down. He's kept the New York office running on his own for years. Doing that remotely isn't an easy task. I'm learning that firsthand. Things are piling up back in San Francisco that I need to take care of in person."

He's trying to help my brother by giving him an out.

"Newlyweds shouldn't spend half their time apart." He chuckles. "I don't want that for Drake. He should be all-in on this marriage. Selling the apartment and setting up an office in London is the way to make that happen."

Shocked, I stare at him. "You're setting up an office for Cabbott in London so Drake can move there?"

"I'm helping your brother live the life he deserves." His gaze drops to the floor. "He's done more for me than I had a right to ask for, so this is my way of paying him back. A London office has been on our radar for a few years. I can't think of a better time to make it a reality."

I sit in silence, absorbing everything he just told me.

"Selling this apartment is the right move for Drake and me." He inches toward me. "He's lived here for this long because he knew I'd have a hell of a time letting this place go, but it's time."

"I didn't realize the apartment meant that much to you," I say, fishing for more.

"Not to me." He shakes his head. "It meant a lot to someone I cared about, but that was years ago. It's time to hand it over to someone else."

Chapter 24

Case

I wait for her to ask me the question I know is sitting on the tip of her tongue. My gaze drops to her pretty lips.

The fire that was in her when she decided to step up to the plate and go to bat for her brother caught me off guard.

I like that she didn't back down when she thought I screwed Drake over.

"Thank you for explaining all of that to me." Her shoulders push forward. "You're doing a lot for Drake. I know he'll appreciate it."

I didn't expect her to skip past my declaration about this apartment holding special meaning to someone I cared about. I thought she'd press for more details.

Opening up to her about that isn't going to happen. I've been hanging on by the barest thread since I got to New York. I need to leave this place in my past.

"When will you tell him?" She tugs on the hem of the tank top, stretching it taut over her breasts.

I force my gaze to her face. "Tomorrow. On his birthday."

"It's his wedding day too," she adds.

Drake's life is changing at warp speed. I'm happy for him. I don't know anyone who deserves this more than he does.

"So Pam and Rod were looking at the apartment?" Emma nudges her knee closer to mine. "Maya mentioned someone named Anton. Is that another prospective buyer?"

Since I let the cat out of the bag, there's no reason not to share the details with Emma. "Several people have looked at this place. Maya feels confident that she's found a buyer. She'll know more tomorrow."

"It's a beautiful apartment." She lowers her gaze to the coffee table. "The first time I came to visit Drake, I almost fell over out of shock when I walked through the door."

I felt the same way seven years ago when I followed a real estate broker into the apartment.

It was more than I ever imagined I'd be able to afford, but I made an all cash offer that day. It was accepted immediately.

It took sixty days to close on the deal, but once it did, all three thousand square feet belonged to me.

"He told you the place was his?" I've been meaning to ask her about that since the night we met. "What exactly did he say?"

She lets out a laugh. "It's more about what he didn't say. He didn't correct my assumption that he owned this place."

That sounds like Drake. He's always strived for the best of the best. I knew when I walked out of here seven years ago that he'd pass off the apartment as his own.

I don't give a damn.

If it did something for him, I won't cut him down for that.

"He's taken good care of it." I choose my next words carefully. "When I moved to California, I left everything here in his hands. I couldn't have asked for a better friend."

Her eyes scan my face. "You're a good friend to him too. He's told me as much since he talks about you non-stop."

I doubt like hell she knows my full story. Drake once told me it wasn't his to tell, and I've held him to that for years.

If she's baiting me, I'm willing to bite. "What do you know about me?"

"You like surfing," she sounds back.

I'd say it's in my blood, but I didn't pick up a board until a few years ago. I learned the basics and all my time on the water since has perfected my technique enough that I can hold my own.

I'm not in the running to win any competitions, but I can hit the ocean confident that I'll ride a wave or two.

"What else has your brother told you about me?" I ask quietly, wondering whether Drake offered information or if she inquired.

For some reason, I want it to be the latter.

"You've never been married?"

"Is that a question?" I call her out on the way she phrased her words. "That sounded like a question."

She settles back onto the couch, gripping her hands together in her lap. Her cheeks blush. "You're single. You've never been married."

True. I convey that to her with a silent nod.

"What about you, Emma? Married, divorced, engaged, dating someone?"

I don't waste the opportunity to pry into her life. I've been curious since I first saw her.

Her gaze drops to her left hand. "I was engaged. I'm not anymore."

Who the hell is the idiot who put a ring on her finger and didn't seal the deal?

"You were engaged? To who?" I blurt out.

Her brows pop up. "Beauregard Garrington."

He sounds like a pretentious son-of-bitch.

"Our dads are old friends. We work together. It seemed like it all fit …" Her voice trails.

"Until it didn't?" I finish.

She nods. "I broke it off because I knew he wasn't my forever."

"How did Beau take that?"

A smile blooms on her lips. "He hated it whenever I called him that."

Jesus. This guy is not only pretentious; he's a goddamn idiot.

"He said he knew I'd bail." She shakes her head. "He told me I was a disappointment to everyone."

I'd pull her into my arms to comfort her, but she doesn't look like she needs it. She seems content.

"When did this happen, Emma?"

Her mouth twitches. "I gave Beauregard the ring back a week ago. It was the same day he told me to find a new job."

Chapter 25

Emma

I just confessed to Case what I came to New York City to tell my brother.

When I broke up with Beau, I called Drake, but he was in a meeting. He returned my call a few hours later, but I was at a yoga class at the gym. My phone was silenced in my locker.

The voicemail message my brother left me was focused on the fact that he was in the middle of a crisis with a competitor. He was on his way to see one of Cabbott's lawyers.

I listened to the message all the while staring at my bare ring finger, feeling a sense of relief I hadn't in a long time.

Beau was wrong for me even though my entire family thought he was my prince charming. Drake was his biggest fan. My brother worked summers in high school with Beau at my dad's car dealership.

Two years ago, when I told Drake I was going on my first date with Beauregard, he was more excited than I was.

"Bonehead is your boss?" Case shoves his hand through his hair.

I laugh at the nickname. It's perfect. "Bonehead?"

Case's brows pinch together. "I've never met the asshole, but I can tell he's a bonehead. Hell, he's a lot worse than that for the shit he's pulling, but bonehead seems to fit."

"Like a glove," I say. "I work for The Garrington Academy. It's a private school in Seattle. Technically, Beauregard's dad is my boss."

He looks at me for several seconds as if he's debating whether to delve more into my connection to the Garringtons. "What's his stance on your job?"

"I haven't spoken to Archibald yet." I shrug. "He's very by the book, so I don't think he'll fire me because I dumped his son."

"Archibald?" Case grins. "What century were these people born in?"

"The one where you don't have sex until you're married," I quip.

I don't know why I shared that. I knew Beau's stance on sex after our third date, but I continued to see him. I thought he would want to be intimate once we became engaged, but he held tight to his belief that waiting for marriage was right for him.

I respected that about him until he shamed me for the fun I had before we started dating.

That was the day our relationship suffered a crack that was too deep to be repaired.

Case tilts his head back to look at me. "You're a virgin?"

"No. Before Beau there were men," I answer quickly.

"How old are you, Emma?"

I'd change the subject, but I'm enjoying this too much. With each question, he inches closer by a breath.

"Twenty-five," I say softly.

His eyes rake over my shirt. I know that my nipples have hardened beneath the thin fabric. He's looking at me in a way that makes me want to race to my room, climb in bed, and bring myself to orgasm.

I've never seen desire this intense in a man's gaze before.

"You don't need me to tell you this," he pauses for a beat. "But, you were engaged to the biggest dumbass on this planet."

Laughter escapes me.

Case's voice lowers. "Bonehead's loss is my…"

My eyes widen as his voice trails.

Finish it, Case. Please say it. Tell me that Beau's loss is your gain.

The words stall inside of me. I don't say them. Instead, I bite back a curse word when Case's phone starts up on a ring.

"For fuck's sake," he mutters as he darts to his feet and races toward the foyer table.

"It's Drake," he announces. "He wants to video chat. What the hell time is it in Ireland?"

My mind is so consumed by what Case almost confessed that I go blank. I can't do quick math in my head right now, even though it's a skill that I use to semi-impress my students back home.

"It's tomorrow." I wrinkle my nose embarrassed that I can't be more specific. "It's already tomorrow in Ireland."

Case glances at me before his finger swipes the screen of his phone.

"Cason!" Drake's voice booms through the living room. "Guess what today is, buddy?"

Crossing the floor toward me, Case smiles. "Happy Birthday to you!"

"And Happy Wedding Day!" I call from where I'm sitting.

"Is that Em?" Drake's voice takes on a higher pitch. "Let me see her."

Case plops himself down on the couch next to me with his left arm extended and his phone in hand. His thigh is pressed against mine; his right elbow jammed into my side. My breath catches as he leans in until his cheek almost brushes against the side of my face. "Here she is."

I glance down at the front of my shirt, grateful that it's not in Drake's view.

"Up here, Emma." Drake laughs. "Look at me."

I do.

I smile at my older brother. Pure happiness is radiating from him.

"Happy Birthday, Drake," I whisper. "You're officially old."

Case playfully jabs his elbow deeper into my side. "I'm right on his tail. My thirtieth isn't that far away."

We lock eyes for a second before I shift my gaze back to the screen of Case's phone. "Are you nervous about the wedding?"

"Not nervous." Drake pushes his glasses up the bridge of his nose. "I'm fucking excited."

"Is Jane there?" I ask, hopefully.

This isn't how I anticipated meeting my brother's future wife, but I'll take it. I want to congratulate the woman who has made him this happy.

"She's asleep." He rakes a hand through his brown hair. "A few hours from now, I'm going to tell her that we're getting married."

Case huffs out a laugh. "Are you sure she's all right with this? You're not giving her any warning here, Drake."

I don't fault him for the question even though it chases the smile away from my brother's face. If Beauregard had planned our entire wedding and surprised me with it on the day he wanted me to become his wife, I would have run for the nearest exit.

Maybe Jane is different. I hope that she has the same adventurous spirit as Drake.

"She'll be over the moon," he says convincingly. "We're on the same page. A wedding, kids, homes in New York, and London. We've got this mapped out."

Case pushes himself even closer to me. "London? What's that about London?"

Drake sets back in the leather armchair he's sitting in. "Shit. I meant to talk to you about that. I've got this plan, Case. It's good for business. Great for me, but I hope you'll see the value in it."

"I've got a plan too." Case glances at me before he levels his gaze back on his phone. "I'm selling the apartment. I want you in London with Jane full-time."

Drake's glasses are in his hand in an instant. When he looks back at the screen, there are tears in his eyes. "What the fuck? I know what that apartment means to you, man. You're selling it?"

"I'm selling it so we can both move on with our lives." Case exhales sharply. "It's time, Drake. We're setting up an office for Cabbott in London. I need you there. Your wife needs you there. We'll work out the details once you're back on this side of the ocean."

"You're serious?" Drake's voice cracks.

"Dead serious," Case responds in a tone that conveys that message. "Blair Montgomery is taking over your duties here next month. I already gave her the heads-up."

"Thank you, man," Drake says quietly. "I can never repay you for everything you've done for me. Everything you're doing for me."

"Let's call it even," Case shoots back.

Drake nods before he shifts his gaze to me. "Can you believe it, Em? I'm getting married. I'm moving to London. Life is full of surprises, isn't it?"

I turn to catch Case staring at me.

"It sure as hell is," he says in a low voice. "You never know what life has in store for you."

Chapter 26

Emma

Case's words bring goose bumps to my skin. I break his gaze when I hear Drake clear his throat.

"Are you two okay?" he asks with a laugh. "It looks like you're keeping a secret."

I wish we were.

"No secrets here." Case edges his hand closer to mine.

"How's Beauregard?" Drake slides his glasses back on. "Is he planning on joining you in New York, Em? It would be great to see him once Jane and I are back."

Case scoops my hand into his. He squeezes it gently.

I look to him because I don't know if this is the right time to tell my brother that my journey to married bliss is over. This is Drake's wedding day. I don't want to drag my drama into it.

Case dips his chin slightly in a nod. "*Tell him*," he mouths.

"Should I?" I question back quietly.

"Should you what?" Drake asks as he inches closer to the camera on his tablet. "What's going on, Em? I know something is up. You didn't sound like yourself on our call the other night."

I turn my attention to my brother even though Case is circling my palm with the pad of his thumb. It's both comforting and arousing. His touch is light, but there's a promise of something more beneath it.

"I ended things with Beauregard."

Drake's eyes widen beneath the dark frames of his glasses. "What?"

The confused look on his face mirrors what I saw when I told my parents that I called off my engagement. They were shocked. My mom cried. My dad left their house to rush off to talk things over with Archibald.

I was left standing in the middle of their kitchen, watching my mom mourn the death of my relationship.

It wasn't until I told Whitney that I felt the comfort of a hug and heard words of encouragement.

To quote my sister, "*You're too badass for that loser. He doesn't trim his ear hair, Em. He was never the guy for you.*"

"I'm not marrying him." I straighten my shoulders.

"You love him," Drake insists. "You two were meant to be."

I blow out a heavy breath. "I cared for him, but I don't think I ever truly loved him, Drake. I made the choice that was right for me."

Feeling confident in my declaration, I glance at Case. He offers me an encouraging nod.

"You might regret this. What if you wake up a year from now and wish you were still with him?"

The words sting because my brother is questioning my heart's choice. It's almost word-for-word what my dad said to me the day after he spoke to Archibald about the break-up.

I tell Drake what I told my dad. "I can't settle based on what-ifs. I didn't love him. I loved myself enough to realize that before I made the biggest mistake of my life."

Silence surrounds me as Drake mulls those words over, and Case sits next to me, stroking my palm with his fingertips. He's offering me the encouragement I didn't realize I'd need.

My brother's approval has always meant the world to me, but I'm not a kid anymore. I don't need to see eye-to-eye with anyone on this. I have to find peace within myself and I do.

"We'll talk about this more when I'm back in New York." Drake yawns. "I'm dead tired, Em. I need to catch a few hours of sleep before I marry my girl."

I ignore the comment about continuing the conversation, because as far as I'm concerned, the discussion is over. I've made my decision regarding my ex-fiancé.

"You'll hang out in New York until I'm back, won't you?" Drake asks. "Promise me you will."

"As long as you're back soon." I nod. "There are things I need to take care of at home."

"She can stay as long as she likes, Drake," Case pipes up.

I look over at him. His eyes are pinned to me.

"Good." Drake's voice lures my gaze back to the phone's screen. "You should check in with Elias tonight, Case. There's an issue with the new app launch."

I glance down when I feel Case's hand slide from mine.

He shifts the screen of the phone so his is the only face in Drake's view. "What issue? I thought we were on track with the launch of Letter…"

"There's a recurring error in the framework," Drake interrupts.

Case's shoulders tighten. "We're less than three months from our launch date. This is coming up now?"

"It's been ongoing." Drake yawns again. "I left it in the hands of our lead software engineer, but he quit. I've got a new guy on it now."

"A new guy who doesn't know what the hell he's doing?" Case leans closer to the phone's screen.

"He'll figure it out, but Elias dropped me a message to tell me that it's taking longer than I wanted, so it's worth looking into."

Case's clenched fist on his thigh says more than any words can. He's frustrated.

"I'm ending this now to call Elias," he warns my brother. "Enjoy the day, Drake."

"Goodnight to all," Drake calls out.

Case is on his feet as soon as the screen goes dark. "I need to go to the office, Emma. This is important."

"I understand." I move to stand.

As he reaches the foyer table to scoop up his keys, I take a step closer. "I want to thank you for that."

He turns on his heel. "For what?"

"Helping me tell Drake about Beauregard."

A ghost of a smile flashes across his lips as his hand curls around the doorknob. "Your brother needs to accept that Bonehead is not the guy for you."

Are you?

I open my mouth to ask, but before I say the words, Case is stepping out of the apartment. He tosses me a glance over his shoulder. "Goodnight, Emma."

"Night," I whisper even though the door is already closing behind him.

Chapter 27

Case

"I should be saving lives, not listening to you bitch about some framework for a kiddie game."

"It's called Letter Leap." I glance at my cousin. "I thought you said you were done being Dr. Fuller for the day. Your shift ended two hours ago, no?"

Fighting off a smile, he stares at me. "I'm a man of medicine, Cason. My work is never done."

I bark out a laugh. "Is that why you're drinking water and not scotch?"

I hold up my almost empty glass not only to punctuate my point but to get Kendall's attention. I need a refill.

Asking Gavin to meet me at Durie's after I spent three hours with Elias was a good idea, whether my cousin wants to admit it or not.

"You said we needed to hang out while I'm in town," I point out. "I didn't promise the conversation would be great."

Gavin looks to Kendall instead of commenting on my remark. "She's about to cut you off."

I shake my head. "I've had one drink. I'm not even close to my limit."

"The bar shuts down in twenty minutes." He points at his watch. "Maybe you didn't realize that you called me after midnight. You're still running on California time, aren't you?"

"What can I do for you two?" Kendall stops next to Gavin. "Are you still nursing that water, Doctor?"

She lets out a stuttered giggle at her attempt at a joke.

Gavin huffs out a strangled laugh even though I can tell he didn't find it funny. He moves to grab his wallet from the inner pocket of his suit jacket. Pulling out a few bills, he drops them on the bar. "We're both fine. We're set to leave."

Her gaze inches its way up Gavin's arm to his face. "I'm heading over to a club in Midtown after I lock up. Do you want to tag along?"

Gavin's been in this pub with Drake. He greeted Kendall by name when we sat down, but before I could ask how well they know each other, he'd shot me down with a slap on my shoulder and a reminder that he doesn't dick around with anyone Drake has been with.

Their friendship formed because of me, but I'm happy to see that it's still going strong.

"Thanks, but there's somewhere I need to be," he says with a grin.

Home in bed is the place he wants to be. I've heard it twice since he walked in. I can tell that he's dead tired, but after what happened between Emma and me earlier, I needed a stiff drink before I walk back into my apartment knowing she's in bed.

I hope to hell she's asleep.

I don't trust myself at this point not to kiss her, or touch her. With my dick driving my desire, I'd be all in with little regard for my friendship with her brother.

Kendall shrugs. "If you change your mind, let me know."

Scooping up the money, she sets off toward a table surrounded by men in suits.

"I doubt like hell Drake would mind if you took her home," I offer.

"I'd mind." He sets a hand on my forearm. "You're too immature to understand that."

I laugh. "You're what...four or five years older than me?"

"Three." He waves three fingers in my face. "I'm three years older. That means I'm wise enough to know that you didn't drag my ass down here to talk about work. What's going on?"

The change in his tone sets an alarm off inside of me.

I know what he's thinking and he's so far off base that I stop him before he can dive headfirst into the one subject of discussion I want no part of.

Gavin is a healer. It's in his blood. If he sees someone in pain, he wants to step in and do his part.

He helped me when I needed it, but I'm not looking for his sympathy tonight.

"Emma," I spit out her name. "Goddamn Emma Owens."

He sits back on the stool. "You fucked her?"

My gaze darts to his face. "Hell no."

He laughs. "You want to fuck her."

"Hell yes," I admit.

"You're worried about Drake." He points out the obvious. "You think he'll be pissed."

"He will be pissed," I spit each word out slowly. "Do you remember what happened when I took Annabeth Carson to bed?"

"I don't believe you shared all the details." He chuckles. "I vaguely remember you got laid and that ended with a black eye and a broken nose."

I was twenty. Annabeth was a year younger and the sister of a guy I knew named Aaron. Drake was a better friend to her brother than I was, but that didn't matter to Aaron.

The strength behind the punch Aaron threw that connected with my face said it all. He saw my actions as a betrayal.

Drake took Aaron's side in that battle. He railed on me for fucking a friend's sister. It took months for us to get back to where we were before that.

I promised Drake I'd keep my hands off the sisters of all of our friends.

That vow means that I can't get any closer to Emma than I was tonight.

"That was almost ten years ago," Gavin points out. "Drake hasn't exactly been following any fuck rules the past few years. You do know he screwed one of my exes, right? He fucked Kaia."

Every time Drake brought up another conquest, I'd tune him out. I doubt like hell the women he was mentioning by name signed off on him sharing what they like in bed.

The only reason I recalled Kendall's name is that he talked about how they got along when he stopped after work for a beer. She was a friend to him before their one night stand.

"That doesn't give me a pass," I say tightly.

Gavin taps the back of my head with his palm. "Stop this shit."

"What the fuck, Fuller?" I lightly punch him in the shoulder.

"You have the right to go after what you want." He pushes the water glass in front of him to the side so he can rest his elbow on the bar. "Drake's off living his life. You need to do that too. If you feel a connection with this woman, act on it. If it turns into more than a hookup, Drake will have to deal."

"It won't turn into more." I shake my head. "Emma lives in Seattle. I'm grounded in California."

"So, you have fun while you're both in New York." He glances at his watch. "You and Emma are adults. You can handle this and Drake if it comes to that."

I swallow what's left of the scotch in my glass. "It won't come to that. We're going our separate ways in a few days. If anything happens between Emma and I, it ends when we leave New York."

Chapter 28

Emma

Lazybones.

That's one of the nicknames my dad gifted me with.

I held onto that proudly the summer after eighth grade when I couldn't find the energy to get out of bed until noon most days.

That lasted all of two weeks before my dad ordered me to get up as he was leaving for work one day. He handed me a list of chores that needed to be done around the house.

My reward for completing the list was a new wardrobe for high school.

I spent most of that summer at home tending to my mother's vegetable garden and painting the massive picket fence surrounding their property. The hard work and commitment to complete every task on the list taught me the value of getting out of bed early.

I thought that my internal clock would have kept me snoozing until at least nine a.m. New York time, but it's barely past seven and I'm wide awake.

This is solid proof that I've outgrown the Lazybones nickname for good.

I crawl out of bed and dash to the door of my room.

I didn't hear Case come home last night because I fell asleep twenty minutes after he left.

Resting my right ear against the door, I whisper, "I hope you're in your bed."

"Alone," I tack on for good measure before I close my eyes and suck in a deep breath.

Even though the only thing that happened between us last night was some innocent handholding, it was more action with a man than I've seen since I agreed to go on my first date with Beauregard.

Since I hear absolutely nothing coming from outside the door, I stretch. "He's asleep. He's fast asleep dreaming about you."

Sighing, I look around the room.

It's much bigger than the bedroom in my condo. Since I'm all about space and comfort when I sleep, I managed to squeeze a king-sized bed into the room when I moved in. If I want to open my dresser drawers, I have to stand to the side, since they hit the foot of the bed before they are fully open.

I don't plan on staying in that condo forever, but for now, it's an almost perfect fit.

I hear a knock in the distance.

Pressing my ear to the door again, I wonder if it's Case.

Silence greets me.

Swinging around, I grab a pair of black yoga shorts off an armchair in the corner. It's become the collection zone for my clothes. Every morning, I tidy things up, make the bed, and hide my suitcase in the closet.

A persistent louder knock starts up.

I trek across the room and open the door to peer out.

The knock has turned into an all-out series of bangs.

Rushing from the room, I turn the corridor and race into the foyer.

Maybe it's Case on the other side of the apartment door. Did he forget his keys last night? Am I about to witness a walk of shame?

Sucking in a deep breath, I march toward the door and swing it open with a flourish.

"Miss Owens," Lester greets me with wide eyes. "Oh dear. I woke you up."

The dead giveaway is the state of my hair. I know that I toss and turn at night. My hair must look like I haven't brushed it in days.

I try and smooth it down with the palm of my hand, but it's useless. I feel it spring back to its unruly state the second my fingers run over it.

"I was awake," I confess. "I was listening for…"

Nope. I will not tell Lester that I was listening for Case because I have no clue if my roommate came home last night. The man standing in front of me will sell a secret for a dollar.

Lester waits for me to finish, but I laugh. "I was listening to the chirping birds outside my window."

"Birds?" His brows perch. "I've heard a siren or two this morning. A multitude of car horns as expected. I can't say I've heard the sweet sound of a bird, though."

I look down and realize that I'm still wearing the same thin tank top I was last night.

Great. Now Lester has seen me braless.

Wanting this to be over, I glance over my shoulder. "Do you need to talk to Case? I can wake him up."

Hopefully he's in his bedroom wearing boxer briefs *or less.*

I smile at the mental image of that.

"No, no." Lester chuckles. "Mr. Abbott left for the office an hour ago. I'm here with a special delivery for you."

My gaze drops to his hands. "What the fu…?"

"Breakfast," Lester interrupts. "There are bagels. It appears to be a dozen. You'll find cream cheese and a container of fresh berries in the other bag. The perfect accompaniment is this coffee from Palla on Fifth."

He pushes two white paper bags at me, along with a large cup of coffee.

I reach for it all. "Wow. I wasn't expecting this."

With a bright smile, Lester tips his chin. "Mr. Abbott arranged it for you. A courier dropped the bagels at the front desk. They are from an establishment called Bright Bagels, I believe. I picked up the rest myself. The coffee contains one cream and one sugar. I hope it's to your liking."

How am I holding a bag from Bright Bagels right now?

Tears threaten my eyes.

No one has ever gone to this much trouble for me.

"Thank you," I whisper to Lester.

"You're very welcome," he says in a soft tone. "One more thing, Miss Owens."

I glance up at his kind face. "What is it?"

"Mr. Abbott asked me to deliver this message to you." Reaching into his pocket, he tugs out a piece of paper. Its edges are jagged as if it was torn from the corner of a newspaper. I catch a glimpse of something written in red ink.

Clearing his throat, he takes a deep breath. "I hope you enjoy breakfast, Freckles, as much as I enjoyed dinner last night."

Chapter 29

Emma

Two hours later, I'm satiated, showered, and standing on the sidewalk outside Sweet Bluebells.

Even though the bookstore Bella wants to take me to is just a few blocks from where she lives in Brooklyn, she insisted on meeting here. She told me in a text that she's been craving a chocolate chip cookie from the bakery since she woke up, so I happily agreed to make my way here.

The text message I sent to her was my second of the day.

I sent a quick one to Case first to thank him for the feast of a breakfast he arranged.

I slide my finger over my phone's screen and reread it.

Emma: *Thank you for the surprise, Rush.*

He hasn't responded yet, but I know that he's busy, even if it is Saturday morning. Drake has never followed a strict Monday to Friday schedule since he started working at Cabbott. I doubt that Case does either.

I swing open the door to the bakery to find it bustling with people.

I can't say I'm surprised. In addition to the display case full of cupcakes, there are a few wicker baskets near the cash register filled with a selection of muffins and cookies.

I spot Delaney behind the counter.

With a quick turn of her head, she sees me. I'm greeted with a big smile and a wave of her hand.

I reply in kind.

"Emma!"

I turn to the left when I hear my name.

"I'm here," Bella calls out from a table in the corner. "I got you a lemonade and a blueberry muffin."

I start toward her, being careful to maneuver around the people waiting in line to pick out a weekend morning treat.

Once I skirt around a couple sharing a kiss in the middle of the store, I realize Bella isn't alone. A young boy is sitting at the table next to her, his gaze glued to the screen of a tablet.

"Hey," I say softly as I take a seat across from Bella. "You're quick. You came all the way from Brooklyn and beat me here."

She lets out a laugh. "Pregnancy cravings dictate my life. I was on the subway before we finished texting."

"Thank you for ordering for me." I glance at the blond-haired boy. "Who is this?"

"Mickey." The little boy rubs his hand over his jean-covered knee before he offers it to me. "It's nice to meet you, Ma'am."

Bella lets out a little giggle, and I can't help but smile. I take his hand in mine and give it a soft shake. "I'm Emma. It's nice to meet you, Mickey."

His blue eyes flick over my face. "Do you know my mom?"

I look at Bella. I assumed the baby she's expecting was her first, but maybe I'm wrong. I perk a brow. "Are you…?"

"This handsome guy belongs to Delaney." Bella points to the counter. "She doesn't usually work weekends, but she was called in to help with the morning rush. Mickey was in the kitchen when I got here. His mom asked if I could keep an eye on him."

I was looking forward to going to the bookstore, but I'm happy with a morning spent here. Mickey is a little younger than the kids I taught last semester. I'm a floater at The Garrington School, so wherever I'm needed, I jump in to help.

I'm in consideration for a permanent position teaching third grade, but Archibald will have the final say on that before school starts again in the fall.

"Are you playing a game?" I inch my head closer to Mickey's.

"Gem Stars," he answers quickly. "It's my fave."

I'm about to score big points with this little person. "Did you get up to level twelve yet?"

His head pops up. Blond curls bounce against his forehead. "No one gets past level eleven. It's way too hard."

With a brush of his hand over his face, he drops his gaze back down.

I glance at Bella to find a huge smile on her face. I grin back before I turn my attention to Mickey. "I finished the game."

His mouth drops open. "No way."

"Way," I bounce back. "I conquered level twenty and found the prize at the end."

"It's a super gem, right?" His eyes scan my face. "Is that what it is?"

Leaning forward, I look over his tablet. "You'll find out once you get there."

Disappointment mars his expression. "You're like seventeen. I'm six. What if it takes me forever to do it?"

Bella giggles from across the table. "Seventeen?"

I shoot her a wink. "I'm twenty-five, but thank you, Mickey."

He shakes his head as though he can't follow the conversation. "Can you tell me some cheats?"

"I can give you a hint or two," I offer with a grin, not adding the fact that I'm the sister of the man who created the game.

I made the mistake of offering that tidbit of information to a class I was teaching back in Seattle. The students overran me with requests to talk to Drake so I arranged a videoconference with him and the kids.

I thought it would be an informative hour spent talking about the benefits of hard work and dedication in order to reach your career goals, but it turned into chaos quickly.

Most of the kids wanted to know how to overcome an obstacle in the game, or where the hidden treasure boxes were located.

I swore that day that I'd never again mention to any child that my brother is a video game developer.

"Thanks." Mickey smiles before he looks down to his tablet.

"I want those hints too." Bella taps her hand on the top of the table. "I've been stuck on level nine for days. Give me all the tips, Emma. Share your wisdom with me."

I laugh. "I'm happy to."

I glance back over my shoulder to see Delaney with a wide grin on her face. I know that look. It's the same look I see when I tell a parent at school that their child is not only smart, but polite.

I've only spent ten minutes with Mickey, but I can tell he's both.

Chapter 30

Case

I smile when I glance up from Drake's desk and spot Emma standing in the doorway.

"There you are," I say, pushing back to stand.

She flicks her hair back over her shoulder. She's wearing white pants and a light blue T-shirt. It's casual, but she looks incredible in it.

I put on a pair of jeans and a black T-shirt before I took off from the apartment this morning. Elias thought one of the software engineers found a possible fix to the framework issue overnight, so I came in early. We're still working toward a solution, but I'm confident that we'll have a breakthrough soon. It's essential if we're going to keep the game's launch on schedule.

Emma looks me over. "Your text said I should stop by if I found myself close to here."

It did say that. When I finally checked my phone mid-afternoon, I noticed the text that Emma had sent to me. I fired one back to her over an hour ago suggesting she drop in if she had the chance.

"I'm sorry I didn't respond sooner." I approach her. "I'm glad that breakfast hit the spot."

My gaze drops to her stomach. It's hidden beneath the shirt. What I wouldn't give to get a glimpse of more of her skin; more of her.

She tilts her head to the left. "It was delicious. They don't make Bright Bagels in Manhattan. You didn't get them from Seattle, did you?"

The surprise in her tone spurs me on. I don't usually take credit for my good deeds, but I'm willing to make an exception so I can see her reaction.

"I did."

"How?" she huffs out a nervous laugh. "How is that even possible? I just told you about them last night during dinner."

Anything is possible with enough money and determination.

"I had them delivered." I cross my arms over my chest.

Her gaze falls to my arms before it levels back on my face. "You had a bag of bagels delivered from the other side of the country just for me?"

I nod. "Yes."

Her hand leaps to her mouth. Her trembling fingers are trying to mask a smile.

"How much did that cost?" she whispers. "It must have been a fortune."

I move closer, reaching up to glide my fingers over hers. "It was worth every penny to see that smile you're trying to hide."

***

A rap on the doorframe behind Emma draws her back a full step.

My hand falls from her face.
Jesus. I was about to kiss her.
What the fuck is wrong with me?

"Mr. Abbott," Elias says my name tentatively. "I just got back from checking in with one of our software engineers, sir."

I keep my eyes on Emma's face. "Good."

Her gaze shoots over her shoulder. "Hey."

"Hey." Elias takes a step toward her. "I'm Elias."

"Drake's assistant," I add. "This is Emma. She's Drake's sister."

Elias points a finger in Emma's direction. "You're the teacher, right? Mr. Owens has told me a lot about you."

Apparently, Drake didn't hold back when it came to talking about his sister to his assistant. I'm the only one in the dark when it comes to Emma.

"Mr. Owens mentioned you were engaged. How's Beauregard?" Elias drops his gaze to Emma's left hand.

She tucks it into the front pocket of her jeans. "I'm sure he's fine. We're not together anymore."

There's no hint of sadness or regret in her tone.

I'm glad Drake's reaction to her ending the engagement didn't deter her from owning her decision.

"I'm sorry to hear that," Elias says, but the smile on his face tells a different story.

I catch him checking out Emma from head-to-toe, so I tilt up a brow in question.

He shrugs that off and keeps his focus on her. "Do you need a guide to show you around the city? I'm free this afternoon. I'm all yours as soon as Mr. Abbott leaves."

I'll keep him here until she boards a plane back to Seattle.

"There's no need for that," I interject. "I'm more than capable of entertaining Emma while she's here."

That draws Elias's brow up in response. "I'm sure Mr. Owens would be happy to know that since he's very protective of both of his sisters."

He follows that up with a smirk.

Is he threatening me? If he is, he can kiss any chance of a promotion goodbye.

"Thank you, but I won't be in New York very long." Emma lets him down easy with a pat on his shoulder. "I'll be sure to let my brother know that you offered to take me out."

Elias steps back. I flash him a cocky grin because now he's the one being threatened. I seriously doubt Emma meant it that way, but Elias sure as hell doesn't want Drake to think that he's making a move on his sister.

"Just to show you the sights," Elias clarifies. "I forgot to mention that my sister would be going with us. Please make sure Mr. Owens knows that part when you talk to him about me."

With his rail-thin legs quivering, Elias takes a step back. "I'll send you the engineer's latest report on the framework via the interoffice messaging service, sir."

"That'll work," I volley back. "You're free to go."

Emma turns to watch him hightail it out of the office. Once he's out of sight, she glances at me. "Is he always like that?"

"Like what?" I chuckle.

She pivots on her heel until she's facing me again. "Quirky. Awkward. He's kind of cute."

I bite the corner of my lip to curtail a smile. "You like that? Is that your type?"

Shrugging, she looks me over. "I haven't decided what my type is."

I shouldn't give a fuck about that, but I do.

I want to be this woman's type more than I want to be friends with her brother. Maybe it's time for Drake to find a new best friend because I want Emma more and more with each passing second.

Chapter 31

Emma

"What did you do today, Emma?"

I take that question to mean that our flirting session has come to an abrupt halt. I thought before Elias interrupted us, that Case was going to try and kiss me.

"I spent a few hours at the cupcake shop with Bella Calvetti and a little boy who is a huge fan of Gem Stars."

My mention of one of Cabbott's most popular games gets his attention. "Really?"

Why does he seem surprised by that?

At the airport, while I was waiting at the gate for my connecting flight to New York, I could hear the signature music that starts up the game coming from many of the seats surrounding me.

It's an addictive game. I should know. When Drake sent me a link to download the test version, I finished all twenty levels during a weekend.

I gave it a solid two thumbs up.

"It's a fun game," I point out the obvious.

He shoves a hand through his hair. "I've never played it."

"You've never played Gem Stars?" I move toward where he's standing. "Are you serious?"

Chuckling, he shakes his head. "Gem Stars is another pet project of Drake's. I don't have time to chase colorful gems around a make believe world, so he took control of it."

Pursing my lips, I hold back a grin. I did have time to chase gems because I was avoiding a fiancé I didn't love. "I should be having this discussion with Drake. He's the one who needs to know how much Mickey Wilts loves his game."

He narrows his eyes. "That's the name of the kid you hung out with? Is he part of the Calvetti clan? There's a lot of them in Manhattan."

I let out a laugh. "He's not a Calvetti. His mom is a friend of Bella's. She had to work so Bella was watching over him."

A smile inches up the corners of his lips. "It sounds like you've made a few friends in the city."

"I have." I nod. "I'll meet up with them another day to go to a bookstore in Brooklyn called Velvet Bay Books. Have you heard of it?"

"Can't say I have." His gaze drops to his phone when it buzzes.

While he reads his message, I glance around the office. I freeze when I spot a framed photo of my family on a shelf behind Drake's desk.

I've never seen that picture before.

I move around Case to get a closer look. Picking it up, I realize that it was taken in Hawaii last year.

No one would have known that Beauregard was on the other side of the camera. He tagged along on the trip after Drake invited him. I didn't realize Beau would be there until I got to the airport and found him standing with my family waiting outside the security checkpoint.

"That's a great family photo," Case says from behind me. "It meant a lot to your brother to surprise you with that trip."

It had meant the world to Drake.

My parents had planned on honeymooning in Hawaii before they realized that my mom was pregnant with Drake. That curtailed all of their travel plans. They took the money that they had saved for their tropical vacation and bought a crib and diapers instead.

I glance back at Case. "It meant a lot to all of us."

He steps in place beside me. "The beach agrees with you."

I wore bikinis for most of that vacation. The sun and fresh ocean air were exactly what I needed. "I love the beach."

"I live on the beach."

I turn to face him. "You do? The ocean is right there?"

"I hear it when I fall asleep." His gaze drops to the floor. "It's a hell of a lot more peaceful than this city."

I'd laugh, but there's nothing lighthearted in his words.

When he glances at me, I see the same sadness in his eyes that is always there.

"You miss it," I say, not questioning it. I can tell that Case wishes he were on the beach in California and not in an office in Manhattan.

Nodding, he drags his top teeth over his bottom lip. "It's home to me. You must feel the same way about Seattle."

I used to. When I knew that I could hop in my car and be at my parents' house in fifteen minutes, I felt safe and grounded.

That's all about to change.

Soon, I'll be the only member of my family left in Seattle. Even my cousins, aunts, and uncles have all moved out of state.

Not wanting to burden Case with my self-imposed pity party, I smile. "There's no place like home."

"Manhattan right now is a pretty close second."

Is the flirting session back on?

I glance over at him as silence fills the room. His mouth curves when our eyes meet. "I'm glad you made the trip here, Emma."

Turning to face him, I murmur, "I'm glad you made the trip too."

"You're stunning in that picture." He dips his chin slightly. "You're beautiful. You're so fucking beautiful."

"So are you," I say in an unsteady voice.

I don't care if my words sound foolish. He is beautiful. He's incredible to look at, but it's more than that. He's kind to me. Since I got to New York, he has taken care of me in ways that have touched me even if they were simple gestures from someone trying to help out his best friend's sister.

With a short step, he's closer to me. "This is a bad idea."

The picture frame in my hand falls into his. "What is?"

I can't take my eyes off of him even though I hear the frame hit the top of the desk with a thud.

Leaning into me, he circles one hand around my waist.

With my heart racing, I close my eyes as he whispers the one word that changes everything.

"*This*."

Chapter 32

Case

I claim her lips in a soft kiss.

I want more. Fuck, do I want more, but I work to control the need that has been building inside of me for days.

Emma steps into my touch. I tighten my grip on her waist when I feel her hand in the back of my hair.

Instinctively, I reach for her neck, tilting her head to just the right angle before I draw my tongue over her bottom lip.

The sound that escapes her ignites a fire in the base of my spine.

I'm hard. My dick is so fucking hard.

Tugging her closer, I groan when she slides her tongue against mine in a greedy kiss.

"Case." My name has never sounded as sweet as it does at this moment, falling from the lips of this woman.

She feathers kisses over my jaw.

"Emma," I say in a strangled tone that's so full of desire it draws her eyes up to meet mine.

"That was…" whatever the fuck she was going to say gets lost in our need for each other.

I hold her against me, deepening the kiss until I feel her hand glide over my cheek.

Her touch is gentle. It's soothing.

I pull back out of a sheer need to breathe.

Why the fuck is my heart hammering so hard?

"That was the kiss," she mutters. "The kiss."

From somewhere inside of me, I find the strength to talk. "The kiss?"

My question brings a flush of pink to her cheeks. "It's nothing."

Anything this woman does or says is everything to me. "Tell me," I insist as I dig my fingers into the soft flesh above the waistband of her jeans.

She brushes her lips over mine in such a tender way that I swear my knees are about to give out.

"That's a fairytale kiss," she half-laughs.

I won't laugh because I see caution in her eyes. I can feel hesitation in the movement of her fingers over my chin. She's confessing something personal to me. "What does that mean?"

I slide my fingers over her cheek. I want her to feel safe with me.

Her gaze drops to my lips. "It's the kind of kiss you only see in the movies."

I take her mouth again in a slow kiss that ends with a draw of my teeth over her bottom lip.

"That's what I mean," she says breathlessly. "I felt that everywhere."

"I did too."

"It was a fairytale kiss for you too?" she asks with a smile.

It was a once in a lifetime kiss. I've kissed more women than I care to admit, but it has never reached inside of me this way.

Nodding, I inch a fingertip over her bottom lip. "You can kiss, Emma. Jesus, can you kiss."

With hooded eyes, she bites my fingertip. "I can do a lot more."

I close my eyes to ward off the mental image of her dropping to her knees to take me in her mouth.

Slow. I have to take this slow. She deserves that. Hell, I need that.

I'm a kiss away from blowing my load.

What the fuck is wrong with me?

"Was that too much?" She whispers with her lips pressed to my chin.

"Not too much," I growl out. "I have to catch my breath. I need to think."

Think about what I want first. I want to taste her. I want to fuck her. I want it all.

"Is it Drake? Do you need to think about him?" Taking a step back, she lowers her voice. "I know he's your best friend. I know that he wouldn't…"

I stop her with a deep kiss. I linger there, sliding my tongue over her bottom lip, breathing her in.

"Don't talk about him," I whisper, not finding the will to say his name. "Don't."

"Case! Are you here?"

The sound of Maya's voice approaching the open office door sets Emma back two steps. Her hand jumps to her swollen lips.

Panic sets over her expression.

I step toward her, but that only moves her back another three steps with her hand waving in the air between us. "We can't."

Fuck. Just fuck this.

"Oh, hey." Maya appears at the office door. "We need to talk."

Emma half-turns until her blushing face is out of Maya's view. "I should go."

"I'm sorry." Maya's gaze darts from me to the back of Emma's head. "Did I interrupt something?"

"No." Emma lets out an exaggerated laugh. "I came to tell Case about a boy I met today. He loves one of Cabbott's games. I wanted Case to know because they work hard on every single game and app they develop. But I told him, so there's no reason for me to hang around here anymore. I'll go now."

Maya looks to me for guidance, but I stand in silence, staring at Emma as she gathers up the purse she dropped into one of the chairs in front of my desk.

Stress taints her every move. Her hands are shaking. Her smile is pinned on to hide what's really going on inside of her.

Regret. I sense it. She's regretting the kiss already.

"Emma," I call out her name. "I'll see you at home later."

When she turns to look at me, my suspicion is confirmed. Regret swims in her eyes behind the tears that are welling there.

Nodding, she hurries past Maya. "It was nice to see you again," she mumbles before she's out of the door.

Chapter 33

Emma

I ran out of Case's office like a fool.

That's because I am a fool. I'm an infatuated fool.

I kissed Case knowing that I'd feel things. I couldn't have known that those things would be amplified a million times over.

I wanted him in a way I have never wanted a man before, but there's more to it.

My heart felt something when his lips touched mine. It broke open.

I can't fall for him. He lives in California. I have to go back to Seattle soon, and on top of that, he's my brother's best friend.

Drake's words about Case's dating history bounce around in my head as I trudge through the late afternoon crowds in Lower Manhattan.

Jealousy has always been a part of the dynamic of Drake's friendship with Case. Drake complained when Case didn't make him a partner in Cabbott even though it was Case's money that founded the business.

In college, Drake was head over heels for a woman named Annabeth, yet she ended up in Case's bed.

She was the first of a long line of women my brother pined for but never got a chance with because Case made the first move.

It wasn't as though Drake made it known that he was interested in those women. He kept those feelings quiet. When I told him that it wasn't Case's fault that he acted on his attraction first, Drake laughed it off, telling me that there were more than enough women for both of them.

I cringed at that.

Case has a lot more experience than me. If he's still the same guy my brother went to college with, sex is all he's interested in.

After my disaster of a relationship with Beauregard, I want intimacy, but not at the cost of my heart.

I've never had sex without some degree of emotional attachment to the guy.

I don't know if I can do it.

I jar to a halt when I hear my phone ringing in my purse. I want it to be Case as much as I don't want it to be. He seemed concerned with my reaction when Maya showed up out of nowhere, but maybe that was because he didn't want his old friend knowing that he was kissing the sister of another of his old friends.

Am I reading way too much into all of this?

I fish for my phone in my purse and glance at the screen.

I answer it immediately. "Drake?"

"Em." His voice cuts through the traffic noise around me. "I'm hitched!"

A single tear falls from the corner of my eye. My brother is officially a married man. "I'm so happy for you."

"I'm so happy for me too," he says. "I wanted you to be the first to know."

I edge past a group of four people to rest my hip against the side of a brick building. "I'm the first?"

"On our side." He chuckles. "Jane's on the phone to her folks."

Our parents have no idea that their only son just got married. I've honored the promise I made to Drake not to say a word to our family, but I don't know how long I can hold out. "Will you call mom and dad and tell them?"

His laughter edges up a notch. "No damn way. I want to see the looks on their faces. Jane and I are going to fly back to Seattle with you once we land in New York. We'll spend a night in Manhattan before the three of us head home to tell the family. The flight is my treat. Does that sound good to you?"

How can I possibly say no to any of that? Drake knows I live on a budget, so the offer to pay for my flight home is appreciated. "That sounds great."

"I'm texting you a picture of us." He blows out a breath. "Promise me you won't send it to mom, dad, or Whitney."

"I promise."

"I have to run and find my bride." He laughs. "I have a wife, Em. I have the most incredible wife in the world."

"She has the most incredible husband," I say softly. "I couldn't be happier for you."

"I want this for you too, Em," he sounds back. "Someday, I'll find my love."

"Maybe you already have." His voice breaks. "Jane just hung up with her folks. I'll talk to you soon."

I stare at the screen of my phone when the call ends. Maybe I have found my love, but it wasn't in Seattle. It was here in New York, but that's a love story that will never have a happily-ever-after, so it needs to end after that first kiss.

It's a first kiss I will never forget. It's the type of kiss you remember when your hair is gray, and your heart still skips a beat whenever you think of that moment from the past.

I glance down when my phone buzzes in my hand. A text message from Drake pops onto the screen of my phone.

I slide my finger over it, opening the attached picture.

My hand leaps to my mouth as my breath catches in my throat.

With the majestic view of a castle behind them, and lush green grass at their feet, my brother has his hands cupped over the cheeks of a woman with short blonde hair as he leans in to kiss her.

Her dress is long and flowing, crafted from lace and silk.

Drake is suited in a black tux.

Love radiates from them, and even though I can't see Jane's face clearly, I can sense that no one on this earth has made my brother feel more joy than she has.

Chapter 34

Case

"The lip gloss you're wearing has a bit too much sheen in it for your skin tone." Maya playfully circles a finger in front of my face.

Swiping the back of my hand over my mouth, I shoot her the same look I did when we were kids and she'd tease me about my overbite. "Don't go there, Maya."

"Go where?" She asks with a bat of her eyelashes. "From what I see, you went there."

"Don't," I warn with a raised brow.

"You're wearing Emma's lip gloss." She smacks her lips together. "She was flustered when I interrupted. It doesn't take a genius to realize that I have horrible timing."

I won't argue with that.

Emma and I may not have been in the middle of our heated kiss when Maya barged in, but the discussion we were wading through wasn't over.

She's Drake's sister. That's a fact that will not change.

"Don't have second thoughts." Maya swats a hand over my forearm. "You're having second thoughts already."

I arch my neck back. "She panicked."

"Because of her brother?" she questions.

Running the pad of my thumb over my bottom lip, I nod. "I hesitated. She brought up Drake."

"Was your hesitation because of him?"

I go with honesty because that's something Maya can always count on from me. "No."

"No?" she parrots back. "Yesterday, you told me nothing could happen between you two because of Drake. Now you're saying he's a non-factor?"

I take a deep breath. Confessing to Maya that I felt something other than a need to fuck when I kissed Emma would set me up for an hours-long conversation about my feelings, so I dance around it. "I met up with Gavin last night. He helped me see that we're all adults here, and Drake will have to deal with it if something happens between his sister and me."

Hearing the words pouring out of me makes sense. Whatever reservation I had about Emma is evaporating. I can't tell if I'm looking to Gavin for justification to act on my intense attraction to Emma or if I'm ready to toss my friendship with her brother out the window to take her to bed.

Either way, what's happening between Emma and me is ultimately about the two of us.

Maya's quiet for a moment too long. "You felt something when you kissed her, didn't you?"

I try to contain the conversation by downplaying. It's what I do. It's what I've done for years. "It was a good kiss."

A laugh escapes her. "It was a good kiss? It blew your world apart. I see it on your face. You must feel it."

I feel it everywhere. I finally feel alive in a way I haven't in a very long time.

Crossing my arms, I stare her down. "Why are you here?"

"Why are you changing the subject?" She shakes her head. "You can pretend that you're not falling for her, but we both know that's a lie."

"Why are you here, Maya?" I repeat the question because I need to think, and I have to do that alone.

"I'll drop this temporarily." She nudges her elbow against my arm. "Pam and Rod apparently have commitment issues. I thought they'd sign on the dotted line, but so far, nothing."

I shove a hand through my hair. I had hoped that this would be a done deal today. I anticipated an offer in hand by tonight.

"You came here to tell me that?"

Scratching her forehead, she lets out a heavy sigh. "No. I have a client in Boston who is looking for a place in New York. He's very interested in your apartment. He wants to see it in person this week."

"When?"

"He'll let me know once he has a chance to look over his schedule." She glances down at the phone in her hand. "He wants to fly in, do a tour and fly out so I'm going to need some flexibility with time. It could be a last minute thing. Do you think that will work?"

"It'll work," I answer. "I'll make it work."

Sliding to her tiptoes, she plants a kiss on my cheek. "You can make anything work, Case. Trust that you can."

I stare down at her. "Not everything is meant to work."

We both know we're talking about Emma, but if that kiss today leads to more, it ends when we leave this city. A long-term relationship won't work for me. Since Emma just broke an engagement, I don't see her eager to start something serious again anytime soon.

Maya's gaze drops to her wedding rings. "Anything worth having is."

I ignore the comment. Maya's life may have worked out just as she had planned. Mine's never charted the course I set for it, but if I can leave Manhattan with one good memory to drown out all the bad ones, I'm on board.

From what I experienced today, Emma is the woman to help me with that.

Chapter 35

Emma

I knew it was a mistake to call Sandy and tell her about my kiss with Case. I've sat here for ten minutes while she's listed every reason why she believes I should throw caution to the wind and sleep with him. Unsurprisingly, she hasn't mentioned one reason why I shouldn't.

Clearing my throat, I cut her off mid-sentence. "He's my brother's best friend, Sandy. It was just a kiss. It doesn't have to turn into anything more."

"Is this seat empty?"

I look up to find a beautiful gray-haired woman smiling down at me. Glancing around the crowded coffee shop, I pull the phone away from my ear. "It is. Please join me."

As she settles, I turn my attention back to my best friend. "I need to go. Love you," I say before I end the call.

"Thank you, dear." The gray-haired woman sets a small coffee in front of her on the table. "Palla on Fifth makes the best cup of coffee in the five boroughs. I stop in once a week to treat myself."

It's a treat for me too. I never pay this much for a cup of coffee, but it's worth the splurge. After I finished the cup that Lester brought me this morning, I promised myself that I'd indulge again before I left Manhattan.

I had no idea I'd end up here hours later.

"I'm Ruth."

She offers me a pat on the forearm instead of her hand, so I offer her a smile. "I'm Emma."

Tugging on the collar of the pink cardigan she's wearing, she nods. "Are you visiting New York City?"

It's a common question in Manhattan. I've been asked it before when I've visited my brother. I don't know if life long New Yorkers have a sixth sense that tells them when someone is a tourist, but there must be something about me that gives it away.

"I live in Seattle." I sigh. "I came to visit my brother, but he's in Ireland. He got married today."

"Well, congratulations to your brother." She lifts her coffee cup in the air as if she's toasting to Drake's marriage. "Did he neglect to include the location on the invitation? You're here and the festivities are in Ireland."

I stare at her weathered hands and the three rings she's wearing. Each is unique. One is a pearl on a band made of rose gold. Another is a small black onyx stone nestled in a circle of diamonds. The third is the most interesting. It's misplaced considering her shoes and handbag screams of wealth.

A tarnished silver double heart ring is on the index finger of her left hand.

I glance up at her face. "He eloped."

Her blue eyes are warm in a way that reminds me of my grandma. I may have forgotten the sound of her voice or the smell of her perfume, but her eyes always stood out to me. They were a beacon of sunshine when I was a kid. I'd spend one weekend a month at her home with its breathtaking views of Puget Sound. We'd eat ice cream for breakfast and cereal for dinner and talk about anything I wanted.

I've missed her every day since her death.

"That stings, doesn't it?" She runs a finger over the ring with the intertwined hearts. "My oldest daughter pulled that trick on me. I nursed a broken heart until she gave me a granddaughter."

I smile because the grin on her face tells me that she forgave everything when she looked into the face of her daughter's newborn.

"Are you navigating New York alone?" Her hand pats my forearm. "If you are, you're a brave soul."

"I'm not brave." I chuckle. "I've made a couple of friends and I'm staying with my brother's best friend until the honeymoon is over."

"Your brother's best friend?" She leans forward on her chair. "I overheard some of what you said on the phone. That would be the young man you kissed? Is there a spark between you two?"

I draw a finger over my bottom lip remembering how it felt when Case kissed me earlier. It was more like a blazing inferno than sparks. "There was something. I felt it."

She drops her gaze to the table. "I have a heck of a tale to tell about my brother's best friend."

I sit silently, waiting for her to continue because I'm up for any story about a brother's best friend. My fingers are crossed that she'll tell me it all worked out in the end and didn't leave her with a heart that was so broken it never recovered.

Instead of launching into a love-filled journey about a sweet memory, she looks at me. I see tears glisten in her eyes.

"You loved him," I whisper.

"I waited much too long to do that." She swipes one fallen tear away with her fingers. "I liked that boy when we were kids. I loved that boy when I was too old to care what anyone thought."

I already know how this story ends. I see it in the way she touches the ring and the heaviness of her breathing.

"He asked me to take a chance on him when I was about your age." A small smile blooms on her lips. "I told him I couldn't. Family loyalty and all, and it was a different time back then."

I nod.

"I married someone else. Tommy married another girl. I was widowed a decade ago. His wife died two years later." She closes her eyes for the briefest of moments. "We found each other three years ago on Facebook of all places."

That lures a smile to my face.

"We had a glorious two years together before he left this earth." She blows out a quick breath. "If given another chance at this life, I would have taken the risk back when he asked me to."

"Even if it meant you'd get hurt back then?" I ask.

"He was about to be deployed." She straightens in her chair. "I tell you, Emma, in his uniform, you'd never find a more handsome man."

I curl my hand around my coffee cup.

"Don't get me wrong." She shakes her head. "I'm grateful for the life I've had, but I do wonder about what might have been."

I lean back on my chair. "Is your brother still…did he know about you two?"

"You're asking if he knew about Tommy and me back in the day, or did he find out when we moved in together?" Her brows dart up behind her silver eyeglass frames.

"Yes." I take a sip of coffee.

"The day of Tommy's wake, my brother told me that he always knew." A soft sigh escapes her. "He could tell there was something brewing between us before Tommy was deployed."

"So when you moved in together, he was happy for you?"

"He was with Tommy the day he bought this ring when I was twenty-one." She circles one heart and then the other with her fingertip. "My brother had no idea who the ring was for. Tommy kept it all those years hoping one day he'd get the chance to give it to me."

I stare at the ring. "It's beautiful."

Holding her hand up, she admires it in the late afternoon sunlight streaming into the café. "To me, it is. It was to my Tommy too."

I take a breath to ward off the emotions I feel.

"I have no idea what your situation is with the young man you're staying with." She pauses. "What's his name, dear?"

"Case," I whisper.

"Case may be your brother's best friend, but he could be your Tommy." She reaches to cover my hand with hers. "From my experience, what a brother wants most for his sister is for her to find a good man to love."

"I can't love Case." I laugh and shake my head. "We're very different. He lives in California. I live in Seattle. It can't work."

"Love can always work."

I bite my lip. "My grandma used to tell me that."

"Us grandmas are smart like that." She taps her chin. "Wise words from wise women will never steer you wrong."

Chapter 36

Emma

"Miss Owens. It's good to see you." Lester tugs on the handle of one of the lobby doors. "How was your day?"

Long and emotionally draining.

"Memorable," I answer honestly. "What about you? How has your day been?"

He purses his lips together. "Mrs. Fields in 3A has a new dog. Suffice it to say we are not friends yet."

He holds out his hand. I spot a faint red spot near the base of his thumb.

"Did the dog bite you?"

"Nip." He opens his mouth to bare his teeth. "It was a nip, but Mrs. Fields felt terrible about it. I'll be dining on a juicy steak tonight at my favorite establishment uptown courtesy of her."

None of this is my business, but Lester doesn't seem to care about that.

"How is Mr. Owens?" He tilts his head. "Any word on the wedding?"

I slide my phone into my bag. I promised Lester that I'd show him any pictures Drake sent me of his wedding, but guilt is getting in the way of that.

How can I show this man the beautiful photo of my brother and Jane if my parents haven't even seen it?

Silently cursing Drake for putting me in this position, I sigh. "They were married earlier today. Drake couldn't be happier."

"No one deserves happiness more than him." Reaching into the front pocket of his pants, he tugs out his phone. "I'll send him a congratulatory text."

This is my cue to run, so that's what I do.

"Have a good night, Lester," I call over my shoulder as I hurry toward an open elevator door.

"You as well, Miss Owens," he sounds back just as I step inside and press the button for the twelfth floor.

***

Wrestling with disappointment, I stand in the foyer of Case's apartment, taking in the silence.

He's not here.

I haven't heard anything from him since I rushed out of his office earlier.

After spending more than two hours having coffee with Ruth, I walked with her to her apartment on Park Avenue.

We shared a brief hug before we said goodbye.

Our time together taught me a lot about the history of New York and the kindness of strangers.

She relived her youth in this city after I bought her a second cup of coffee. I sat mesmerized by the stories of what Manhattan was like decades ago.

I doubt that I'll ever see her again, but I'll never forget this afternoon.

I'll never forget this day.

I kissed Case.

Tossing my keys in my bag, I start toward the guestroom. I need a bubble bath and some soothing music to help me wind down.

My phone starts up on a ring in my purse. Part of me wants to ignore it, but I fish it out.

Sandy's name flashes across the screen.

I could let the call go to voicemail, but that's not something she'd do to me. Sucking in a deep breath, I answer the call. "Hey, sweetie. I'm sorry I had to go so abruptly earlier, but a …"

"I'm pregnant!"

My bag slides down my shoulder and hits the floor as my body goes numb.

"Emma, are you there?" Her voice vibrates with excitement. "I'm having a baby!"

I grip my free hand on the corner of the wall for balance. "What? With who?"

"Kylan," she spits out the name of her most current ex. "It's our baby."

"But…I thought you two…how?" I fumble through a series of questions, not able to get one coherent one out.

"We spent the night together before he left for Michigan two months ago," she confesses. "We've been chatting since, Em. Things are better. No. Things are amazing. I'm moving in with him, and we're having a baby."

"You're moving to Michigan?" Tears prick the corners of my eyes.

Sandy was the last thread that kept me tied to Seattle. The only thing left for me there is a job if I even have that to go back to.

"Not for a few months." She sighs. "I have to finish out my contracts here, and then I'll make the move before the baby arrives."

I'm suddenly grateful to all of her current interior design clients.

"We'll celebrate as soon as you're back." Her voice takes on a lighter tone. "Sparkling apple juice and pickle sandwiches."

An unexpected laugh bubbles out of me. "I'll pass on the pickle sandwiches."

"Whatever works, Auntie Emma."

My hand leaps to my mouth to hold back a sob. Sandy has always wanted a baby. Her dreams are coming true. Everyone I love is creating the life they've always wanted.

Maybe it's time I did the same.

Chapter 37

Case

"A man can't live on…" Gavin drops a white paper bag on my desk. "Whatever the fuck you've been eating."

I glance up and nod a silent thank you to him. "Nothing. I haven't eaten all day."

My appetite up and left when Emma ran out of my office with regret storming inside of her.

I should be at my apartment talking to her, but instead, I'm still at the office, trying to find someone who can pinpoint the issue with Letter Leap.

Our stringent testing protocols failed this time. I've gone through Drake's notes on the development of the game, and I see gaps where there should be accountability in the form of test runs.

I don't know if he was preoccupied with planning his surprise wedding or if he put too much trust in the team he assigned to the project, but there was a fracture, and our release timeline fell victim to it.

"It's almost midnight, Cason." Gavin drops into one of the chairs in front of Drake's desk. "You're pulling worse hours than me."

I shrug. "I've got too much invested in this game. I have to put everything into it."

Shoving a hand through his hair, he leans forward. "Is that really what's going on here?"

This conversation can either stay on the track I want it to, or it can venture in the direction that Gavin's leaning, which is seven years in the past. I'm not on board for that, so I take the wheel to steer it. "If this app fails, it's on me. I have a lot depending on it."

Gavin's interest in Cabbott has never been more than a comment or two. Usually, some form of *'I saw your name in Forbes again, you rich bastard'* or *'no one needs an app for that.'*

He's as skilled in his profession as I am. The difference is that when I go to sleep at night, I'm not doing it with the knowledge that I've saved a life. I entertain, sometimes I inform, but I don't hold anyone's future in my hands.

"Eat the sandwich." He pushes the bag toward me. "You might want to think about getting some sleep too."

I would if I could concentrate on anything but the way Emma's lips tasted or how it felt to have her hands on me.

"Are you daydreaming?" He huffs out a laugh.

"What? No," I answer too quickly.

"Let me guess." He taps a finger on the corner of the desk. "It's Emma Owens, right?"

Peering into the bag, I nod. "She was here."

"And that's got you looking all starry-eyed?" He shakes his head. "What happened when she was here?"

I'm knee-deep in this, so I dive all the way in. "We kissed."

He leans back on the chair. "Just a kiss?"

I rub my eyes, exhaustion finally setting over me. "I've never had a kiss like that before."

A smile creeps over his mouth. "Was the feeling mutual?"

I hang my head. "It was until she remembered that I'm friends with her brother."

Gavin digs in the bag and pulls out a paper-wrapped sandwich. Opening it, he grabs one half and takes a bite. "Kiss her again, and she might forget."

Laughing, I pick up the other half of the sandwich. "Thanks for sharing your dinner with me."

"I wasn't about to let it go to waste." He motions for me to eat. "Finish up and go home, Case. If Emma felt anything from that kiss, she's sitting in your apartment, waiting for you."

***

I spent another two hours after Gavin left my office trying to focus on work. I failed. I'm finally in the main bedroom of my apartment.

Emma has to be fast asleep.

I stopped outside the door to the guestroom, but there was nothing but silence behind it.

I expected as much.

Heading to the bathroom, I drop my clothes along the way.

A shower will soothe me, and help clear my mind. I hit the control panel and step in. As the cool water beats over me, I close my eyes, but all I can focus on is that kiss.

Who the fuck kisses like that?
I swear I felt it in every part of me.
I still do.

It's the first time I've felt anything but numbness in years. I don't deserve it, but *fuck*, I crave it.

I rake a hand through my hair and exhale audibly. I need to try and sleep if I'm going to face my life tomorrow.

Resting my hand over my heart, I take a moment to recite the same silent prayer I do every night hoping that if there is peace to be had, that every soul here on earth and those lost, will find it.

Chapter 38

Emma

I heard Case come home late last night.

After learning about Sandy's baby and seeing the picture from Drake's wedding, I thought about how different my life would be if I had stayed engaged to Beauregard.

Settling for someone I don't love would have trapped me in a marriage that would have ended at some point.

I walked away because I knew it wasn't right for me.

The kiss with Case was proof of that.

I felt more in that moment than I felt the entire time I was with Beau.

A knock at the apartment door lures my gaze in that direction.

I'm already dressed for the day in a pair of faded jeans and a simple blue sweater. My hair is in loose waves, and I only applied the bare essentials for makeup today. The pale pink lipstick and mascara I'm wearing will have to suffice. I don't have the energy for more.

I swing open the door and find the face I was expecting.

Lester smiles. "Miss Owens, a good morning to you."

"And to you." I slide my hand into the front pocket of my jeans, hoping I have at least a few dollars in there.

I come up empty.

Lester watches my movements before he shoves a coffee and a bouquet of brightly colored flowers at me.

My heart skips a beat. It's not because I'm in desperate need of a caffeine fix. It's the flowers. They're breathtaking. My gaze lands on the small white envelope. Case must have sent these. I've never received flowers from any man before other than my dad. He sent me a beautiful bunch of daisies the day I graduated from college.

"I took a walk over to Palla on Fifth and thought you might enjoy a coffee."

Does that mean the coffee was his idea, and not Case's?

"Thank you," I offer because good manners are a gift to others.

I tell my students that. It's wisdom passed on from my grandma.

"And these were just delivered." He takes in the fragrance of the bouquet with a sniff of his nose over the blossoms.

Opening my palm, I wait for him to hand the flowers over.

"It looks like they came from Wild Lilac. It's the favorite florist of many of our residents." He glances at the flowers before his gaze settles on me. "The delivery person suggested I call you to come down to the lobby to get them, but I offered to bring them up."

I don't need to be hit over the head with a flashing neon sign. Lester wants a tip for his trouble.

I shift the coffee to my right hand so I can fish in my left pocket.

I tug on the bill I feel in there.

Before I have it out, Lester's hand is in front of him.

My eyes drop to the twenty dollar bill I'm holding.

Dammit. I paste on a smile as I hand the ransom for my flowers over to him.

"Thank you very much," he says, half-bowing in appreciation. "Enjoy the coffee and the flowers."

With a kick of my foot, I close the door once he's on the other side.

I place the coffee on the foyer table before I furiously rip open the envelope attached to the wrapping paper on the flowers.

With my heart pounding in anticipation, I read the card aloud. "Em. Consider these a thank you for keeping our secret. We can't wait to tell the folks we're married. Love, Drake and Jane."

Disappointment mars my excitement over the floral gift.

I shouldn't have jumped to the conclusion that Case sent the flowers. I can't wish something into existence regardless of how badly my heart wants it.

I head to the kitchen with the flowers in hand, in search of a vase.

I rifle through the cabinets until I find a tall silver beaded trumpet vase. I had no idea my brother had such excellent taste.

After cutting the tips off the stems with a pair of scissors I find in a drawer, I arrange the flowers in the vase.

Standing back, I admire their beauty.

This calls for a picture.

I race to my room to grab my phone, stopping to scoop up the coffee cup off the foyer table on my back to the kitchen.

After I take the bouquet photo, I type out a text message to my brother thanking him for the flowers.

Emma: *I got the flowers, Drake. Thanks to you and Jane. xo*

Just as I'm about to drop my phone on the counter, it buzzes.

I pick it up and scan the screen, but the message isn't from Drake. It's from Case.

Case*: Emma, how are you? How did you sleep?*

There's just enough concern in the message to suggest he cares, but not enough to indicate that the kiss has lingered with him the way it has with me.

I respond without putting any thought into it.

Emma: *I'm good. I slept okay. How are you? Did you sleep at all?*

I wait as he types out a reply.

Case: *I'm fine. I squeezed in a couple of hours. It looks like I'll be stuck at work for the day.*

If he wasn't facing an issue with the release of the new game app, I might think he's avoiding me after the kiss.

But, Case is honest. I know he lives his life that way, so I need to accept that he's actually focusing on work.

Emma: *I'm going to hang out here.*

When a reply doesn't come, I tuck my phone in my pocket and head back to the guestroom with my coffee and the vase, debating whether to surprise Case at his office.

By the time the coffee cup is empty an hour later, I'm settled on the bed with my laptop, watching a movie.

I glance at the window and the rain beating down on Manhattan.

I take it as a sign that I need to stay inside today, so I snuggle under the covers and fall victim to a romance movie where the heroine falls in love with the hero in a small town with a big heart.

Chapter 39

Emma

I read the text message Case sent me this morning for the third time.

Case: *How are you today? I'm still chained to my desk.*

I meant to answer before I got on the subway, but I was in such a hurry that I dropped my phone in my purse, locked the apartment door, and darted out of the building.

Lester tossed me a wave, along with something about wishing me well.

I smiled back, hoping he didn't think I was rude.

I don't have any pocket change left to line his glove.

"Are you playing Gem Stars?" Mickey cranes his neck to try and see what I'm gazing at.

I'm at Velvet Bay Books in Brooklyn with Mickey, his mom, and Bella.

When Bella texted me to ask if I was free to meet up with the trio for a bookstore tour and a lunch date, I jumped at the chance.

I spent most of yesterday watching romance movies and staring at the flowers Drake sent me. I'm feeling an unrelenting sense of guilt over the fact that I haven't told my parents that they have a daughter-in-law.

I went to bed late, hoping that Case would make it home before midnight.

He didn't. I heard him sneak in shortly before two. He took off before I woke up.

"No." I smile at the little boy. "I got a text message from a friend."

Delaney inches up behind me to steal a peek at the screen. "From a boyfriend?"

"Ew." Mickey covers his ears. "I don't want to hear that."

Reaching for one of his hands, Bella laughs. "Come with me. I saw a new book about dragons that you need to see."

As they take off to the other side of the store, Delaney rests a hand on my shoulder. "I didn't mean to pry."

I turn and face her. "You're not."

"You haven't been your cheerful self today." She pushes a lock of hair behind her ear. "Does that have anything to do with the guy who texted you?"

I nod. "It's my brother's best friend. I'm staying with him right now because my brother took off to get married."

Her eyes widen. "What's the story between you and the best friend?"

I inch a fingertip over my bottom lip. "We kissed a couple of days ago and…"

"And it was epic?"

I laugh. "So epic."

"What's the problem?" Her smile widens. "I haven't had an epic kiss in years."

We haven't discussed her situation.

On the subway ride here, Mickey watched intently as a man bounced his son on his lap. Delaney must have noticed too because she hauled her little boy onto her lap and did the same.

Mickey laughed the entire time.

I caught a case of the giggles too as I watched them together.

There's no denying that their bond is strong. I hope to have that with a child of my own someday.

"It's complicated," I say. "I don't want to hurt my brother, but I can't deny what I'm feeling. That kiss was unreal."

"I've only felt that feeling with one guy." She darts a finger into the air. "When he kissed me for the first time, I swear time stopped."

I glance at Mickey when I hear him let out a squeal.

"Was the kiss with Mickey's dad?" I ask tentatively.

She nods. "He was my first love; my only love."

Just as I'm about to press for more, her son comes running at us full speed. "Mommy, come and see this book. You have to read it to me."

Delaney skims her hand over the top of his head before her gaze levels on me. "A kiss like that is rare. Don't ignore what you're feeling because it might upset your brother."

As she walks away, holding tight to Mickey's hand, I type out a response to Case.

Emma: *I'm good. I'm at Velvet Bay Books with my friends. Work sounds like a battle right now. How are you holding up?*

His reply takes a moment. I watch as the three dots dance on the screen as he types. There's a pause before they bounce again.

Case: *I'm fine. Enjoy your day, Freckles.*

My response is as quick as a beat of my heart.

Emma: *You too, Rush.*

Chapter 40

Case

I end the call with my assistant in California just as I step into my apartment.

The lights are out. Stillness sits in the air.

I don't know why the hell that surprises me. It's after midnight. I've been knee-deep in Cabbott bullshit for the past two days.

The framework issue still hasn't been fixed. I've got my most skilled software engineers on the job. Back in California, I'm facing the resignation of two of my top executives.

They emailed me within thirty minutes of each other to tell me they were leaving Cabbott at the end of the month. Who the hell quits their job when the boss is out of town?

Lionel Burkhard and Shaun Melcor do.

Replacing them won't be easy. I'll have to pull from the New York office to fill the vacancies temporarily.

I'd offer Drake an incentive to postpone his move for a few months, but he already has other plans. I need to clue Emma into those.

I should wake her up and do it now.

What the fuck is wrong with me?

Anything I need to say to her can wait until morning. It's waited this long. It's been days since we kissed.

I haven't seen her or spoken to her. Text messages have been our only line of communication for the past few days. Yesterday, I checked in, and she told me she was hanging out here. Earlier today, I texted her to see how she was, and she replied that she was at a bookstore in Brooklyn with her new friends.

She asked how I was doing. I typed out a response about missing her, but before I pressed send, I deleted it and replaced it with my typical generic answer of *I'm fine*.

It was bullshit; both times I sent it.

I glide a finger over the smart home panel's screen, hoping to activate the light above me. I hit the mark this time.

"Case?"

I turn when I hear her voice behind me. "Emma."

She's wearing a light pink tank top and a pair of black shorts. Her hair is a tousled mess. I don't know if I woke her when I walked in or not, but I'm grateful that I get to see her like this.

I'd place my entire company in her hands for the chance to feel her arms around me.

"I didn't know when you'd come home tonight."

I considered sleeping at the office to ward off the need I feel for her, but hiding from it won't chase it away. I've slept here the past two nights, but it's been no more than a two to three hour stretch at a time.

I drop my keys, wallet, and phone on the foyer table. "Work never ends. I need to grab a few hours of sleep and head back to the office."

She rubs at her eyes. "You should go to bed."

You should join me.

I shove my hands in the front pocket of my jeans to resist the temptation to reach for her. I still haven't stopped thinking about the kiss. Fuck, that kiss.

It ruined me. It cracked open something inside of me that I can't hide from anymore.

I felt again. I haven't felt anything but numb in seven long years.

I know she has reservations. I do too, but mine aren't tied to my relationship with her brother anymore. She just broke up with her fiancé. I don't want to hurt her. I can't start something that has an expiration date if she's not on board with it.

I want her, but not if it costs her a broken heart.

"Drake sent me a text just now." Her gaze drops to the phone in her hand. "It woke me."

"I got a text from him too," I confess. "Your brother just keeps piling on the surprises."

Her eyes narrow in the dim light of the room. "What do you mean?"

Shit. I assumed Drake filled his sister in on his grand plan, but maybe he didn't get that far.

I tread lightly. I start at the most logical place. "Do you know that Jane told her parents about the wedding?"

"I know." Her gaze falls to the floor. "My parents have no idea that their son is married. I can't talk to them because I make a promise to them that I'd never lie, and this would be a lie of omission. Drake wants me to fly back to Seattle with him and Jane to tell my family, but how am I supposed to keep this secret for another day?"

I can see that all of this is gutting her.

Her brother put her in an impossible position. Whether or not he realized how fucking selfish it is doesn't matter at this point. Emma gave him her word, and I sense that she honors that at all costs.

She looks past me to the apartment door, but I catch the twitch in her eye.

I want to put her at ease. Shit, I want it so badly that I'm about to arrange for her family to be flown to London to surprise Drake and his bride.

This is between her and Drake, though, so I push the idea aside.

Her phone buzzes in her palm.

She looks at the text before she reads it to me. "We're making a pit stop in London before we head back to New York, Em."

"Her folks want to buy them a house in London as a wedding gift." I tilt my head back. "Jane and Drake are meeting up with them to figure that out."

When her meet mine, I can tell that she's as shocked as I am by her brother's latest revelation. "When did he tell you that?"

"Ten minutes ago," I answer.

It's the break of dawn in London. He's already there, planning the next stage of his life. Apparently, he finally found time to fill Emma and me in.

"I should go back to Seattle." Her hand drops to her hip.

I can't take my eyes off of her. "Give it a few days. I'm stuck here too. I've got a problem that I can't run away from."

I let myself believe I'm talking about the launch of Letter Leap, but that's not it.

The problem is that ever since I kissed her, nothing has made sense to me.

My desire to fuck her is clouding everything. I can't think straight.

"How long will you be staying in Manhattan?" Her voice lowers.

"As long as it takes."

The gruffness in my tone shocks us both. She steps back. I scrub the back of my neck. I need to temper the need I feel for this woman.

Her phone lights up with another text message.

"Dammit." Her tongue darts over her bottom lip. "It's Drake again. I should respond."

I move closer to press my lips to her forehead. Breathing in the sweet scent of her skin, I whisper, "Try to get some sleep tonight."

Her eyes find mine. "You too. You need to rest."

I need to come.

I keep that to myself as I brush past her and head to my bedroom alone.

Chapter 41

Emma

Glancing at the flowers on the nightstand, I turn over on my side. My brother had little to say when I texted him back. He told me he'd fill me in more when he had time. I reminded him that I'd prefer if that would be during daylight hours in New York.

I roll over again and kick the covers back from the bed.

I'm burning up.

Sitting up, I fist the sheet with my hands to keep them from shaking.

Not only did I drink my body weight in coffee today, but I'm on fire from the way Case looked at me before he went to sleep. The roughness of his voice went straight to my core.

"*As long as it takes.*"

I've been replaying those words in my mind since I dropped into bed an hour ago.

As long as it takes to satisfy his need for me?

As long as it takes to fuck me over and over again?

As long as it takes until we wear each other out?

My hand darts to the outside of the white silk panties I'm wearing.

I'm desperate to come, but I'm savoring the high of the desire I'm feeling.

Fanning a hand in front of my face, I look to the open window. It's doing nothing to quench my need for cool air.

I may be feeling flushed because of Case, but it's more than that. The air conditioning hasn't come on. This room has to be upwards of eighty degrees.

Swinging my bare legs over the side of the bed, I stand.

My brother installed a smart home system in this apartment before my last visit. He gave me a primer on it the day I arrived, but I didn't have to use it during that trip.

Drake pre-programmed everything in, so my coffee was ready in the morning when I woke up and the lights in my room were set to dim in the evening.

The air conditioning runs off the panel, so I start toward the door of the guestroom.

I inch the door open, peering out into the darkened hallway.

No light is escaping from under the door of Case's bedroom. The air conditioning must be working in there, or he's so accustomed to the heat in California that this feels lukewarm to him.

I tread down the hallway toward the panel. The only light illuminating the space is seeping in from the windows of the main living area.

Manhattan never fully shuts down, so there's always some degree of muted light when you gaze out a window, even in the dead of night.

I suck in a breath as I stare at the panel. I remember Drake saying that if you tap the screen, it will illuminate in the darkness.

I jab a finger into the middle of the screen.

The blare of loud classical music sends me stumbling back two steps. "Oh, fuck," I mutter.

I tap the screen again to stop the music. Silence immediately surrounds me. I glance at Case's room, but the door is still closed.

The screen darkens again before I have a chance to find the button that controls the air conditioning.

"Damn you," I spit out.

I lean closer. I know there's a voice-activated feature. Drake proudly showed that off when he ordered it to turn on a football game, and he requested that it preheat the oven even though neither of us was going to cook a thing.

"Air conditioning in the guest room," I whisper.

Nothing happens.

"Turn on the air conditioning in the guest room," I say louder.

Still nothing.

I cup my hands around my mouth and direct my voice to the panel. "I need air conditioning in the guest room. Please. Now."

I stomp my foot when the panel doesn't light up.

"Screw you," I seethe. "I'm hot."

"So fucking hot."

I almost trip when I jump at the sound of Case's voice.

I glance toward the open door of the main bedroom. My breath catches as I take in the sight of him dressed in nothing but a pair of jeans that are undone, the fly partially open.

Holy hell.

He leans against the doorframe with his arms crossed over his chest. "What do you need, Emma?"

Words can't find their way out of me, so I squeak. I literally let out a small squeaking sound.

"You can't sleep. I can't sleep." His eyes trail over my body. "We're both wide awake. What should we do about that?"

Shock grounds me in the spot I'm in even though I want nothing more than to drop my panties and tank top and follow him into his bedroom.

He straightens and starts toward me. There's no masking that he's naked under the jeans. The deep ridges of his abs lead down to a light dusting of dark hair and the swell of his erection against the fabric.

This is the sexiest thing I've ever seen.

I pinch the inside of my arm to make sure I'm not dreaming.

"You're holding back," he tells me. There's no question in the statement. He can sense what I feel. "Is it because of your brother?"

He avoids using Drake's name just as he did in his office when we kissed.

I shake my head.

"Bonehead?" he says the nickname of my ex with distaste on his tongue. "Are you considering getting back together with him?"

That's laughable, so I add a chuckle to my headshake.

"You've never fucked just to fuck, have you?" He circles me like I'm his prey.

I glance down. "No."

"You don't want to risk getting hurt for a good, hard fuck. Is that it?"

I close my eyes against the rush of desire that consumes me with those words.

He stops in front of me. His hand drops to his stomach. It slowly trails down his skin to the opening of his jeans. "If you don't take the risk, you'll never experience the reward, Emma. I can promise you one hell of a reward."

My gaze stays glued to his hand as he glides it over the fabric. I can see the outline of his erection. He's large. He's perfect.

"Emma." My name leaves him in a breathless rush. "If we set rules and stick to them, a good time is had by all."

I slide my eyes up to his handsome face. "Rules?"

"We fuck while we're in New York. Once you-know-who comes back to town, I head back to California. You go to Seattle. We part ways with great memories."

I want this. I crave the feeling of a man's body again. It's been too long.

It's been so long.

If I don't take this chance, I'll regret it. I know that I will.

"It's over when my brother gets back to New York?" I question, so it's crystal clear.

He trails the pad of his thumb over his bottom lip. "Yes."

I can handle this. My heart can do this. The last thing I need right now is an emotional complication. The one thing I need is to be in his bed.

I stare at him. This gorgeous man is offering me the chance to have a hot as hell summer fling before going home to sort out my life. With Drake relocating to London, I'll likely never see Case again after this trip.

"I want you, Emma." He steps closer. "I've barely slept since I got to Manhattan because I've been thinking about your body and all the things I want to do with you."

I close the distance between us with a step of my own. Reaching forward to trace a finger over the center of his chest, I look up and into his eyes. "Show me."

Chapter 42

Emma

His gaze caresses my face, his eyes lingering on my mouth.

"Kiss me," he orders in a strangled moan. "Kiss me."

I slide my hand up to his bicep, trailing my fingertips over the firm muscle before I glide my fingers along his skin and into the hair on the back of his head.

Urging his head down, I rise to my tiptoes. I lock eyes with him. "Meet me halfway."

He does.

His mouth lowers onto mine. The kiss is gentle and tender as if it's hiding the promise of what is waiting just beneath it.

I tighten my grip on his hair, tugging it, coaxing him.

I'm impatient.

It's been so long since I've been with a man. The need I feel is pouring out of me.

He deepens the kiss. With his hand on my waist, he twists me around until my back hits the wall. His knee edges my legs apart.

"You're ready," he whispers as his lips feather over mine. "You want this."

"So much."

His hand falls to my thigh. His fingers trace small circles over my flesh. Each move brings him closer to my core.

I groan when his touch drifts up.

"Case," I whine into our kiss. "Please."

I won't beg for this, but if a kiss can bring a woman to orgasm, it would be from this man.

I pull back when he tugs on the hem of my shirt. In a heartbeat, it's over my head and on the floor.

His gaze drops to my breasts. Natural and full, the nipples are perked from my need for him.

"Jesus." The word escapes him in a rush before he bows his head to take one nipple between his teeth. He holds it there, the bite of pain stirring my desire more. I try to edge my legs together, but he pushes me harder against the wall, his knee rising between my thighs.

His tongue lashes my nipple again and again. I gasp when his hand finds my other breast. He circles that nipple lightly, tenderly. The sharp contrast to his teeth on the other is almost too much.

Closing my eyes, I sink my nails into the skin of his shoulder.

The ache between my legs is so much I reach down.

He stills. His body stops. His mouth leaves my breast as he watches my fingers glide over the silk of my panties.

"Show me," he spits out in a tone laced with dark promise. "Show me all of you."

I edge my other hand down when he moves back. His gaze is latched on my body.

His hand falls to the front of his jeans. His cock is straining. His need for me is reflected in mine for him.

My fingers graze the top of my panties. "You want to see me," I say brazenly.

"I need to," he breathes. "Show me."

I slide the panties down my legs, watching him as I do. The expression on his face shifts when I straighten, and I'm fully exposed.

"Fuck," he growls. "I've never seen anything more beautiful than you."

His hands are on me, tugging me closer to him, trailing heat over my skin as he urges me up.

I reach for his shoulders. He lifts me effortlessly, pressing my body against his. With my legs around his waist, he kisses me before he leads me to his bed.

***

He hovers over me, his gaze trailing a path over every inch of my face. The only light in the room is seeping in from the half-closed curtains.

I push my back into the soft sheets of his bed. "Case."

"Emma." His mouth softens. "I'll take care of you."

I believe him, but still… "You have condoms."

His brow edges up. "You assume I do."

I glance down at his body. He may still be wearing his jeans, but it's obvious he's gorgeous everywhere. The man must have all kinds of crazy hot sex.

"You do," I say with confidence. "We need one."

He glides down my body until his lips are pressed between my breasts. "Your tits are so soft."

One hand cups my right breast.

"Condom," I remind him. "Please."

He kisses my nipple before he takes it between his teeth again. I close my eyes against the assault of pleasure that hits me full force.

Who knew pain could feel this good?

I moan when he nips me. Again, when he rolls his teeth over my other nipple.

I reach down to pull on his hair. "Condoms, Case."

"Shhh," he whispers. "We don't need one yet. Just feel."

My head falls back into the pillow as he trails kisses down my body, stopping to circle my belly button with his fingertip.

As he nears my cleft, I wind my fingers through his hair. "I'm sensitive."

His eyes dart up to meet mine. "Good. I want you to come for me, Emma again and again."

Settling between my legs, he pushes them open until I'm fully exposed. I blush beneath the darkness in the room.

"You take my breath away," he says softly before he presses his lips to my inner thigh. "I've wanted this more than you know."

I stifle a moan when he licks a slow path over my swollen folds, but the groan that escapes him cuts through me.

My back bows from the sheer pleasure of his reaction to my body.

"That's it," he growls. "Feel it. Feel it all."

I look down and watch as he lowers his head again, closes his eyes, and brings me more pleasure with his mouth than I've ever felt before.

Chapter 43

Case

I wipe my lips over the skin of her navel.

Emma squirms beneath me, her movements slowing as I work my way up her body.

"Twice," she mutters under her breath. "That was twice."

She'd come once and then again under my tongue. I wanted more. Almost begged her for more, but she fought me with her hands in my hair and her ass dragging along the bed, trying to edge her pussy away from my lips and tongue.

"For now." I flick my tongue over her nipple. "I want that again tonight, Emma."

Her eyes fall to my face. "I want more."

She wants to fuck.

The driving need to be inside of her is dictating every movement of my body.

I'm hard as nails. I fought back the urge to stroke my dick when I was eating her. I could have come just from the taste and the sounds pouring out of her.

I move when I feel her pull away.

Pushing to my feet, I stand next to the bed. I gaze down at the front of my jeans before I turn back to face her.

"One of us is overdressed." She rolls to her side, resting her head on the pillow. Her hand runs over her side. "Here's a hint. It's not me."

I rake her from head-to-toe. Her body is made to be fucked.

By me. Only by me.

I dip my chin to clear my head. "I don't have any condoms."

I doubt like hell I've ever uttered those words before. I've had a condom tucked into a pocket or hidden in my wallet since I was a teenager. I didn't bring any with me on the trip because screwing a random woman was not on my schedule.

I expected to be in and out of Manhattan within a couple of days.

I had no clue that Emma Owens would drop into my orbit and end up in my bed.

Her gaze darts from my face to the bedside table.

She won't give a voice to it, but she's silently asking if there are any condoms in this room.

There aren't. I checked. Twice.

Shaking my head, I shove a hand through my hair. "Tomorrow. I'll pick up some tomorrow."

She stretches an arm in front of her. "I have one."

Anger shoots through me. I have no right to feel it, but it's there. "You have a condom?"

"Just one," she says as if that explains it all away. "I thought maybe I'd meet someone while I was here."

I drop my hand to my jeans. One swift dive inside, and I'm circling my cock with my fist. "To fuck? You thought you'd meet a guy and fuck him?"

Rolling onto her back, her hand glides to her mound. "That's what happened. Luckily I'm prepared."

I squeeze my dick harder. "Here? You thought you'd bring a man here to screw?"

Her back arches when her hand trails over her smooth folds. "Or somewhere. It's been a long time."

Too fucking long. I wish I'd met her years ago.

"Where is it?" I bark out through a stuttered breath. "I'll get it."

Her eyes close as she shifts her hand to her thigh. "I can get it."

"Go."

My order draws her gaze to my face. "I will, but I want to do something else first."

I watch in awed silence as she moves along the bed with an effortless grace that stops my breath.

She crawls closer to me, but before I can get my jeans to my thighs, she's on her back, her head hung over the edge of the bed.

Fuck.

"Please," she whispers. "I want to. I want to do this."

I drop my jeans to the floor and move closer, convinced that I'll blow my load all over her tits before I feel her tongue on me.

I guide the crown of my cock over her soft pillow lips until she parts them and takes me inside.

Cupping a hand over the front of her neck, I fuck her mouth slowly at first.

She's eager, and when I increase the pace, she works my cock to the back of her throat.

"Jesus," I hiss, feeling every swallow under my hand. I watch each thrust of my dick between her lips.

She moans. Her fingers glide over her soft flesh, diving between her spread thighs. I give her more with each hard drive of my cock. I give it all to her until I come down her throat as she takes everything I offer.

Chapter 44

Emma

I cross the hallway and enter Case's room with the condom in hand.

Sandy handed it to me when I was packing for my trip. I laughed it off at the time, telling her that I wouldn't need it, but she insisted I take it.

I'm glad I did.

Case told me he needed a second to catch his breath after he came. He collapsed on the bed beside me, his hands grabbing for me.

I pushed my elbow into his chest and asked if he liked what I'd done.

I didn't need the confirmation but hearing him tell me that I'm incredible buoyed my soul. The soft kiss on my lips that followed his hearty, "Fuck, Emma. I've never felt that before," left me completely satisfied.

My footsteps stall as I peer at the bed and the sight of him fast asleep.

He moved up to his pillow and now with one arm over his head, and the other resting across his toned stomach, he's drawing deep, easy breaths. I take in the sight of his naked body.

Crawling in next to him is what I want to do, but I can't.

We didn't agree to share a bed beyond sex.

Placing the condom on the nightstand, I lean down to press a kiss to his cheek.

"Thank you," I whisper against the softness of his light beard. "Thank you for a night I'll never forget."

"Get in bed," he murmurs under his breath.

I trail a finger over his shoulder. "Are you sure?"

"I need ten minutes of shuteye, and then it's on, Freckles."

Laughing, I fall on the bed next to him. "What's on?"

He cracks open one eye. "You on my cock."

A shiver runs through me at the promise of that. "Ten minutes of sleep and then sex."

"That's our agenda." He runs a fingertip over one of my perked nipples before he wraps his arm around my waist. "Close your eyes and dream a nice short dream."

"About you fucking me?" I ask playfully.

Edging closer to me, he brushes a kiss over my lips. "You'll need a hell of a lot longer than that to dream about me fucking you. I told you once that I take my time. With you, I want to take forever."

I shut my eyes to soak in those words.

Forever.

If this is what forever with him feels like, I want it.

***

Sitting straight up, I struggle to place where I am. The room is flooded with sunlight. It's morning. I must have drifted off to sleep at some point.

I glance to my side, but the bed is empty.

Case.

I was with Case.

A loud thump echoes through the hallway outside the door of the main bedroom.

"I'm coming." Case's voice carries through the space.

The door? Is someone knocking on the apartment door?

Whoever is on the other side of it doesn't understand the meaning of the word patience. A series of dull thuds fill the silence as I swing my legs over the side of the bed in a panic.

My panties and tank top are in the hallway where I left them after I stripped for Case last night.

His jeans aren't on the floor where he dropped them. He's at least half-dressed, which is fifty percent better than being nude like I am.

I tug on the sheet, thinking I can wrap it around me, but it doesn't give. Whoever comes in to take care of cleaning this place has bed-making skills that put me to shame.

I toss my duvet over my bed at home every morning, throw my pillow back in place and call it a day.

"I need a robe," I mutter to myself as I hear Case talking to someone.

He wouldn't let that person in, would he? He knows that I'm in his bed.

I quickly pace around the room, searching for anything that I can use to cover myself.

Relief washes through me when I spot a white button-down shirt draped over the back of a chair. I grab it, slide it over my arms, and do up two buttons that are level with my navel.

It's a look I'd never willingly choose, but all the sensitive parts of me are covered.

My parents would be proud.

I laugh at that. I slept with a man I haven't known very long. I did things that I've only ever fantasized about. My parents would be mortified.

I inch along the floor on bare feet, hoping that the second voice I heard is gone.

It's not.

"Miss Owens is a lovely young woman, isn't she, sir?"

Lester. I smile, knowing that the unexpected visitor is the doorman. He may be nosy, but the hallway is out of the view of the foyer, so there's little chance he'll see my panties and top.

"That she is," Case answers brusquely.

"I do hope you'll both enjoy the coffee." Lester sighs. "I recall that you were a five cup a day fellow when you first moved in."

"I've cut it down to one every twenty-four hours now," Case answers.

"That's good to hear." Lester's voice lowers a touch. "You've come a long way since that time. It's good to see you looking well. I worried over you when you left the city so abruptly years ago."

"I'm fine." I hear the brush off in Case's tone.

Whatever Lester is referring to, Case doesn't want to talk about.

"Mr. Owens worried too," Lester continues, oblivious to the obvious annoyance Case is feeling. "He told me you left without a thing. I remember him carting boxes of your clothing and other items out of here to donate."

"My New York wardrobe didn't fit in California." Frustration taints Case's words.

"Digging out of a hole as deep as the one you were in takes a great deal of strength, Mr. Abbott. You should be proud of yourself for that."

"I should get ready for work," Case counters. "I'm leaving for the office within the hour."

I should be disappointed that Case has to leave soon, but curiosity has got a grip on me.

What happened all those years ago that caused Case to move across the country and leave everything behind?

Chapter 45

Case

I close the door behind Lester, hoping to hell that he didn't wake Emma with the incessant kick of his foot against my door.

With a coffee in each hand, he walked in and dragged my past into the light of day.

For fuck's sake.

I don't want to explain any of the shit that just poured out of his mouth to Emma. I wouldn't know where to start.

I suck in a deep breath before I turn and start toward the bedroom.

When I round the corner and find her panties and tank top in the hallway right where she dropped them last night, relief washes over me.

I take that as a good sign.

Another few steps bring me to the doorway of my bedroom.

My shoulders tense again.

She's awake.

Her back is to me as she gazes out the window. Her dark hair is a stark contrast to the white shirt she's wearing. *My shirt.*

I've never liked it when a woman has helped herself to anything that belongs to me, but I want her to keep the shirt. It looks fucking fantastic on her.

The cups in my hand almost drop when she turns to face me.

Her nipples are pressing against the fabric of the shirt. Since she only fastened a couple of buttons, I can see the top of her thighs and the skin between her breasts.

"Hey." She lifts a hand before she drops it to her side.

"Emma," I growl out her name. "You're awake."

I'm pointing out the obvious, but I want her to lead this. I need to know whether she heard Lester talking about the worst days of my life in the foyer during his unexpected coffee delivery.

"I just woke up." She runs a hand through her messy hair.

Nothing in her expression or body language contradicts that, so I step toward her. "Lester brought you a coffee."

Her lips curve into a smile. "From Palla on Fifth? He's spoiling me."

I'll buy the goddamn café to put a smile like this on her face every day of the week.

Gripping the coffee tighter, I chase the thought away.

This ends when I head back west. My rules. Those are my fucking rules.

Stepping closer, she reaches out a hand. "Which one is mine?"

I hand her the one that has Miss Owens written on the side in red ink. "Here you go, Freckles."

A pale pink blush rushes over her cheeks. "Thank you."

I watch as she takes a tentative sip before her eyes close. "There's nothing quite like that first taste of coffee in the morning."

It can't compare to the taste of her last night.

Nothing compares to that.

My gaze wanders to the nightstand and the condom we didn't have a chance to use. I never sleep more than a couple of hours in one stretch. I thought I'd doze off for a few minutes, sheath myself, and feel her wrapped around me.

"Maybe we can make use of that."

Her voice jars me back to reality. I shoot her a look. "Tonight."

"Not now?" She raises a brow.

"I won't rush our first time." I lean forward to press a kiss to her soft lips. "I need to go to the office, but tonight we'll meet back here."

Her fingertip trails a path over my bottom lip. "I might be persuaded to do that."

I nip at her finger.

She draws it back with a pout. "That hurt."

"Don't play games." I take her hand in mine. "Agree to be here tonight, Emma."

"I'll be here most of the day naked and waiting."

My cock swells at the thought of her roaming my apartment with nothing on, but Maya has plans with the potential buyer from Boston. Today is the day he wants to look at the place.

I press a kiss to her palm. "Maya's bringing someone over at four, so…"

"Go hang out somewhere else for a couple of hours," she finishes for me.

Nodding, I take a sip of the coffee. "I can arrange for you to see a matinee of a show on Broadway, or I can book you a table at Nova for a late lunch."

Her eyes widen. "That's all tempting, but I have something I need to take care of, so I'll handle that today."

As eager as I am for details, I don't ask. I won't pry into her life because I don't want her to pry into mine.

"I'm going to hit the shower." I nod toward the bathroom. "I wouldn't mind the company if you wanted to join. I'd love a front row seat to one of your shower concerts."

Her chin dips as a wide smile blooms on her lips. "You can hear me when I sing in the shower?"

"Most of Manhattan can," I jest. "It's music to the ears of all New Yorkers."

"Funny." She slaps a hand across my bare chest. "Let's save the shower concert for another time."

Cupping a hand over her cheek, I stare into her eyes. "Promise me that will happen."

Her hand darts into the air as if she's taking an oath. "I promise that before we leave New York and go our separate ways, I'll sing you a song in the shower."

And I promise I'll let you go.

I keep those words to myself even though it's a promise I don't want to keep. I don't have a choice. When her brother gets back to town, this ends. It has to end.

Chapter 46

Emma

"Is that a new game?" Mickey cranes his neck to get a better look at the screen of my phone.

"Mick." His mom gives him a playful tap on the shoulder. "Don't be nosy."

I laugh off the idea that any child his age could be nosy. "I tell my students back home that it's good to ask questions and to be inquisitive."

"According to Miss Owens, you are a very good boy." Delaney directs her words to her son but offers me a soft smile.

When I stopped in at Sweet Bluebells, I didn't expect to see Delaney and Mickey huddled together at a corner table.

They spotted me just as I was about to order a cup of lemonade to go. When they waved me over, I couldn't resist joining them.

I turn my phone's screen around and place it on the table in front of Mickey. "This is an app I use to organize and print my photos. It's called Printe."

His gaze scans the screen before he taps his index finger on an image. "That's Bella."

I caught her in a moment of bliss as she was looking down at her small baby bump yesterday. I showed her the picture, and she insisted I send it to her. The tears in her eyes when she thanked me for taking it made the image a keeper.

"I'll print that one for my scrapbook back home." I slide my finger over the screen. "Today, I'm going to get a larger print made of a very special picture."

"Who is that?" Mickey leans closer to me.

"My brother and his wife." I turn the phone toward him. "It's a pretty great, isn't it?"

He shrugs. "I guess it is if you like weddings."

"I love weddings." Delaney shifts her chair closer. "Can I see?"

I hand her the phone.

"Emma, this is gorgeous." Her eyes dart up to look at me. "Where did they get married?"

"Ireland."

"Going to Ireland is now on my bucket list. Maybe I'll add getting married in a castle." Laughing, she hands me back my phone.

"Take one of the three of us." Mickey bounces in his seat. "You can put it in your scrapbook too next to the picture of Bella."

"Mick." Delaney runs a hand over his hair. "I'm sure Emma has taken a million photos during her trip. She doesn't need one of us."

"I'd love one," I interject before Mickey can plead his case. "I'm trying to capture all the best moments of my trip, and I think this ranks high up there."

Mickey darts up from his chair, pushing to his tiptoes. His hand flies into the air above his head. "Does it rank up here?"

I follow his lead and stand, raising my hand above his. "Way up here."

Delaney rises to her feet. "Let's take it by the display case. What's better than having cupcakes as a backdrop?"

"Two new friends," I say with a smile.

Her arm falls over my shoulders. "Two new lifelong friends. The next time you're back in Manhattan, your first stop needs to be here."

I don't know if I'll ever come back to New York City again, but I grin as Mickey grabs for my hand. With a skip in his step, he leads me across the bakery.

***

Grateful that Lester apparently has the afternoon off, I plop myself down on a bench in the lobby.

The temperature outside has to be closing in on one hundred degrees, and I didn't dress for that. I'm wearing jeans and a pink patterned lightweight blouse. The sandals on my feet may be uncomfortable, but they're a much better choice than the boots I almost wore.

I can't wait to get up to Case's apartment to shower.

A glance at my phone screen tells me that Maya is likely already gone, but I want to give it until quarter past five before I hop on the elevator.

I drop my phone in my purse and peer into the shopping bag at my feet.

I picked up an antique brushed gold frame for Drake's wedding photo after I ordered a large print on the Printe app. My brother couldn't have known when he developed the app, that I'd use it to print a picture of him kissing his bride a year later.

After typing Case's address into the order form, a wave of guilt washed over me because in the very next breath, I typed Case's name into a search engine on my phone.

My quest was focused on one thing. I wanted information on what chased Case out of New York City seven years ago.

I found nothing connected to that.

All that I did find were pictures of the man I spent the night with and an array of stellar reviews for his work in the app market and stories about his philanthropy.

The list of charities that he's donated money to is staggering.

The combined amount is astronomical, yet he never took direct credit for any of it.

Each contribution to a worthy cause was in the name of a foundation he'd set up through Cabbott Mobile.

He's a good person who suffered through something so devastating that it drove him across a continent with only the clothes on his back.

"Emma?"

I turn at the sound of Maya's voice.

As always, she looks every inch the professional in a tailored blue pencil skirt and white blouse.

"Hey." I push to stand. "How are you?"

Her face brightens. "I'm doing well."

I shift from one sandal to another. I want to go up to the apartment, but I can't be rude.

"I'm meeting my sister and Case for an early dinner." Her gaze drops to the watch on her wrist. "Or late lunch."

I steal a glance at it. It reads five minutes after seven. That's two hours from now.

As if she can read my mind, she lets out a giggle. "I buy vintage watches because I love the style. They are notoriously bad at keeping me on time."

"Being on time is overrated." I lean closer. "I would never tell my students back home that."

"It'll be our secret." She tugs the strap of her navy blue tote up her forearm. "Why don't you join us for dinner? I'm sure Tilly, my sister, would love to meet you."

The offer is tempting, but I want to take some time to pamper myself before Case comes home. "I'll pass this time, but thank you for thinking of me."

"I'm not the only one thinking of you." Her hand lands on mine. "It's been a very long time since I've seen Case smile. You have everything to do with that."

I dip my chin to hide the wide grin on my face. "He makes me smile too."

"I promise we won't keep him out too late." She looks toward the lobby doors. "His time in New York is limited, so I want him to spend a few hours with Tilly and me before he goes home. It's not often we get to reminisce. We never know when we'll see him again."

A pit settles in my stomach as I watch her walk away.

She has something I'll never have.

Hope.

Once Case leaves for California, Maya knows she'll see him again one day.

I can't say the same for me.

Chapter 47

Case

It took every ounce of restraint within me to sit through a meal with Maya and Tilly. All the two of them wanted to do was play catch up. I wanted out of there.

Three hours later and I'm finally done.

I stand at the door to my apartment with my key in hand.

Earlier this afternoon, I stopped by to drop off a box of condoms. I was sure to be in and out before Maya arrived so I could avoid the inevitable questions about my relationship with Emma.

Maya shot a few questions at me over dinner, but I expertly avoided them by changing the subject. Once I mentioned that Drake is moving to London, Maya picked up the conversation detailing how she hopes to surprise her husband with a trip there next year.

By the time dessert was placed in front of us, I was itching to call it a night and get back here.

An unexpected phone call from my assistant in California gave me an excuse to leave. I paid the check, kissed both women on their cheeks, and took off.

I step into the apartment and stop when I hear Emma's voice.

Shit.

I know she's made friends in the city, but I don't want them here tonight.

It takes me a second to realize that the pause in the conversation is filled with silence. She's on the phone.

Judging by the volume of her voice, I place her in the guestroom with the door ajar.

It's not my place to wonder who she's talking to, but Beauregard comes to mind. If she's willing to give the chaste fool another chance when she heads back to Seattle, that's her choice.

I tell myself that even though my gut is knotting from the thought of another man kissing her. I can't picture another man fucking her without wanting to slam my fist through the wall, so I don't go there.

She's mine right now.

It's temporary, but I'm going to enjoy every second of it.

"I'm grateful that you took the time to call me, Archibald," she says evenly. "I'll give your offer some thought."

I take a step toward the hallway but stop when she continues. "No, I haven't talked to Beauregard. I'm sorry to hear that, but..."

Her voice trails.

I inch closer to the hallway, hoping to catch her coming out of her room. I want her eyes on me when she's talking about her ex-fiancé. I want her to think about a man who craves her. Hell, I can barely contain the desire I feel for her.

Beauregard Garrington has no idea what he lost.

"When do I have to make a decision?" Her voice quickens. "I should be back in Seattle in a few days. Can we talk then?"

A few days?

I want weeks, months. If life were different, I'd be all in for...

My mind can't go there.

I don't get to think about weeks from now or months. Some people won't see tomorrow. I can't lose sight of that. I will never lose sight of that.

"Okay." Emma's voice carries from the guestroom. "Thank you again, Archibald. Good night."

I wait until I hear her footsteps approaching before I round the corner to the hallway.

She lets out a gasp when she sees me.

Her hand leaps to the center of her chest. "You scared me. I think my heart stopped."

Mine sure as hell did.

She's wearing a white strapless dress that skims the floor. Her dark hair is flowing around her shoulders.

She is so fucking beautiful that I literally ache inside when I look at her.

I drop my gaze.

I need to get a grip if I'm going to fuck her.

"Did your overhear me talking on the phone?"

Lying serves no purpose at any time, so I glance at her. "You were talking to Archie."

That brings a bright smile to her lips. "I like that. I'd never call him that, but I like it."

I like you. Jesus, I really like you.

I swallow those words because I'm not a fourteen-year-old kid with a crush. I'm an almost thirty-year-old man with an aching cock who wants to strip this woman bare.

"He offered me a job." She shrugs. "It's not the job I was hoping for, but I'll be back at the Garrington Academy in September."

"With Bonehead?"

She chews on the corner of her bottom lip. "He'll be working in the classroom next to the one I'll be in. I'll be a teaching assistant, but it's a prelude to taking over the class in the next year or two."

It sounds like Archie isn't willing to trust her to lead the kids on her own. What a fucking fool.

"Are you going for it?" I ask, wondering why I give a fuck about this.

I know why. My heart wants to know because it's screwing me around.

I tap the middle of my chest.

Her hand follows my movement. "Do you have heartburn?"

Is that what you call this ache in my chest?

I shake my head. "It's something like that."

"How was dinner with Maya and her sister?" She changes the subject even though I'm far from done talking about her September plans.

"Fine," I answer simply.

"I made a salad for dinner." She bounces up to her toes. "It was très magnifique."

I exhale a deep breath because every word out of her mouth is fucking adorable, including the French words she just said with a roll of her tongue.

"You're all that and more." I rake her from head-to-toe.

She tugs on her skirt with her hand, twirling in a circle. "I have to admit that it was delicious."

I stalk toward her, catching her in my arms mid-twirl. "So are you."

Her eyes skim my chest before they meet mine. "I bought condoms today."

Of course she did. She's practical. She wants to be safe.

"Me too," I whisper as I skim my lips over hers.

"You can never be too careful," she quips.

I've lived my life by that motto for the past seven years. I've been careful with every decision I've made. I've been mindful of how each of my actions impacts the people around me.

I've been so careful that I've stopped feeling.

She wraps a hand around the back of my neck to pull my head down until her lips brush against the curve of my ear. "You're really handsome. Do you know that?"

Dipping her back, I trail my lips over her neck before I take her mouth in a soft kiss. All the air leaves my lungs when she presses a hand to my cheek. "You are the most beautiful woman I've ever seen, Emma Owens."

Her gaze travels over my face, stopping on my eyes. "I'm glad I came to New York."

I straighten her, holding tightly to her waist. "I'm glad you came too."

Running a fingertip over my jaw, she sighs. "I think tonight will be one of those nights I remember for a very long time."

I'll remember it until I take my last breath on this earth.

Chapter 48

Emma

I can't take my eyes off of Case as he lies next to me. His breathing is stuttered. His gaze is feral. I watch intently as his tongue slides over his bottom lip.

"Case," I say his name. "You're driving me crazy."

He barks out a laugh. "I'm driving you crazy?"

He rakes my nude body before he looks at his groin. "You've been stroking my dick for ten minutes straight. I'm so hard that I'm in pain here."

I lean forward to press my lips to the corner of his mouth. "I told you that touching you would make me wet."

"My mouth can make you wet a hell of a lot faster."

I kiss him again, deeper this time. It draws a groan from inside of him.

"I need to fuck you, Emma."

I need that too, but…

My heart won't get out of the way. I'm feeling so much already, and he isn't even sheathed. Once he's inside me, I'm scared that I'll never feel the same again.

Can you fall for someone this hard, this fast?

He moves to reach behind him to the nightstand and the pile of condoms we dumped there.

I emptied the box I bought. He followed with his box. We laughed at the sheer number of foil packages.

He told me we'd use every last one before we go our separate ways. The promise dropped me onto the bed.

I watch as he tears a package open before he skillfully slides the condom over his erection.

It's raw and uninhibited. Each motion of his hand is necessary but primal.

He glides his fist over his cock once and then again.

Before I can catch a breath, he's on top of me. His weight is held up by one hand pressed on the bed next to my head.

His other hand dips between my legs.

I whimper when he rubs my clit.

"Jesus, Emma. You're so wet." The words fall from his lips in a groan.

I stop him with a hand to his chin. I don't have anything to say, but my lips part as if I'll find the words to tell him that this is everything. This moment is more to me than a fuck. I'm reclaiming a part of me that I left behind in my search for love.

"I'll take it slow." He laughs. "Or not."

Locking eyes with him, I smile. "Or hard and fast."

His eyes darken as he shifts his body until the crown of his cock is sliding over my sex.

I cry out when he pushes into me in one solid thrust.

"Easy," he whispers. "Nice and easy."

I wrap my legs around him, trying to lessen any distance between us. I want to feel all of him. I want this man to feel all of me.

His hand snakes beneath my ass to tilt my body to just the right angle before he thrusts once, and then again. And then over and over until I'm lost to every sensation and every sound we make.

He squeezes the flesh of my ass, his fingers digging into me as he takes me with hard, measured strokes.

Each pump of his cock sinks deeper than the last.

I moan as he kisses my neck. I lose my breath when he pins my shoulder to the bed and grinds into me.

"Feel it," he bites out through clenched teeth. "Feel me inside of you. So fucking deep."

We lock eyes as I clench around him. I can't control anything. I feel everything, and when his teeth latch onto my nipple, I fly over the edge and climax in a shudder that leaves me breathless.

"Fuck," he grunts as he rides me through my orgasm.

I hold tightly to him. His eyes lock on mine as his jaw tenses, and he lets out a guttural sound that shoots straight to my core.

I come again just as I feel the heat of his release.

"Please," he breathes through slow strokes as he empties himself into the condom. "That was too much. Fuck, that was so much."

It was everything.

Resting his lips against my neck, he draws in heavy breaths as I cradle him in my arms and wish, more than anything, that I could stop time and stay in this moment forever.

Chapter 49

Case

I crack open an eye to find Emma with her phone in hand.

"Are you trying to grab a dick pic?" I perk a brow. "You could at least wait until it's semi-hard, Freckles. I don't want a picture of my limp cock making the rounds in Seattle."

Shaking her head, she lets out a laugh. "No."

"That's a shame." I drop a hand to circle my now semi-hard cock. "This one deserves to be admired."

Her gaze follows the movement of my hand. "I won't argue with that."

I brush my fingers over her hip before I roll on my side to face her. "What's with the phone in the bed?"

Her eyes search my face. I can tell a question is sitting on the tip of her tongue, waiting to be asked.

Cupping her chin in my hand, I lower my voice. "Tell me what's on your mind, Emma."

"I take pictures of things I want to remember for my scrapbook." Her bottom lip trembles before she sinks her teeth into it to halt it. "Can I take a couple of you? Maybe from the waist up?"

I want her to remember me. I want to be a constant in her memory to even things out because I know I won't get through another day of my life without thinking about her.

Resting my head on the pillow, I gaze into her eyes. "I'm in as long as you do something for me."

"You don't have to negotiate that." She bats her hand over my bicep. "I was going to suck you right after the photo shoot. Maybe in the shower?"

My dick hardens.

We both gaze down.

"I see you like that idea." She laughs, leveling her phone so the camera is centered on my face.

"I fucking love that idea, but I want that and more."

I want it all. I want her.

I tuck my forearm over my face and peek at her as she snaps a photo.

"I want to see all of you, Rush."

"Sing to me." I inch my arm down.

The faint sound of the shutter of the phone's camera fills the air.

She looks past the phone to lock eyes with me. "You want me to sing to you?"

With the back of my hand grazing my lips, I smile. "Do it."

She does. She starts a song about love and affection. Her voice is carrying the tune in a way it hasn't before.

Or maybe I wasn't listening to the lyrics the last time I heard her sing.

It's beautiful. It reaches deep inside of me, and when she takes the last picture, I'm staring at her in awe.

The song winds down with a pound of her fist into the bed's sheet as she almost hits a high note.

I'm on her then. My hands glide over her skin, my lips are on her mouth, and as I hold her next to me, I breathe in the sweet scent of her.

I don't deserve this moment in time, but I'll take it.

I'll savor it, and I'll remember it forever.

***

Reaching around to cup her tit in my hand, I drive my dick into her.

Her cheek pushes into the tiles of the shower stall. "Fuck me."

She first whispered the words when I yanked her up from her knees as I was on the brink of blowing my load down her throat.

I wanted inside her, so as desperate as I was, I marched through the bathroom and into the main suite of my bedroom to grab a condom. Water dripped from me with every step.

With shaking hands, I sheathed myself on the way back, and without a word, I pushed her against the wall of the shower as hot water beat over us.

I took her hard, and unashamedly, not caring if she was ready.

She was.

I slid in easily, and when I found my rough rhythm, she met it with thrusts of her own, each punctuated with a moan.

"You're so fucking tight," I hiss out the words.

Her head falls against my shoulder, so I cup a hand around the front of her neck and draw her closer. I'm desperate to feel my mouth on hers.

A fierce kiss on her lips sends her hips back. "Harder, Case."

I sink my fingers into the flesh of her waist as I pump harder and faster until she comes with a powerful shudder, her hands reaching back to claw at my skin.

My release is one thrust behind as I rest my head against hers and groan her name.

Chapter 50

Emma

I gaze down at the pictures I took of Case this morning. I see joy in his eyes.

I don't know if it's because of the sex. I hope part of it is just because of me.

"Who the hell is that?"

I look up to find Bella standing over me. I drop my phone into my lap. "No one."

"No one?" She takes the empty seat across from me. "That's him, isn't it? That's your brother's best friend?"

I glance around the interior of Calvetti's. It's just after noon.

I came here after Bella sent me a text this morning asking what I had lined up for lunch. Since Case had to go to work, I messaged her back, agreeing to meet at her grandma's restaurant.

Case arranged for Drake's driver to bring me here even though I insisted that I was enjoying learning the intricacies of the subway.

Our plan is to meet at his office later.

"It looks like he's shirtless in that." Bella wiggles her fingers at me. "Is he in a bed? Give me your phone. I want to see."

Shaking my head, I glance toward where her grandma is standing. "Let's talk about something else, this feels…"

"Marti knows about sex." She laughs. "How do you think she ended up with so many kids?"

Chuckling, I scoop the phone back into my palm and hold the screen toward her so she can see the last image of Case that I took.

Leaning forward, her gaze darts from the screen to my face. "He's gorgeous, Emma. Do you see how he's looking at you?"

I turn the phone back so I can stare at the picture. "He looks happy, doesn't he?"

"I don't know him, but that is the face of a very content man." Leaning her elbows on the table, she lowers her voice. "You slept with him, didn't you?"

Even though I only met Bella recently, I feel close to her.

There's something about her that is disarming. I know I can trust her.

"Last night."

The corners of her lips curve up. "You look happy too."

Shaking my head, I let out a sigh. "It was the best. I mean, by far, the absolute best I've ever had."

"It's incredible when that happens, isn't it?" She lowers her chin. "My first time with Barrett blew my mind. I couldn't think straight. I could barely walk straight."

My knees trembled after I came in the shower this morning, so Case carried me back to the bed. He toweled me dry before he crawled between my legs and ate me to an orgasm.

After he dressed in a navy blue suit and a white button-down shirt, he watched me choose a pair of jeans and a red blouse. I felt nothing but happiness as he helped me dress, kissing the skin between my breasts before he buttoned my blouse.

This morning couldn't have been any more perfect than it was.

"I'm glad you went for it." She glances at Marti as she approaches. "My grandma always says that you can't win if you don't take the chance."

They're wise words, but I can't win.

Soon, I'll board a plane and head back to Seattle with only the memories of last night.

"What can I get for you beautiful girls?" Marti slides a hand over Bella's hair.

"I could go for the avocado pesto linguine." Bella looks at me. "How about you, Emma?"

"That sounds delicious."

"You'll both have the lamb ragu." Marti starts toward the kitchen. "I made it myself."

Watching her walk away, I laugh. "Did she just veto your order?"

"Our order," Bella corrects me with a wink. "Consider yourself an honorary Calvetti. You know you're part of the family when my grandma feeds you what she thinks you need, instead of what you want."

***

I wait to approach Elias until he ends the call he's on.

He's not the same assistant that my brother had last year, but I like him. I know he's been helpful to Drake and that matters to me.

"Emma." He pushes back from his desk, adjusting the collar of the striped blue button-down shirt he's wearing. "It's good to see you again."

"You too." I glance past his shoulder to the open door of Drake's office. "Is Case busy?"

Nodding, he shoves his hand into the front pocket of his gray pants. "He's in a meeting with Human Resources. Give him another twenty minutes and he'll be back."

I can wait. I want to wait.

"You're welcome to take a seat in your brother's office." Elias gestures to the open office door. "I'll grab you something to drink. There's coffee or tea in the break room. I can get a soda from the machine down the hall if you want."

"Thank you, but I'm good."

Breezing past him, I walk into Drake's office. I should sit in one of the chairs facing his desk, but I plop myself into the chair behind the desk so I can see Case as he approaches.

Dropping my purse on the floor, I lean back and take in the office.

It's expansive. The furniture is modern and sleek.

There's no way that Drake chose any of this. This looks like it was plucked out of Sandy's brain. My best friend has the magic touch when it comes to interior design. The things she could do with an apartment in New York would blow my mind.

An apartment in New York where I'd build a life with Case.

I chase that thought away with a sigh. That can never be. He lives in California. I belong in Seattle.

Or I did once.

I'm not sure where home is anymore.

Chapter 51

Case

I could get used to seeing this.

I watch Emma as she sits behind her brother's desk. She's twirling a pen between her fingers as she hums a tune that sounds like pure heaven to me.

It also sounds a hell of a lot like the theme music to Gem Stars.

I only know that because Drake played it over and over for me before he finally approved it.

I join in, humming a few beats.

Her head pops up. The smile that blooms on her lips grips my heart. "Hey, you."

"Hey, you," I repeat back in a soft tone. "I didn't expect to see you for a couple of hours."

Her gaze drops back to the desk and the open file folder in front of her.

It's the blue folder that contains some of the most brilliant ideas her brother has ever come up with. I was skimming through it again before I was called to HR.

"How has your day been?" I keep the conversation light because Elias is less than ten feet away with his ear tuned to us.

This guy gives Lester a run for his money.

If he's reporting anything back to Drake, I want it to all be rated PG.

"I had lunch with Bella." Her gaze drifts up. "Calvetti's has spoiled me for Italian food. How will I ever go back to a chain restaurant that serves warmed up pasta again?"

"I'll courier Marti's lasagna to you in Seattle whenever you crave it."

It's meant as a joke, but her expression shifts. She covers it quickly with an awkward grin. "Or I could just ask Bella for the family recipe."

I laugh. "I think Marti will take all her recipes to the grave."

Emma half-shrugs a shoulder. "I'll experiment in the kitchen when I get home."

I almost volunteer to be her taste tester, but that's not going to happen.

Her hand pats one of the papers in the folder. "Drake keeps notes on the things we talk about."

I take two measured steps into my office so I can shut the door and cut off Elias's access to this conversation because *what the fuck did Emma just say?*

Lowering my voice, I ask the obvious question. "What do you mean?"

Her lips curve up. "Drake and I brainstorm sometimes. My educational expertise helps him flesh out ideas. I'm happy to help."

I skim the paper in front of her. It's the detailed notes on an app for kids. The premise is genius. The child gets to dictate the direction of various stories with their gameplay. It's based on the child's reading level. As they progress, more words are added to the game's vocabulary.

"You helped him with that idea?" I point to the paper.

She nods. "This is Vary Tales. I wouldn't say I helped him with the idea. This one is all mine."

With a swipe of the pen in her hand across the top of the paper, she writes *Vary Tales*.

"Vary Tales?" I ask, curious where the idea was born.

"Our grandmother's maiden name was Vary, and she always made up stories to tell us." She traces a fingertip over the words she just wrote. "I thought it was fitting that we name the app after her since she was the inspiration. It's an obvious play on fairy tales. Whenever I come up with a new story idea for this I send it to Drake. I've sent dozens over the last six months, but he only has a few written down on this paper."

If we take this to market, she deserves credit and compensation.

This is her idea.

She's the creative mind behind it.

I stare at the folder, realization hitting me like a freight train. "Did you have a hand in any of the other ideas in there?"

Her fingers flip through the papers in the folder. She yanks one out and places it on top. "This one is mine."

Before I can get my eyes on what it is, another paper is on top of it. "This one too."

Scrubbing a hand over the back of my neck, I curse under my breath.

"Oh, and this one." She pats her palm on yet another paper.

Every fucking paper in that folder that has some tie to education is Emma's idea.

"My favorite idea isn't here." Her lips dip into a frown. "Drake was so excited about it. I'm surprised he didn't keep the notes I gave him."

He probably already developed the damn thing and collected a huge bonus from me for all '*his*' hard work.

I drop into one of the chairs in front of Drake's desk. "Tell me about that."

"It's an app to help kids learn basic reading comprehension. It's a simple concept."

I want more details, so I roll my hand in the air. "Go on."

"If they line up the letters to spell a word, they uncover a picture related to another word that starts with the same letter. It's all about sound association." She smiles. "Spell Snake was the working name because I thought it would be adorable to have an animated snake guide the kids through the game."

I feel like I've jumped into the deep end of a pool without any sense of which direction I need to swim to hit the water's surface.

"The app would mainly help kids prepare for kindergarten and first grade, but there are levels beyond that." Her gaze drops back to the desk. "Drake thought it might be too simplistic, but I think it has merit."

It has millions of dollars invested in its launch weeks from now.

Letter Leap is expected to gross more than any educational product we've developed based on early interest in it. Our preliminary testing showed that kids love the animated frog that narrates the game.

That app wouldn't exist if it weren't for Emma's ideas.

I need to make this right and that happens now.

Chapter 52

Emma

Case slides to his feet and rounds the desk toward me.

Are we about to have sex?

Is he going to swipe an arm over the desk to clear it before he strips me and takes me right here and now?

He points at the drawer right in front of me. "There's a tablet in there I need. I want to show you something."

My dream of office sex won't be coming true today.

I roll back to give him room to open the drawer.

He yanks out a tablet. He swipes a finger over the screen to power it up.

"I want you to look at something for me."

I glance up to his face. He's not smiling. If anything, he looks worried, or concerned.

Anxiety roots itself in my stomach in the form of a knot. What could he possibly have to show me? Please don't let it be related to Drake coming back to New York.

I may have been eager for that to happen a few days ago, but now I want my brother to take his time.

I'm not ready to say goodbye to Case yet.

'This is Letter Leap." He places the tablet in my hands. "We're working out a glitch, but you shouldn't run into a problem if you play the first few levels. Give it a try."

I scan the screen, taking in the brightly colored graphics.

When I gaze back at Case, he's scrubbing a hand over the back of his neck. Something has shifted dramatically since he walked into this office. "You want me to play a game? Do you want my opinion on it? Drake sent me an early copy of Gem Stars."

His eyes close briefly. "Please just start the game, Emma."

Nodding, I set my focus on the screen. I tap the start now button and take time to set up the features, including adding my name. I choose the skill level of a first grader since I've worked with many during my time at Garrington Academy. I assume this is the point where a parent would hand the tablet over to their child to play.

An animated frog pops on the screen.

He croaks out a greeting to me. "*Hi, Emma. Welcome to Letter Leap.*"

Working my way through the first few puzzles, I feel my pulse quicken. This is surreal. I can't believe this.

I stop to glance up at Case standing next to me. "This is Spell Snake. All of it is exactly what I envisioned. I gave Drake all the details right down to the old talking apple tree with the crooked teeth and the long eyelashes."

I expect a smile to creep over Case's lips, but instead, I see fury behind his eyes.

I place the tablet on the desk. "What's wrong?"

Case sets a hand on the corner of the desk, and the other on the back of the chair so he can lean closer to me. "Did he tell you he was using your idea?"

I shake my head. "No."

"*Fuck*," slips from between his lips.

"I don't mind," I try and smooth out his anger. "He's my brother. It's fine. I got him to help me with an English paper when I was in high school."

His jaw tenses. "This isn't the same, Emma."

"It is to me."

He crouches to look me directly in the eyes. "Did you come up with the concept for this game on your own?"

"I'm not sure," I answer tentatively because I have no idea what's running through his head. "I thought a snake was a great idea, but obviously, Drake thinks a frog is better."

"You need a lawyer, Emma."

Panic shoots through me. A lawyer? What the hell do I need a lawyer for?

In the scramble to rush to my feet, I almost knock Case flat on his ass. He stands, giving me room to do the same.

"What's going on?" I knit my shaking hands together in a fist in front of my stomach. I feel nauseous. "Drake told me about people pitching ideas to Cabbott that were replicas of apps that belong to other tech companies. Do you think that's what I did? You think I stole the idea for this app from someone?"

Case reaches for my hands. He quiets them immediately by drawing them to his chest. "I think your brother stole the idea from you."

I laugh. "That's not what happened. I suggested an idea, and he developed it."

Case exhales sharply. "You are the creative mind behind Letter Leap. You're entitled to compensation and recognition for that."

I try to wrap my brain around what he's saying. "What kind of compensation?"

He brings my hands to his face to skim his lips over one of my palms. "A royalty. We'll work that out. You need to get a lawyer to negotiate terms, Emma, but Cabbott will be generous. I promise we'll be more than generous for this idea and the development of Vary Tales."

My head is spinning as I take it all in. "You're going to develop Vary Tales?"

His eyes lock on mine. "I'd like you to consider joining the development team as a narrative designer for that project and others in our educational division."

"What does that mean?"

"It means a full-time job at Cabbott." He glances at the tablet before he levels his gaze back on me. "I'll explain more if you're interested."

I'm interested. How could I not be, but... "I don't know anything about coding or software development or the other terms Drake is always talking about."

"You don't need to be skilled in any of that." He squeezes my hands. "Essentially, you envision the concept of the game or program and our software developers will help you bring it to life. It's what we've done with Letter Leap. Your vision is now a reality."

I shake my head. "I don't know. I became a teacher because I want to help kids learn. It's what I love to do."

His hands move to cup my cheeks. "You will be helping millions of kids learn through these apps, Emma. You can make a difference in so many lives."

Biting my lower lip, I suck in a deep breath. "Will I make as much as I do teaching?"

He cracks a wide smile. "The salary for a narrative designer is substantial, but you should know in terms of royalties on these games, you're looking well into seven figures, if not higher the first year of release."

My knees go weak for the second time today.

Case is there to catch me again. He circles his arms around me. "Are you okay?"

I shake my head. "No, I am... seven figures... that's in the millions, right?"

His lips brush my forehead. "Yes."

I hold tight to him because the earth just shifted under my feet.

Holy hell.

My entire life has changed in an instant.

Chapter 53

Case

I sit Emma back down in the chair because all the color has drained from her beautiful face.

A dozen thoughts crowd my mind, but all I can focus on is the fact that I can tell her that the job is based in San Francisco.

I could build a life with her.

We'd take Cabbott to the next level hand-in-hand.

"Are you mad at Drake?" Her question breaks through my fantasy.

"Disappointed," I answer truthfully.

I was seething a few minutes ago, but I've placed the weight of the world on my best friend's shoulders. I dropped my business into his lap seven years ago and expected him to take the reins until I found my footing again.

I gave him the impossible task of sorting through details of the life I left behind here in New York. No one should expect another to take care of some of the things I pushed at him.

But he did it. He never complained or questioned me.

He cared enough to give me a clear path to heal after the worst experience of my life.

How can I rail on him for this?

"I don't think he meant to steal anything from me," Emma says quietly. "Drake isn't like that."

Drake is as devoted to Cabbott as I am. Breaking into the educational app space is a big step for us. He looked to his sister for inspiration, so it's on him to sort that out with her on a personal level. I won't get into the middle of that, but I will do what I can do look out for Emma's best interests.

I can fool myself into believing I'm doing this to cover Cabbott Mobile's ass since Drake took her idea and ran to the bank with it.

That's not why I'm going to have contracts drawn up that guarantee Emma will be well compensated for her creative ingenuity.

I want her to get what is due to her.

She deserves this.

"I'll talk to Drake about this," I offer. "You'll get to work finding a lawyer. I want all of this handled as soon as possible."

Her gaze drops to her lap. "I know a lawyer in Seattle. He helped me with my contract when I signed on with the Garrington Academy."

"Did Archie recommend him?"

She glances at me with perked brows. "Yes. Beauregard said he handled the estate planning for his grandparents too."

"He's not going to work for this." I lean against the edge of the desk, crossing my feet at the ankles. "You need someone who specializes in contract work. I can have Elias put together a list of attorneys in Manhattan who are skilled in that area."

"Someone in your back pocket?" She winks, or her nervous tic has got a hold of her.

"The only lawyers in my back pocket work for Cabbott." I look her in the eye, so she understands I'm serious. "I won't steer you wrong on this, Emma. I want this above board for obvious reasons."

She drops her head into her hands, shielding her face from my view. "Is this really happening?"

"It is."

Her hands fall to the desk, but she keeps her head bowed. "Where will I work? I mean, what city will I work in? I know you have different offices."

With expectation swimming in them, her eyes meet mine as she waits for me to answer.

The urge to say '*San Francisco*' is almost overwhelming, but I stop myself.

"We'll figure out those details in the contract."

With a faint nod of her head, she glances at the desk. "When I came to New York, I didn't think my entire life would change."

Neither did I.

The moment breaks with a knock on the door. *Fuck.*

"What?" I bark out, knowing that it has to be Elias on the other side.

He opens the door with a flourish and a smile. "We got it, sir! The framework issue on Letter Leap is fixed."

"Thank Christ," I mutter under my breath.

Emma slides to her feet. "We should celebrate."

Elias nods a little too exuberantly for someone who isn't getting near any celebration that involves Emma. "I'll get some champagne."

"You'll get the hell out of the office." I shoot him a look. "Give Emma and I a minute alone, and then I'll head down to check out the fix."

He laughs like I'm jesting.

Fool.

"Out, Elias." I take a step toward him. "Get Drake on the phone. I want him informed of where we are on this."

"On it, sir."

Once the door is shut, I tug Emma closer to me. "I need some time to check on this."

"I need some time too."

She doesn't expand, and I don't pry. I just dropped a future in her lap that she didn't see coming.

I wish to fuck I could offer more. I want to give her everything she deserves.

"I'll see you at the apartment later?" She runs a hand over my bicep. "Or do I need to steer clear of the place?"

"Maya won't show up today," I assure her with a smile. "You are more than welcome to get naked and wait for me."

Her lips brush mine in a soft kiss. "I might have to put that on my agenda."

I scan the watch on my wrist. "I'll do my best to make it back by seven."

"I'll do my best to not touch myself until then."

A groan escapes me. "Fuck. You'll make me hard if you talk like that."

"Just think about it." Her finger trails a path over my chin. "I'd give almost anything to feel this on my thighs again."

I grab her hand and press it to the light beard covering my jaw. "This?"

With a perch up to her tiptoes, she kisses me again. Her tongue strokes mine, tempting me. "And that. I want to feel that again."

"You have yourself a deal." I cup the back of her neck with my hand. "I'll see you later, Freckles."

"You can count on it, Rush."

Chapter 54

Emma

I could have stayed in Drake's office and waited for Case to finish up with his work, but I needed time alone to digest what happened today.

I'm being handed a chance to change my life completely.

Although it couldn't have come at a better time, something inside of me is mourning the life I had a month ago.

I don't miss Beauregard. That's not it at all.

I'll never be able to drive over to the house I grew up in to hang out with my parents. I won't braid Whitney's hair while she complains about a guy she secretly wants to date.

Sandy and I will never again convince the woman who runs the theatre near my condo to let us sneak in just to buy a bag of popcorn because it's the best we've ever tasted.

Beyond all of that, I'll miss the kids I worked with.

I know most of them by name since I've floated in and out of their classrooms.

Life changes. I know that. I accept that.

I want that.

I move from where I've been standing near the window in Case's apartment that overlooks Madison Avenue.

When I got here an hour ago, I let myself in and dropped the envelope in my hand on the dining room table.

Lester gave it to me as I was passing through the lobby on my way up here.

It's the print I had made of Drake's wedding that I ordered through the Printe app. I look at the envelope, suddenly wondering if Drake was actually the person who created the app or not.

I've never doubted my older brother, but I do now.

Faulting him for taking my idea and passing it off as his own won't splinter our relationship. The only thing it's proven to me is that he's human.

He has flaws.

We all have flaws.

Setting myself into one of the dining chairs, I open the envelope and slide out the picture.

The quality is impressive. The colors are vibrant.

I've never ordered anything from the app other than snapshot size prints for my scrapbook.

My phone's sudden ring jars me enough that the picture falls from my hands onto the table. I stare at it, marveling at how happy Drake looks even though he's not facing the camera.

I fish in my purse for my phone and pull it out.

"Drake," I whisper his name before I slide my finger over the screen to answer the call.

"Hey," I say quietly.

"Em," he pauses. "Fuck, Em. I'm sorry."

Tears don't come because I'm not sad. I'm feeling something that borders on relief combined with acceptance.

Drake is just a man. He's not the superhero I've always made him out to be in my mind.

"I know," I reassure him.

"You don't know," he counters. "I feel like shit. I should have discussed it with you. I should have gone to Case and explained that the idea for Letter Leap didn't belong to me."

"Case is handling it," I say it with conviction. "I'm handling it."

"I'll make this up to you."

How? He made a mistake. He's apologized and since I'll be working in the educational division at Cabbott, I'll be in control of what I bring to the table. I'll take ownership of that.

The blind trust I had in him may be fractured, but time can rebuild it to a place that's more balanced.

"We found a house," he blurts out before I can say anything.

I shut my eyes, trying to grasp what he just said. "What?"

"It was the first one we saw." His voice climbs to a chirpy tone. It's suddenly more cheerful. "We'll put an offer in tomorrow morning."

"Don't you want to see a few others before you commit?"

"When you find something that's perfect for you, why bother looking for anything else?"

I glance up when I hear the apartment door open.

Case's smile is the first thing I see.

"You're right," I say to my brother. "Why keep looking once you've found perfection?"

***

"Did you give him hell?" Case asks as I place my phone on the table after ending my call with Drake.

I didn't tell him I love him. Drake didn't offer the words to me either, but the sentiment is there even if it's buried under other emotions.

"Did you?" I counter.

"That and more." He slides his suit jacket off. "I'm hiring someone to oversee him in London. Drake will be second in command there."

It's a demotion. It's likely temporary but warranted all the same.

I sense that if anyone else in Cabbott's organization tried to get away with what Drake did, they'd be fired.

"Is the London office an option for me?"

A slow smile spreads over his lips. "You're not ready to take on the role of being your brother's keeper, Emma."

I laugh that off. "That's not what I meant."

He works to unbutton his shirt. "I know."

He doesn't expand on that, so I press for more. "Is New York going to be my home base?"

My breath catches when he opens his shirt because the man is gorgeous, and the sight of him takes my breath away every time.

"We'll talk about that."

I'd ask when but I can tell he wants something else right now. I step out of my sandals. Before I can drop my hands to the buttons on my blouse, he's on top of me.

"How are you so beautiful and so smart and so everything, Emma Owens?"

Biting the corner of my bottom lip, I shake my head. "That's a secret I'll never share."

"Do you have secrets?" He pops a brow.

"Do you?"

His gaze falls to the floor as he swallows hard. "Doesn't everyone?"

"You know mine." I try to lighten the mood. "I was celibate for a long time."

His hands grip my waist. "A woman like you should never be denied what she wants."

I slide my fingers over his cheek until they're resting on his chin. I tilt it so his eyes meet mine. "I want you."

His heated gaze travels over me. "I'm yours."

Forever?

That question lingers on my tongue, but I know I can't ask it because the answer will spear me. It will break me.

"Take me to bed," I whisper.

Without a word, he takes my hand in his, kisses it, and leads me down the hallway.

Chapter 55

Case

She moans when I stroke my tongue over the seam of her sex.

I take that as a challenge to lure another orgasm from her. She came once as I licked her. It was intense with her fingers clawing at my hair, tugging it, pulling it, and drawing pain to the surface.

But it couldn't compete with what's happening inside of me.

My heart is aching.

Never in my life did I think I'd fall in love. That has to be what this is.

I'd sacrifice everything for Emma. I'd step in front of a moving bus if it meant she'd get another minute on this earth.

"Case." My name escapes her in a long-drawn-out sexy-as-fuck groan. "You need to stop that."

"Never," I say.

It's a lie. It's the only lie I ever want to tell her.

I can't promise her anything more than tonight or a day or two more.

"Stop," she whines. "Please."

I do because I sense that she needs my arms around her more than she needs this.

I crawl up her body, taking my time to plant kisses on my journey.

One on her hipbone and another on the curve under her belly button. I press my lips to the tender spot between her breasts before I glide my tongue over her neck.

"I came," she announces in a whisper. "Could you tell?"

I settle in next her, drawing her into my chest. "I'm bald. You pulled out all of my hair."

That lures a laugh from her. "You're not."

"I wouldn't care if I was." I rest my cheek against hers. "If it brought you pleasure, I'd walk around without any hair."

Her breathing quiets. "It's your turn, but don't pull out my hair. I like it."

I huff out a laugh. "Is that how this works?"

I feel the nod of her head against me. "That's how it works."

"I don't want it to be my turn." I kiss her forehead. "I want to feel you come again. I want to be inside you."

She inches her way over me, her lush body pressed against mine until she's on top of me. "We can try it like this."

Staring up, I take in the vision of her nude body. Her nipples are swollen into hard points. Her cheeks are flushed pink from the orgasm.

My heart rams against the wall of my chest.

Love hurts. It's true – love fucking hurts.

I reach to the nightstand to grab a condom. Ripping open the foil packet, I feel her eyes glued to my every movement.

Sliding back onto my thighs, she gives me space to sheath myself. She watches intently, her eyes glued to my cock.

I reach out to guide her back when I'm ready, but she's already moving. Before I can register what's happening, her tight heat is enveloping me.

"Oh, God," she moans. "This is…"

"Fucking amazing," I groan. "More, Emma."

She sinks lower, taking more of me. "It's so good."

It's damn good. It's so damn good that I have to shut my eyes because watching her face as she sinks onto my cock is chasing me to the edge.

She starts on a slow rhythm. It's gentle glides of her body over mine.

I hold her waist to temper her movements, because *fuck me*, this is more than any man can bear.

"We have to do this again," she purrs. "Over and over."

I can't form a response because every nerve ending in my body feels exposed. I'm close to coming already.

I crack open an eye to see her brushing her tongue over her bottom lip. Her eyes are closed. Her head lulled back in ecstasy as she rides my cock.

Small moans escape her with every movement she makes.

I spear up into her. That sets her back into an arch.

My hand slides to her clit. I finger it, pushing, circling, luring her closer to the edge because there's no way in fuck I'm going to last.

"Case." My name spills out of her in a breathless rush. "I'm going to…"

Before the word falls from her, I come. I curse as she follows me into it, and when her pussy clamps around me, my eyes tear because this is everything.

This is pure and honest intimacy with a woman who has opened my heart and given it another chance to feel.

I pull her onto my chest and hold her there so she can hear the pounding of my heart.

It's her heart.

It belongs to her, and regardless of what happens tomorrow or a year from now, that's a fact that will never change.

Chapter 56

Emma

"You left me in bed so you could play a game on your phone?" Case accuses with a laugh. "What the fuck, Emma?"

I glance over my shoulder to see him coming down the hallway toward me. He's wearing only a pair of black boxer briefs.

Wow.

I turn my phone's camera to face him. "I should get a picture of this."

He stretches his arms out at his sides. "Have at it. I have no shame."

I snap a quick picture before I add it to my Printe order.

Drake will probably be coming back to Manhattan soon. That means I'll be heading to Seattle with him and Jane to fill my folks in on everything that's happened.

I want to print out the pictures I've taken on this trip to add to an extra scrapbook I have at my condo. I'll label it my life-changing scrapbook since the life I'm facing in the future is completely different than the life I had before this trip.

Case drops onto the couch next to me, craning his neck to see my phone's screen. "Is that the Printe app?"

I turn my phone toward him. "It is. I'm putting in an order. Do you have a coupon code?"

He huffs out a hearty laugh. "Hold off on that order until you're on staff. Free Printe prints are a perk for Cabbott employees."

I glance back at the screen and hit the *order now* button. "I can't wait."

Dropping my phone on the leather couch between us, I glance at his face. "You were fast asleep. What woke you up?"

His lips part, but he doesn't say anything. Instead, he shoves a hand through his hair. "What woke you up?"

I don't have an answer to that question either. My mind quieted enough after we made love that I was able to sleep for almost two hours.

When I woke up, I needed space, so I came into the main living area.

My time with Case is coming to an end unless he offers me a job at the Cabbott office in San Francisco.

"I'm not sure," I answer with a shrug.

He leans forward to scoop my bare legs into his lap. I'm wearing his white shirt again, but this time only one button is done up.

Running a hand over my skin, he sighs. "I had a dream about you."

My mouth curves up into a smile. "Tell me about it."

Glancing at me, he grins. "You were singing, of course."

"Of course?" I question with a fake scowl. "What does that mean?"

"You always sing to me in my dreams."

My breath catches in my chest. "Do you dream of me often?"

"Since I met you, yes." He glances at the windows that overlook Madison Avenue. "Before that, I had other dreams."

"What dreams?" I question even though I doubt he'll answer.

He's holding something painful inside. I see it whenever I look deeply into his eyes. It might be masked by happiness now because of us, but it's still there below the surface, gnawing at him, consuming him.

His gaze drops to my legs. He runs a finger over one. "Dreams about my brother."

"What's his name?"

His hand stops. I see the sudden shake in it. Reaching forward, I place mine over it.

"Apollo," he whispers. "My brother's name was Apollo Easton."

***

I wait for more, but the only sound that fills the silence is the beat of raindrops against the window.

I rest my head on Case's shoulder, trying to comfort him, so he knows that I'm here. I'll listen. I'll understand.

"In my dreams, he's eighteen." He closes his eyes. "I think when someone dies, they never age in your dreams. They always look and sound the way they did the last time you saw them."

I bite back the urge to cry because that's not what he needs. He needs strength. "What was he like?"

"He was nothing like me."

I smile because I doubt that. Case must have an influence on every person he meets. He's had an incredible impact on me.

"It was a long time ago." His hand inches over my knee. "I don't want to forget him. I never want to forget him."

"You won't," I offer even though the memory of my grandma has faded over time.

He looks at me. "He would have liked you, Emma. He probably would have liked you more than he liked me."

I can't help but laugh. "That's hard to imagine. You're pretty likable."

His gaze wanders to the window again before it levels back on me. "Come back to bed. The rain will help us fall asleep."

I place my hand in his. "Lead the way."

He does.

We crawl into his bed, and with his arms wrapped around me he drifts off. I watch him sleep with a new understanding of why sadness has taken root in his beautiful green eyes.

Chapter 57

Case

I swore that I'd never tell a woman about my brother.

Guilt has kept his story locked inside of me for years.

I couldn't even get the words out to the people I worked with at Cabbott Mobile.

Drake handled it.

He handled everything after I found Apollo's lifeless body. He let me stay at his apartment until I moved into this place. He made sure I ate at least once a day. It was Drake who sorted through my brother's belongings and took care of all the arrangements I couldn't think about.

I glance up from where I'm sitting at the dining room table when I hear Emma's footsteps approaching down the hall.

I left her in my bed. She was curled up, fast asleep.

I got up to work on my laptop, but that requires concentration, so everything that needs my attention is still waiting.

"Good morning," she whispers when she rounds the corner.

Good morning indeed.

She's a vision wrapped in another of my button-down shirts. This one is light blue.

I'm tempted to ask her to toss all of her clothes out and only wear mine.

"How are you?"

The compassion in her voice slices through me. She's a kind soul. Her heart is in the right place.

I knew that the conversation that I started last night wouldn't end when we fell asleep. She'd want to know more. I want her to know more, but it's going to take time, and we don't have a hell of a lot of that left.

Drake will be back in Manhattan soon, and I'll take off for California.

I imagine Emma will need to settle up her life in Seattle before she starts working at Cabbott.

I glance at the screen of my laptop and the information that I'm gathering in a document to send off to one of Cabbott's lawyers. She'll plug the details into a standard contract for Emma to sign.

I decided on the salary we'll offer and the perks.

It's the location of the job that I'm stuck on.

I want her in San Francisco. I want to continue what we've started. Maybe, last night was the first step toward that.

"I'm fine," I say. "How are you, Emma?"

"Tender." Her hand dives to cover her mound. "Last night was intense."

"In a good way." I wave her over. "Sit in my lap."

She pads over on her bare feet. With a yank on the hem of my shirt to pull it down, she settles on my lap. The only thing separating us is the boxer briefs I'm wearing.

Her hand falls into my hair. Running her fingers through it, she smiles. "I know last night wasn't easy for you. I mean the sex was easy."

I let out a chuckle. "Pleasing you is easy. I'd do anything to make you feel good."

"I want to make you feel good too." Her lips brush my forehead. "Your body and your heart. I want to make every part of you feel good."

Including my conscience?

When I glance up and into her eyes, I see that she means everything she just said. "When we first met, I wondered if you knew about Apollo. I wondered if Drake had told you."

Her fingers trace a path across my forehead. "He didn't say a word. I had no idea that your brother had passed away."

The words are as peaceful as Apollo's death was.

What came after was the brutal part.

"He moved to Manhattan six weeks before he died."

Her breathing stutters. "He moved into this apartment with you?"

Fuck. I wish that had happened. I wish every goddamn day that we would have had time here together.

"I was living in a walk up on the Lower East Side." I close my eyes, willing the wave of memories to retreat.

I rented the apartment when I first settled in New York. It was a month-to-month two bedroom with a sticky lock on the door and a refrigerator that couldn't keep anything cold.

I had money in my pocket, but fear kept me from spending it until my younger half-brother wanted something.

"Apollo came to Manhattan after he was accepted to Fordham University." I take a breath. "The kid was an ace at baseball. That was his ticket to the scholarship he earned."

Right after Apollo died, everyone who visited my grandfather in San Francisco to offer condolences, rushed him through his memories of Apollo. They wanted to know what took his life. The death of someone so young is often more about that one moment than all the time they spent living.

"What position did he play?"

The question catches me off guard. I've never been asked that. Drake never bothered to ask that.

Emma is putting value in who Apollo was; not on how he was taken. "Pitcher."

"Some would argue that's the most important position on the team."

That lures a smile to my mouth. "Pol would agree with you."

"Pol," she repeats his nickname. "Did he like it when you called him that?"

"He fucking loved it." I tilt my head back to steal a breath. "His dad left before he was born, so it was my grandpa and me that raised him. I was Rush, and he was Pol."

There's no question about my parents waiting to be asked. Drake must have told Emma that my father was killed in a motorcycle accident was I was three. My mother left when Pol was a year old. She fucked off with some random she met who had a fat wallet and a dislike for kids.

My grandfather stepped in and saw to it that my brother and I had everything we needed.

I've returned the favor the past few years. He lives a half-mile from me in his own beach house. It's smaller, but it suits him fine.

It's the ocean that is the draw for both of us. It's where we feel closest to Pol.

Silence settles between us, but it's comfortable. Emma rests her head against mine.

I want her to know what happened to my brother as much as I want to forget.

"I went to work early one Tuesday morning." I squeeze her tighter, wanting to keep her in place while I get the words out. "When I came home from work that afternoon, he was gone. He was still in his bed."

She presses a kiss to my forehead. "I'm so sorry, Case."

"He was supposed to go to Fordham that day for orientation, but he never made it." My voice cracks. "Pol died in his sleep of a seizure."

Chapter 58

Emma

I hold Case in my arms.

Words can't do justice to the loss that he experienced, but if I can offer comfort through my touch, I want to do that.

"Apollo wanted to live here." He tilts his head until our eyes meet. "His dream was to live in a fancy place with a doorman and a killer view of the city."

I run my fingers over his cheek. "This apartment fits that bill."

"We looked at it together." His gaze surveys the room. "Two minutes into the tour, he was nudging me in the side and telling me this was our new home."

I don't have to ask why. Case's brother was as impressed with the apartment as I was when I first saw it.

"I put an offer in that day. It was accepted," he pauses briefly to shift me in his lap. "Sixty days after that, we were supposed to move in."

Apollo died in the interim.

I glide my hand to his neck and then his shoulder.

"I tried to get out of the deal after he died, but Drake convinced me to move in." He swallows. "He thought it was a good way to honor Pol's memory, but every day I lived in this apartment felt like hell on earth."

"I'm sorry." I rest my head against his. "I can't imagine how painful that must have been."

His lips find my cheek for a soft kiss. "I tried to drown the pain. I drank too much at the bar across the street, and then I'd bring a woman home and…"

I don't ask him to finish the sentence because I don't want to hear about him and other women.

"I reached my breaking point one morning when I woke up next to a woman I didn't know. I picked her up at the bar across the street the night before."

I listen intently because I know that confessing this can't be easy for him.

"She was going through my wallet." He dips his chin. "She had a picture in her hand of Pol and me. We had taken it in one of those photo booths in Santa Monica when we went surfing about a year before he died."

He's quiet for a minute before he clears his throat. "I lost it. I told her to get out. I grabbed the picture. She held tight to it, and it ripped in two."

I gasp.

His eyes linger on mine as if to reassure me that it's all right. "I still have it taped together in my wallet."

"Good," I whisper.

"That picture represented something." He shakes his head. "I don't know how to explain it, but it was a day to end all days. It was one of the best days of my life."

Tears well in the corners of my eyes. I feel his loss. My heart breaks because I know how devastated I would be if Drake died.

He reaches up to swipe a fingertip over my cheek to catch a tear. "I know you understand."

I nod. "I think I do."

He slides his hand to one of mine. Cradling it, he continues, "I hit a brick wall emotionally that day. I couldn't take it anymore. I left Manhattan with Pol that afternoon, and I never looked back."

My breath stalls as I take that in. Maybe I heard him wrong.

Pushing a piece of hair behind my ear, he looks into my eyes. "Pol was cremated. I took him home to California. My grandfather and I spread his ashes in the ocean. He loved to surf, so it's what he would have wanted."

***

A dark cloud has settled over Manhattan again.

I stare out the window as rain beats against the glass. People on the sidewalk below are searching for cover. They want solace from the rainstorm.

It's what Case wants too. He wants a break from the storm that has been raging inside of him for years.

I understand why California is home to him now.

His family is there. His grandfather and in a very important sense, his brother is too.

"You're sure I can't get you anything, Emma?"

I turn to watch him walk back into the living room. He put on sweatpants and grabbed a glass of water.

After he told me about Pol's ashes, he kissed my cheek and told me he needed a minute.

I didn't question him, even though all I wanted was to hold him forever.

I can't erase his pain, but I can help him carry it.

Burdens are heavy if they rest solely on your shoulders.

"I'm good, thank you." I make my way closer to where he's standing next to the dining room table.

He lifts the glass and downs half the water in one swallow. "How are you doing? This was a lot for you to take in."

I close the distance between us until I'm standing next to him. "I'm good. I'm glad you shared that with me."

"You are?" he asks before he finishes the water. "Why?"

Watching him place the glass on the table, I take a minute to sort my thoughts. "It helps me understand you. I knew you were in pain."

"It's that obvious?" His gaze darts to me.

"It's in your eyes," I say softly. "There's a sad story there."

With a nod, he reaches to run his finger over my chin. "Beautiful, compassionate, and insightful Emma Owens. I didn't stand a chance, did I?"

"A chance?" I search his face for clarity. "What do you mean?"

Is he falling for me too? Is his heart in free fall the way mine is?

He glances at the table again. With a step forward, he taps his finger on the edge of the picture of Drake and Jane. "I haven't seen this. Drake sent it to you?"

Frustrated that our conversation has shifted in an entirely different direction, I sigh. "He did. I had that printed. I'm going to frame it for a wedding gift."

Reaching down, he carefully picks up the print. He tilts it slightly to the right and then the left. "Is this the only picture you have of them?"

Stepping closer, I nod. "Yes. Why?"

With a slight shake of his head, he looks at me. "She looks familiar."

"Jane looks familiar?" I lean in so I can gaze at the picture too. "You know her?"

He moves the picture again. This time he brings it closer to his face. "It's hard to tell."

Anxiety pricks its way up my spine. I don't know anything about Jane other than she's now my sister-in-law. "I can ask Drake for another picture of them at the wedding."

I offer that to appease not only Case's curiosity but mine too.

"We'll meet her soon enough." He drops the picture. "I've never met a woman named Jane, so I think it's safe to say I don't know her."

It's not safe to say anything. A month ago, I would have said it's safe to say my brother would live in New York forever and stay single for years.

"Enough about Drake." Case tilts my chin up. "I need to go to work, Emma."

I glance at the picture one last time before I focus on him. "I'll frame the wedding photo and find something else to do."

"I'll have the contract to you by the end of the day."

Startled, I search his face for a clue about where exactly I'll be working. "By the end of the day, today?"

He nods. "I want you to have dinner with me so we can discuss it."

This sounds too business-like to be an invitation to move to San Francisco with him.

My heart drops inside my chest. "Okay. You'll let me know where and when?"

He presses his lips to my cheek. "I'll text you as soon as I have the contract in hand."

Why does this feel like the first step in a very painful goodbye?

"I'll be waiting to hear from you," I say softly.

With another soft kiss to my cheek, he turns and heads down the hallway to his bedroom. When the door shuts behind him, I look toward the windows.

As raindrops hit the glass, tears flow down my cheeks.

I knew this would hurt, but I had no idea how badly.

Chapter 59

Emma

I march up Park Avenue on my way to nowhere.

After I left Case's apartment, I sent a group text to Bella and Delaney to see what they're up to.

I know both of them have to work today, but I'm hoping at least one of them can spare me an hour at lunch.

I don't know that I'll confess anything to them about what I'm feeling concerning Case and me, but I need a friendly face and a chance to escape from the sadness I feel.

My time with Case is going to be over soon.

Drake and Jane will come back to New York, and then the three of us will fly to Seattle to finally tell my parents about the secret wedding.

I'll share my news too.

I'm going to work at Cabbott. I'll be moving to a new city.

This is the next chapter in my life. I should be over the moon, but I'm feeling nothing but loss.

I maneuver around a couple standing in the middle of the sidewalk. Their embrace is beautiful and tender in a way that speaks of deep love.

I slow as I move past them, taking in the expression on the man's face as he stares at the woman.

It's pure joy.

"Emma? Is that you?"

Startled to hear my name, I stop in place and spin in a circle.

I don't recognize the voice until I hear it again. "I'm over here."

I glance to the left to find Ruth with her hand in the air. She's exiting the same building she disappeared into the other day.

"Ruth." I approach her with a smile on my face. "I didn't expect to see you again."

She steals a look at the couple. They're now walking down the sidewalk hand-in-hand. "Did you see that? The way he looked at her reminds me of Tommy. He always had that same look on his face right before he kissed me."

I want memories like that too.

I have some with Case, but I want more. I want a lifetime's worth.

"They seem very happy," I reply. "How are you?"

"Late," she confesses on a laugh. "I'm headed to the airport."

I glance down at the suitcase by her side.

Laughing, she jerks a thumb over her shoulder. "The doorman is bringing most of my luggage. I'm planning on staying in Ireland for a month."

"Ireland?" My gaze flicks over her face.

"You're the inspiration for this trip." She slides her hand over my shoulder. "When you mentioned your brother getting married in Ireland, it reminded me of a promise I made to Tommy."

"What promise is that?"

"I promised him I'd make our dreams come true." She glances down at the double heart ring on her finger. "We planned to see the world, but that didn't happen, so it's time for me to make those dreams a reality."

Speechless, I stare at her.

"You helped me see that it's never too late to do what makes you happy." Her arms reach around to pull me into a quick hug. "I wouldn't be taking this trip if it wasn't for you."

I take comfort in knowing that I helped her chase after a dream.

"I hope you'll do the same." She reaches for my hand. "If a life with that young man is your dream, make it happen, Emma."

She can't know how much I want my dream to come true. I want a life with Case. "What if it's not his dream?"

"Ask him." She smiles at the doorman as he passes us by with the luggage cart. "My car is here so I do need to run, but promise me you'll tell him how you feel."

I can't promise that.

I don't want to burden Case with my feelings. He has enough to wade through.

"I promise I'll think about it," I say to appease her. "I hope this trip is everything you want it to be."

"With my Tommy in my heart, it'll be the trip of a lifetime." She rests a hand against her cheek. "I'll go to a pub and toast to my love."

She spins around and starts toward the waiting SUV. Just as she's about to slide into the back seat, she turns one last time to face me. "Tell him how you feel, Emma. I wish I would have done it when I was as young as you."

I wave a hand in response as she gets in the car, and it drives away, disappearing around the corner.

***

"My cousin Chloe Scott is the woman for this job." Bella's gaze darts up from her purse. "I'm sure I have one of her business cards in here."

"She's a lawyer?" I ask. "Does she handle contracts?"

"Yes, and yes." Bella punctuates her answer with two nods of her chin.

When I mentioned to Bella that I had been offered a job at Cabbott, she squealed. That turned into a groan when I told her that I might not be working in New York.

Marti rushed over to see what the fuss was, but Bella played it off as nothing.

Her grandma didn't buy any of it, but she's now in the kitchen of Calvetti's preparing us each a plate of cheese ravioli with meat sauce.

"Marti will want to push another of my cousins on you if she thinks there's a chance you're about to become a New Yorker." Bella chews on the end of a breadstick. "I'd tell her you're not single, but you haven't said a word about where things stand with you and Case."

I pick up a breadstick from the basket in the middle of the table too. "He lives in San Francisco, and I don't think he's offering me a job there."

"But you don't know for sure, right?" She tugs her phone closer to her. "I have Chloe's number. I'll call and give her a heads-up that you'll be reaching out to her."

I'm grateful that Bella is helping me find a lawyer. I didn't know where to start. Elias sent me a list of names, but I haven't looked it over yet.

"For selfish reasons I'm hoping the job is in Manhattan." Bella sighs. "But, I want it to be in California, Emma. I want you to have a chance with Case."

"Lunch is served." Marti approaches from the left. "Two plates of spinach lasagna for two beautiful girls."

"Marti." Bella looks up at her grandma as she places the dishes of steaming hot pasta in front of us. "I thought you were bringing ravioli."

"Surprise, my Bella." She laughs. "This is delicious. You'll thank me later."

I laugh as I dive a fork into the cheesy goodness. "I'll thank you now, Marti."

"You're welcome." She leans down to press a kiss to my forehead. "You enjoy every last bite."

When she walks away, Bella circles the fork in her hand in front of my face. "You have a pink lipstick imprint front and center on your forehead."

"Good." I laugh, reaching for my phone to snap a selfie. "It's a perfect reminder of how incredible your grandma is."

"Take the picture and then eat." Bella points at my pasta. "After lunch, we're going to connect you with Chloe, so you have the best of the best on your side when you negotiate with Case."

I don't want to negotiate with him. I want us to be on the same page.

Working with Case in California is what I want more than anything, but I don't want a lawyer to help me get that. I want the offer to come straight from Case's heart.

Chapter 60

Case

As I sit at Drake's desk, I read Emma's contract over for the third time.

"Is it correct, Case?" Maureen Townsend, the lead counsel for Cabbott Mobile, taps her pen against her palm. "You've been staring at it for thirty minutes."

That's because I'm taking a leap of faith.

I feel like I'm about to attempt a jump over the Grand Canyon without a running start and no safety net.

I read the paragraph about the location of the position again.

It's the address for Cabbott Mobile in San Francisco.

Emma's office will be next to mine.

I want her next to me in bed when I wake up every morning.

"The salary is generous," Maureen says.

She wants to fill the silence. It's the same thing she did after Pol died. She talked and talked about nothing when I asked her to come to my office a week after he died.

I needed her to work her magic to cancel my purchase of the apartment on Madison Avenue. Before she could do that, Drake worked his magic, and I agreed to move in.

I'm thankful for that now.

It brought Emma into my life. There's no way in hell Drake would have tried to pass the two-bedroom walkup on the Lower East Side off as his own.

"It's fine," I finally say. "I need to order pizza and pick up some cupcakes."

Her thin lips perk up in a grin. "Cupcakes? Don't you detest sweet things?"

I laugh. "I've changed, Maureen."

She takes a step forward. "You should thank whoever is responsible for that."

Pushing back from my desk, I stand so I can give her a hug.

"What was that for?" She smiles.

"For helping me get through the darkness seven years ago." I point at the contract on my desk. "And for helping make my dreams come true."

She pats my cheek. "I'd do it all again in a heartbeat. I know it hasn't been easy, Case."

"Loss never is."

She contemplates my words. "Grief runs on its own schedule. I get the sense that you're edging toward brighter days."

Before I can say anything in response, her hand is in the air. "I'm not saying that you'll ever stop grieving, but you're turning a corner. I can see it, and nothing could make me happier."

"I am turning a corner," I affirm with a nod. "I have someone special to thank for that."

"I think I know who." She presses a finger to her lips. "I'm bound by client and lawyer privilege. No one will get those details out of me, not even Drake."

I raise a brow in response. "He'll know soon enough."

He will. I plan on telling my best friend that his sister owns my heart.

"Are you as surprised as I am that he's marrying Jane?" She lets a laugh spill out of her. "I thought they hated each other."

My brows perch together. "I have no fucking idea who Jane is."

The laughter slows as her eyes skim my face. "You know Jane."

"I don't." I shrug. "I've never met a Jane."

Something shifts in her expression. "She was an intern at Cabbott, Case. It was years ago."

"Seven years ago?" I question.

Her gaze drops. "I guess it was around that time, yes."

"Shit." I drag a hand through my hair. "Why don't I remember her?"

"You had very little to do with her." She rests a hand on my shoulder. "She was assigned to Drake. They couldn't get along. She finally left after a couple of months."

I try to drag up a memory of Jane, but I come up blank. Grief might be to blame for that, but it's no excuse.

"She stopped in last fall to see Drake to apologize for giving him a hard time." A smile tugs on the corners of her lips. "It wasn't love at first sight, but there was something there. You know what they say about there being a fine line between love and hate."

"Does he seem happy?"

"Happier than I've ever seen him." She drops her hand in front of her. "Almost as happy as you are."

I'll be happier if things go my way tonight.

"Have a copy of the contract sent to my apartment." I adjust my suit jacket. "Seal the envelope. I don't want the doorman getting his eyes on it."

"Done." She nods. "Anything else?"

"Take the rest of the day off." I surprise both of us with that statement.

"That I can do." She sets off out of my office with a spring in her step.

I look down at my phone. I type in the name of the bakery Emma loves into the search bar.

Sweet Bluebells is on the Upper West Side.

I'll head there, grab two red velvet cupcakes, and then make my way to the apartment.

I plan on having a large pizza delivered along with a bottle of red wine from the restaurant I took Emma to.

It's not the best food, but it holds meaning for us now.

We shared our first meal there, and she taught me that it was all right for me to laugh again.

I felt happiness for the first time in years as I sat at that table and ate pizza with her.

Tonight, I want to sit in my apartment and plan my future with her.

I send Emma a simple text message.

Case: *How do you feel about staying in tonight? I want to talk to you at the apartment.*

Her reply is instant.

Emma: *I like that idea. I'll be there waiting for you.*

***

I look up to see the sun breaking through the clouds as I swing open the door to Sweet Bluebells. A woman exiting the bakery brushes past me with a large white box in her hands. "You're a lifesaver. Thank you for holding the door."

"It's my pleasure," I say with a smile.

I take a step inside, and I'm instantly assaulted with the smell of cake. I can see why Emma hangs out here.

I approach the counter. An older woman with brown hair gifts me with a bright grin. "Welcome to Sweet Bluebells. How are you?"

"I'm great," I say for the first time in a very long time. "How are you?"

"Good. Good," the woman repeats the word twice. "Tell me what you'd like."

I survey the cupcakes in the display case.

I came in thinking I knew what I wanted, but I suddenly wonder if Emma wants to try something new.

"I think that the woman I love would want one of each," I say, realizing that I just put a voice to what I'm feeling.

"Why don't I pack up a dozen assorted for her?" She perks a brow. "Does she have a favorite that I should include?"

I bend to get a better look into the display case. With a tap of my finger on the glass, I smile. "Put two red velvets in for her. I know she can't resist them."

The woman nods before she reaches for a white rectangular box.

"Rush? Is that you?"

I freeze in place. Only a handful of people have ever called me that.

I turn toward the soft voice as she says it again, "Rush?"

I look at the blonde woman standing next to me. Her hands are shaking. Tears are streaming down her face tracking her mascara with them.

I reach for the counter to steady my balance because I can't place her. I have no fucking idea who she is, but I can tell she knows me.

I caused her pain. I see it. I fucking feel it with every sob that comes out of her. Whatever I did to this woman, I need to make it right. That has to happen now.

Chapter 61

Case

I had a taste of happiness and *fuck*, was it sweet.

It didn't last because that's not my ticket in life.

My brother died on my watch. The pain that caused reached far beyond what I felt or what my grandfather endured.

The night that I found Apollo dead in his bed, I stood on the street outside of our apartment building. I was numb to everything going on around me.

I have hazy recollections of police cars blocking the street to oncoming traffic. I remember a neighbor trying to assure me that time would help. She said time always helps.

She was a liar.

Off in the distance, I could hear the sound of a young woman screaming. Her pain mirrored what I was feeling.

She was calling for Pol. Over and over again, she wailed his name as her friends held her upright.

When I stumbled over to her after she yelled at me, she beat on my chest with her fists.

She tore through me because I'd let my brother down.

The memory of her face got lost in my grief, but I saw it again today at Sweet Bluebells.

Her big blue eyes, and her long blonde hair.

Delaney is her name.

I didn't bring that up from memory. She had to remind me of that today as she told me that she'd never forgiven me for not keeping a closer eye on my brother. She wanted to know if I had called him that day. I told her I hadn't because that was the truth.

She'd called him six fucking times because she knew something was wrong.

When he didn't answer, she went to the building and begged someone to let her in. No one listened to her that day.

Deep down inside, she knew.

I didn't have a goddamn clue.

I worked until noon. Then I hit up a bar and then a hotel with a woman I met at the bar because I couldn't take her back to my apartment out of fear that my brother would find her.

During the six weeks he lived with me, I found him with four different girls. Not one of them had blue eyes and blonde hair.

Delaney loved Pol, but Pol loved everyone.

He was young, and he wanted to experience life for the first time. He was finally out from under the watch of our grandfather, so he made friends with the girls who turned his head.

Seeing the pain that still consumes Delaney was enough for me. It was too damn much. She reminded me that my brother never got the chance to be happy. She told me that it killed her to hear me say that I was buying cupcakes for the woman I love because my brother will never love anyone again.

How the fuck do I deserve more than him?

I reach into the pocket of my pants and pull out the key to my apartment.

I walked out of here this morning in love and on top of the world.

Tonight, I'll break my own heart into a million pieces.

***

I walk in to find Emma standing at the dining room table. She's wearing a short blue sundress that's bouncing around her thighs.

I drop my gaze because I can't look at her if I'll never touch her again.

"Hey," I offer when she doesn't say anything to me.

"Hi."

I expected more because I want more. I want something to hold with me forever because I'm going to walk out of here tonight without my heart.

"The contract came." Her tone is stiff. "I'll be working in New York."

I hate the sound of it. I could barely get the words out when I called Maureen and told her to get back to the office to make the switch.

She suggested I sit on the decision for a day or two. I insisted she make the change and get the contract to Emma as quickly as possible.

I finally look up to see her tear-stained face.

Fuck. Just fuck.

She wanted to move to San Francisco. She wanted me.

"I'll go to Seattle with Drake and Jane once they come back, and then I'll find a place to live here." She twists her hands together in front of her. "Bella can help me with that. She'll know of a good neighborhood where I can find something reasonable. I can have my furniture shipped to Manhattan, I think. I've never done that before, but it can't be that complicated."

She's rambling because she's falling apart inside.

I want to take her in my arms. I want to tell her I love her.

Apollo will never get the chance to love a woman the way I love Emma.

"You're welcome to stay here for as long as you need. I'm leaving for California tonight."

Her hand grabs for the back of a chair. "You're what?"

I'm running away.

I keep those words in and fall back on a believable excuse. "I need to take care of things there."

Her head drops. "I thought you were going to stay until Drake came back."

"I can't," I lie. I fucking lie to the most beautiful and kindest woman I've ever met.

"I guess this is goodbye?" She turns to face me. "I know it's what we agreed to."

I take a step toward her. "I'll never forget you, Emma."

"You will." She half-laughs as her eyes fill with tears again. "It's okay."

I stalk toward her, stopping just short of taking her in my arms. "Listen to me. I will never forget you, Freckles."

That breaks her. Her hands dart up to cover her face. "I'll never forget you, Rush."

"Emma." I reach out a hand, but stop it mid-air.

"Let's leave it at that." She swipes a hand over her cheek to chase away a tear. "I'm not good with big goodbyes."

I can't ask for anything, so I nod in agreement. "I'll pack up my stuff and head out."

"I'm going to my room to look this over." She picks up the contract. "I'll have my attorney get in touch with yours when I'm ready to sign it."

As she breezes past me, a tear spills from my eye. I take a breath as I hold it together until I hear the guestroom door shut with a click.

Chapter 62

Emma

"Emma?" Bella places a cup of coffee in front of me. "I got you a large."

I look up into her blue-gray eyes. "Thank you."

She takes a seat in a chair next to me. We agreed to meet at Palla on Fifth. Bella arrived first. She was drinking an herbal tea when I walked in.

She put it on the counter and ran to me. Gathering me in her arms, she gave me the hug that I've desperately needed for the past seven days.

It's been that long since Case left Manhattan.

Our only communication has been through our lawyers. Chloe negotiated a settlement deal with Cabbott Mobile that compensated me well for my share of the future royalties for Letter Leap.

That comes with a substantial advance.

Chloe wanted that in my hand so I'd be able to find a comfortable place to live in Manhattan.

I haven't received the check yet. It's due to arrive in the next few days. I haven't signed the employment contract with Cabbott yet either. It's not that the terms aren't fair or generous. They are, but I freeze up every time I imagine working for Case's company.

"Have you talked to your brother?"

I push my palms along my jean-covered thighs. "I did. Their flight lands in a few hours."

"Are you excited to see them?" Bella always finds brightness where darkness has settled.

She texted me the morning after Case left to see how our evening went. When I told her that he had left to go back to California, she insisted that I meet her at her apartment in Brooklyn.

I had dinner with her and her fiancé. Barrett Adler loves Bella completely. He looked at her the same way Case looked at me before he left New York.

Or my wishful heart wants to believe that he looked at me that way.

"I am," I admit.

I need something to anchor me to this place. I have Bella, but family is what I crave. Drake and I have some issues to resolve, but I need him right now. I can't wait to feel his arms around me.

She takes a sip of her tea before adjusting the collar of the red dress she's wearing. "I saw Delaney and Mickey yesterday."

The change of subject is welcome. My mind has been so focused on Case for the past week that I haven't let anything else steal my attention away. I've replayed our last day together over and over again.

I assumed we had crossed an emotional barrier when he confided in me about his brother, but I was wrong.

Case stuck to the plan of leaving New York without me.

He even did it sooner than I expected.

"How are they?"

"Mickey is great." Her smile brightens. "He's struggling a little with some of his summer school work."

My ears perk. "What kind of school work?"

"I'm not sure." She shrugs. "But, I know that Delaney would thank you in free cupcakes if you could lend a hand."

"I'd love to."

"Good." She leans back in her chair. "Delaney didn't seem like herself."

"Why?" I ask, even though I think I know the reason.

I've interacted with many parents because of my work. I've seen the struggles they face. I know there's an extra layer added to that for single parents.

"She was vague about it."

"Vague?" I finally take a sip of the coffee, and it's as good as I remember.

When Case left for California, Lester stopped dropping by the apartment with a morning coffee for me.

I've restricted myself to a coffee from the café next to Durie's. It's bland, but not overpriced.

"All she would say is that it had to do with Mickey's dad. It was literally that one sentence and then she changed the subject." She looks to the counter. When the woman working the cash register notices her, she raises a hand in greeting.

Bella smiles and waves back.

"Do you think she heard from him?"

Bella's head slowly turns until our eyes meet. "He died before he knew Delaney was pregnant."

***

"She was eighteen when Mickey was born." Bella shakes her head. "I'm twenty-four and some days I don't think I'm ready to have a baby."

"The only thing I worried about when I was eighteen was which dress to wear to prom." I tap my fingernail on the table. "Delaney was thinking about giving birth and raising a child all by herself."

"Her family helped." Bella curls her hand around the cup in front of her. "Her aunt owns Sweet Bluebells. She's the one who gave Delaney the job."

"Did Mickey's dad's family help at all?"

Bella shrugs. "She never talks about any of them. I've only ever gotten bits and pieces about that time in her life. Once, I asked how they met, and she burst into tears, so I don't press."

It must have been desperately hard to lose him and then to have his child alone.

"She told me he was her first love."

Bella's lips curl into a smile. "She told me that too."

I glance at my watch. "I have time to stop at Sweet Bluebells before Drake's flight arrives. Is she working today?"

Bella pushes back from the table. "I don't know, but let's go find out."

"You have time to go with me?" I shoulder my purse before I stand.

"I always have time for a cupcake." She skims her hand over the front of her dress. "This little lady loves those strawberry cream ones the best."

My brows perk. "It's a girl?"

She waves her hand in front of her. "I don't know yet, but I feel it. I think we're having a sweet little girl."

"She'll be beautiful, Bella."

"Or he will be." She chuckles. "Barrett is convinced it's a boy, so who knows."

I laugh along with her. "Either way, that baby is going to be well-loved."

"That's what matters the most, isn't it?"

I stop and look in her eyes. "I think it is. I think every child needs to feel loved every single day of their lives."

Chapter 63

Case

"You're a fool!" my grandfather yells as he approaches. His bare feet are moving at a snail's pace through the sand.

"Good to see you too, old man." I adjust my surfboard under my arm. "Did you catch my form out there?"

Holding the straw hat on his head in place, he nods toward the ocean. "You're getting there, Rush. Give it time."

I huff out a laugh. "You've been saying that for years."

"I didn't say how much time you had to give it." He gestures toward my house. "What say we head up and grab a beer?"

I tug on the waistband of my board shorts. "It's not even noon."

I'm still running on New York time even though I've been home a week now. I thought I'd find solace on the beach and under the California sun, but all I've found is emptiness.

"Is that a problem?" He takes two steps in the sand. "The first one to the fridge buys the beers."

I follow behind him. "I already paid for them."

With a glance over his shoulder, he winks. "That's how it should be."

"You're going to explain that fool comment at some point."

Trudging up toward the side door, he gives me a look. "What's there to explain? You ran away from your future."

Cadby Easton has been more than a grandfather to me. He's been my lifeline. I confided in him when I returned from Manhattan because I was carrying a burden that I couldn't bear.

I wept as I told him about Delaney, and before I could catch my breath, I confessed that I was in love.

He's been telling me to go back to New York every day since.

Once he's inside the door, he tosses the straw hat toward a chair. He misses just as he does every damn time.

With a skim of his hand over his smooth head, he goes straight to my kitchen.

I stop to lean my surfboard against the house's siding before I follow him through the open door.

I take the beer he's offering even though I'm not in the mood for a drink.

I'm not in the mood for anything, but Emma.

"I booked you a flight to New York," he announces with a wink.

"Cancel it." I march across the white tile floor to land my ass on one of the stools next to the island in the kitchen.

"I'm going with you."

That draws my gaze up to his. "You're what?"

"You have unfinished business there," he points out with a tip of his beer bottle toward me. "I have things I need to say to that girl."

I don't need him to say her name.

Delaney has been on his mind for days. She's been on mine too, but Emma's been the one stealing my thoughts.

I miss her.

I fucking miss her so much that I ache inside.

I shake my head. "We're not going."

"You listen to me, Rush." He leans his elbow on the marble-topped island. His green eyes focus on mine. "You will never find a woman you love as much as Emma."

I fucking know that. I don't need a reminder.

"Do you think Apollo would have wanted this for you?" His arm does a full sweep in the air. "If your baby brother were here, he would kick your ass all the way to Manhattan. He'd tell you to be happy. He'd want you to drop to your knees and beg Emma to forgive you."

"He'll never get the chance to love," I point out. "Do you know how that makes me feel inside?"

"Guilty." He raises a hand to punctuate the word. "You feel guilty because he died, and you didn't."

I drop my head. "Why did he have to die?"

"Why did I get to live?" His voice quivers. "Do you think I didn't take on some of that guilt too?"

I look up at him with tears clouding my vision. "You weren't there."

"I should have been." His hand slams the top of the island. "I should have been there to hold him when he took his last breath. Your mother looked to me to take care of you both, and I failed."

I'm on my feet and in front of him in an instant. "Fuck no, you didn't. You took care of us. Your daughter ran for the hills, and you took on her two boys. Don't ever doubt what that meant to Apollo and me."

He takes me into his arms in a shaky embrace. "I want to tell that girl that I'm sorry that she lost Pol."

I step back and cup his cheek in my hand. "She believes Pol loved her."

"He did." He nods. "In his own way, he loved her. She doesn't need to know about the others."

Silence is a weapon in itself, but sometimes it's a gift.

Delaney needs to heal, and we have to help in any way we can.

"Does Emma know you love her?" He taps my bare chest.

Shaking my head, I hold back a rush of emotion. "You should have seen her face. I swear I could see her heart breaking in two in front of me."

"You're going to fix that."

I stare at him. Wisdom has always shone from my grandfather's eyes. It's there now.

"What if it's too late?" I ask on a whisper.

"Then you get your ass in gear and show her that you're the man for her." He pats my cheek. "Go pack. We're leaving in two hours."

"Two hours." I huff out a laugh. "You were sure you'd get me to say yes to this trip."

"I'm sure you love Emma," he says matter-of-factly. "If you want her back, you get on the plane. It's as simple as that."

Chapter 64

Emma

"That's my newest creation." Delaney slides a plate with two cupcakes into the middle of the table. "The cupcake is lavender, and it's a honey cream frosting."

Bella eyes the plate. "Unless you get your hand on one of those now, Emma, I'm eating them both."

I tilt my head back in laughter. "I want one."

"There's more." Delaney motions to one of the display cases. "It's our flavor of the day."

Bella takes a hearty bite. Her head nods as she chews. "I need to take two to go. Barrett is going to love this."

Delaney looks to me, so I pick up mine and take a bite. My eyes almost roll back in my head because it's that good.

"My brother and his wife are coming back tonight." I point at the cupcake. "I'll take two as well for them."

"I'll pack them up." Delaney turns to walk away.

"Wait." Bella reaches out her hand. "Emma wants to help Mickey with his schoolwork."

That drops Delaney onto the empty chair at our table. "It's his reading comprehension. He gets stuck on certain letters."

"I'd love to help." I take another bite of the cupcake. "Maybe we can meet up tomorrow morning? I'm going back to Seattle the day after tomorrow to sort out some stuff there."

"But you're coming back, right?" Bella's eyebrow edges up. "You're taking the job at Cabbott."

It's a statement not a question, but I don't want to mislead her. "I'm still thinking about it."

Delaney's gaze volleys from Bella to me. "Am I missing something?"

Bella takes the lead before I can say anything. "Emma was offered a job in Manhattan."

"You should take it."

I turn to Delaney. "It's a big step."

"It doesn't have to be forever." She glances at the windows of the bakery. "I love living here, but I don't think Mickey and I will stay here forever."

"Where would you go if you left here?" Bella asks before she takes the final bite of her cupcake.

"California." Delaney's gaze drops to her lap. "I want Mickey to see the ocean one day. His dad loved the ocean."

Case loves the ocean.

The bite of pain I feel whenever I think of him gnaws at my heart.

With a deep breath, she smiles. "Apollo loved to surf. Mickey wants to learn how someday."

Time stops for a brief second as I try and absorb those words.

Apollo?

Her Apollo can't be Case's Apollo.

311

With a lump in my throat, I turn toward her. "What was Apollo's last name?"

Her eyes search mine. "It's the same as Mickey's middle name. Easton."

I can't stop the flood of emotion that hits me. I drop my head into my hands and let out a sob.

"Emma?" Delaney reaches to grab my shoulder. "What's wrong? What happened?"

I try and focus my gaze on her, but it's blurring with tears. "I love his brother. I love Apollo's brother."

That sets Delaney up on her feet so fast that the chair she was sitting in tumbles to the ground.

Bella stands too. Her expression is clouded with confusion as she tries to make sense of what I just said.

Delaney shakes her head. "Rush? You're not talking about Rush, are you?"

"Who is Rush?" Bella glances at me. "What's going on, Emma?"

I push to stand, even though my knees are shaking. I look to Delaney, but all I see is sadness so profound that it takes my breath away.

"He was here," she shouts at me with her finger pointing at the display case. "He came in here last week to get cupcakes for the woman he loves."

It's me. He loves me.

I don't say it, but Delaney connects the dots as she looks at me. Her hand darts to her mouth. "Oh my God, Emma. That's you. Rush loves you."

"Loved," I whisper. "He left me. He went back to California."

Her shoulders sag forward as her hand searches for the edge of the table. "It's my fault. It's all my fault. I told him he didn't have a right to be happy because he let his brother die."

Bella falls back on her chair. She doesn't say anything.

I don't either because there's nothing left to say.

***

Ten minutes later, I'm sipping a glass of water as I watch Bella give Delaney a hug.

They went to the bathroom in the back of the bakery together for a few minutes. I could have followed them, but I had to sort through my thoughts.

Case is Mickey's uncle.

Why didn't he say anything when I mentioned Mickey's name?

"I'm going to go home." Bella scoops up her purse from the table. "I'll text you later."

She leans down to wrap her arms around my neck from behind. With a whisper in my ear, she puts a voice to what I've been thinking. "Case left New York because of this. It was guilt, Emma."

I pat both her hands with mine. "It's a lot to take in, Bella."

She presses a kiss to my cheek. "He needs you. Delaney does too."

I glance over to where Delaney is standing. "I'll talk to her."

"I'll leave you two." She straightens. "Call me if you need anything."

I nod as she walks away, leaving Delaney and me alone.

Chapter 65

Emma

I wait while Delaney speaks to the brown-haired woman behind the counter. We've never been formally introduced, but I suspect that she's Delaney's aunt.

Delaney drops her apron on the counter before she grabs a gray crossbody bag and slings it over her shoulder.

By the time she's in front of me, her tears are gone. "Can we walk, Emma? Let's walk and talk."

Nodding, I get back to my feet.

I scoop my phone into my palm before I drop it in my purse. "You lead the way."

She holds the door open for me, so I step through and onto the bustling sidewalk.

"There's a playground by Mickey's school." She glances up the sidewalk. "It's a couple of blocks over. They have benches there."

I fall in step beside her. She's taller than me, and her legs are long, but I keep up as she hurriedly maneuvers through the late afternoon foot traffic.

"Mickey is with his sitter today." She smiles as we wait for a light to change before we cross the street. "He absolutely adores her."

"That's good," I offer because I can't think of anything to say.

I'm still reeling from earlier.

I can't believe that I didn't know that Mickey was related to Case.

As we near the playground, she tugs her phone out of her bag. With a quick scan of the screen, she sighs. "Sometimes, Mick will send me a message using the sitter's phone, but they must be busy today."

This small talk is lovely, but it's a precursor to what's to come.

I have dozens of questions.

I know Delaney must have a few too.

"Is Rush your brother's best friend?"

I didn't think she'd lead with that question, but I'm happy to answer it. "He is. Drake has been friends with him for years."

"Drake," she repeats my brother's name. "He's the man in the wedding picture that you showed me?"

"That's him."

She stops just as we're about to enter the playground. When she turns to face me, her eyes lock on mine. "I met your brother, Emma."

I don't know why that takes me aback. Nothing should surprise me at this point. I ask a simple question in response to her declaration. "When?"

"Right after Apollo died." Her words are sharp and to the point. "Drake looked a lot different. He had a beard, and his hair was past his shoulders."

I look toward a vacant wooden bench. I need to sit. I feel like the universe is closing in on me.

Delaney picks up on my cue and makes her way to the bench. She takes a seat before I do.

"Apollo took me home a couple of times. It was an apartment on the Lower East Side." Her eyes wander to three children playing on the swings. Their mother stands nearby, watching over them.

"I never met Rush." Her voice lowers. "I saw him talking to Apollo on the sidewalk one afternoon. When I asked who the guy in the suit was, he said it was his brother Rush."

"Case," I say.

"What?" Her brow furrows.

"Rush is his nickname." I straighten my shoulders, trying to find some inner strength to draw from. "His name is Case Abbott."

"Case Abbott," she repeats his name slowly. "It's no wonder I couldn't find him. I've been looking for Rush Easton for years."

***

I raise my hand to wave at a little girl playing in the sand. I've never seen her before, but children only see the good in the world. They want to bring a smile to a face that has a frown, so they'll grin or wave if they think it will make a difference.

It made a difference for me.

I was on the verge of tears when Delaney told me that she'd been searching for Case but didn't know his real name.

"Why did Apollo call him Rush?"

I glance at her. "Case's middle name is Rushton."

Her chin bobs up and down. "Did they have different fathers?"

317

The pained expression on her face as she asks the question tells me that she's embarrassed. She doesn't know a lot about Apollo's family. It's as much as I know about them.

"Yes." I keep the answer simple.

She takes a breath. "I went to the apartment a few days after Apollo died, and Rush wasn't around. Your brother was there clearing out the place. There were a couple of other people helping him. I told Drake to tell Rush to call me. My number was in Apollo's phone, but I never heard from him."

"You never heard from Case?" I question back.

"No." Her head shakes. "He didn't call me."

I turn to face her directly. "Ever?"

Her eyes lock on mine. "When Rush or Case … when he walked into Sweet Bluebells last week, it was the first time I'd seen him since the day Apollo died."

Frustration taints her tone. I don't blame her. I can't blame her.

A little boy with blond curls runs past us. He resembles Mickey, but he's shorter, and his eyes are a deep brown.

Delaney must spot the resemblance too because the next words out of her mouth are about her son. "Rush doesn't know about Mickey. When I saw him at Sweet Bluebells, I didn't tell him that Apollo has a son."

Chapter 66

Emma

I try Case's number again, but the call goes immediately to voicemail for the third time. I curse under my breath before I leave yet another message that's exactly the same as the two I just left him.

"Please call me Case as soon as you can. It's an emergency."

"He's still not answering?" Delaney is pacing the patch of grass in front of the bench. "Why do you think he's not answering?"

A few hours ago, I would have thought it's because he doesn't love me, but I know that he does.

He said it when he was in Sweet Bluebells a week ago.

After he spoke to Delaney, guilt settled over him, and it drove him back to California.

"I messed this up so badly." Delaney rakes a hand through her hair. "I should have told him about Mickey. I shouldn't have yelled at him. I screamed at him, Emma."

I stand to take her shaking hands in mine. "You have been holding this in for years. You were angry with him."

"I was so pissed that he never bothered to call me back." She looks up at the blue sky. "I didn't want him to be happy if I couldn't be."

I want to tell her that she can be happy. She can open her heart back up to love.

She can move to California and teach her son how to surf because she has a built-in family there. She has Case and his grandfather.

I glance down at my phone's screen. "I wish he'd call me back."

Her finger flies in the air. "Text him. Maybe try and text him."

It's worth a shot, so I type out a quick message to him.

Emma: *Case, please get in touch with me immediately. It's very important!*

I stare at the screen waiting for the delivered message notification, but it doesn't come.

"What's wrong?" Delaney cranes her neck to get a better look.

"It's not delivering the message."

"His phone is off." Delaney shakes her head. "Maybe he's in a meeting? Can you call someone else there to get a message to Rush…I mean Case?"

I smile. "I call him Rush too."

Her gaze drops to her phone when it buzzes. "Mickey's sitter is taking him for a walk. I'm going to tell them to swing by here to say *hi* to us. Is that okay with you?"

My hand darts to my mouth. "He's Case's nephew."

Tears fill Delaney's eyes. "I need Case to know that. I let my anger keep me from telling him, but I want Mickey to know his uncle and his future aunt."

I laugh through my tears. "You're not talking about me."

"I am." She swipes a hand over her cheek. "Case loves you, Emma. I saw it when he was talking about you at Sweet Bluebells. He's crazy about you."

"I feel that way too," I confess. "I love him, Delaney."

"We're going to make a family out of the mess I made." She looks to the left to see her son approaching with an older woman with red hair. "There's Mickey. Let's wait to tell him about his uncle until you talk to Case."

"Agreed," I nod curtly. "I'll say hi to Mickey, and then I'll try the Cabbott offices in San Francisco."

I'll find Case. I need to. He has a nephew that he has to meet.

***

Two hours later, I fall into my brother's arms when he walks into Case's apartment.

"Emma." He runs a hand over my back the way he always has. It offers comfort. I need it more than I thought I did. "Damn, I've missed you."

I step back when I see the woman standing in the foyer. She came in behind Drake, but I was too focused on my brother to notice.

"You must be Jane." I move around Drake to greet her.

"I've only heard the best about you, Emma." Her hands fist in front of her.

I won't push for anything more than I think someone will offer, so I give her a smile instead of a hug. "It's good to meet you, Jane."

Drake surveys the interior of the apartment. "I hear that there's an offer on this place."

I try not to look shocked, even though I am.

"You've got sixty days to clear out, sis." Drake laughs.

I don't share the same amusement because we have things to talk about that are far important than where I'm going to live.

"Where's Case?"

Drake's gaze volleys from my face to Jane's. "Remember Case, babe?"

"Yes." She nods. "I can't say they're all good memories."

"Jane interned at Cabbott eons ago." Drake keeps his eyes trained on his bride. "Case wasn't exactly Mr. Friendly to her."

This seems like a good time to start my confessions, so I jump right in. "I love him."

A nervous laugh falls out of my brother. "You love who? Beauregard? Did you realize that you two belong together?"

"Case," I correct him curtly. "I love Case."

Anger flares over his expression. "What the fuck is going on? What did he do to you?"

I won't go there. Instead, I toss the question back to him. "What did you do to him?"

"What are you talking about?" He brushes past me to drop his laptop bag on the couch. "Tell me what's going on between you two."

Ignoring Jane, I turn my back on her so I can face my brother. "A girl named Delaney asked you to give Case a message seven years ago. You never gave him the message, did you?"

He chuckles. "I don't know what you're doing right now, Em, but if you're trying to cover up the fact that you slept with my best friend, you're doing a shitty job."

"I did sleep with him," I confirm with a nod. "And we fell in love."

He drops onto the couch. "I'm going to kill him."

"Why?" I bark out a laugh. "He's happy. I'm happy. You don't get to dictate who either of us loves."

He's quiet. His face falls into his hands.

"What were you saying about someone named Delaney?" Jane steps into my view. "I remember meeting a girl named Delaney when I helped Drake move some boxes out of an apartment years ago. I hated every second of it. It wasn't what I thought I was getting into when I took the intern position."

Drake's head pops up. "It's fine, babe. This is between my sister and me."

I shake my head. "What do you remember about her, Jane?"

"She was so sad." Her hand drifts to her cheek. "She was tall and very thin. I remember she looked like she'd been crying for days. She asked Drake to give Case a message for her. I remember that."

I twist back around to face my brother. "Did you give him the message?"

Drake darts to his feet. "Why the fuck would I do that? His brother had just died, Em. He couldn't walk straight. Do you know how many times that girl called Apollo's phone? I turned it off because it never stopped ringing."

"You what?" I seethe. "You had Apollo's phone after he died?"

"I had to handle all of it, including his cremation," he stresses the last word. "I erased everything from the phone and tossed it."

Anger barrels through me. "You had no right to do that. You should have given the phone to Case."

"Case couldn't think straight. He didn't need any of that teenage drama in his life," he spits the words out. "Why the hell are we even talking about this?"

This is Drake's fault. It's my brother's fault that Case has never met his nephew. He's the reason Delaney and Case haven't connected to help each other through their shared grief.

"I have to find Case."

"Call Cabbott in San Francisco." Drake tosses that out with a flick of his wrist.

"I tried that."

"Gavin Fuller would know." Jane clears her throat. "I overheard Drake telling his assistant that Case is close to his cousin. Elias loves to gossip with your brother."

"Give me Gavin's number." I point at my brother. "If you have it, give it to me now."

His finger slides over the screen of his phone. He steps closer to me until he drops it in my hand. "I have no idea what the fuck is going on here, Emma, but I need you to know I love you and I love Case. For what it's worth, I'm sorry if I screwed up."

I take the phone from him and press the call icon next to Gavin's number. I can only hope that he'll help me get in touch with the man I love.

Chapter 67

Case

Five long hours on a flight next to my grandfather is not how I thought today would play out.

I wanted to sit quietly with my thoughts. He wanted to replay his championship run when he pitched for Fordham University decades ago.

By the time I was old enough to throw a ball, I knew how the season had ended.

His team placed second, and he met my grandmother after the final game when she came onto the field.

She was a California girl with blue eyes and golden blonde hair. They married a year after they met, and the rest is a history filled with more laughter than pain. The smiled every day until she passed away.

"You need to slow down, Rush," he calls from behind me as we make our way through the terminal at LaGuardia. "My old legs take twice as long to get anywhere these days."

"Hop on my back." I pat my shoulder. "I'll give you a ride."

He tosses me the same look he always has when I overstep.

Pushing my luck, I keep at it. "There's a car waiting for us if you can make your way out of here before the crack of dawn."

"You should be wearing a suit." He lands a hand on my forearm. "Men always travel in suits."

He's wearing the same tan-colored three-piece number that he's worn for every special occasion for the last decade. He had it on when we took Apollo's ashes out to the ocean to lay him to rest.

My brother didn't want a formal service. He told us that when he was fifteen. He made us both promise that if anything ever happened to him that we'd skip the pomp and circumstance and take him to his favorite place on earth. He was a kid of the ocean.

"A T-shirt and jeans is a lazy man's suit," he scoffs as he drags his feet behind me.

I glance at him. "It's a rich man's suit. Do you know how much I'm worth?"

"I read Forbes." He laughs.

I hold onto his hand as we step on an escalator to take us down to the ground level. I didn't bother calling Drake's driver. Gavin arranged for a car for us when I gave him a heads-up that we were headed to Manhattan.

I can't stay with Emma, so I followed my call with Gavin with one to Julian, Maya's husband.

He owns a chain of luxury hotels, so my grandpa and I are set with two suites.

Cadby balked about it. He wanted to share a room, but I need space. It's the reason he lives next door to me, and not with me.

As we reach the bottom of the escalator, my eyes land on a beautiful woman standing near the baggage carousels.

I stop mid-step and stare.

"Rush." My grandfather yanks on my hand. "Move it."

I let him drag me forward as I keep my gaze pinned on Emma.

How the fuck am I looking at her right now?

It's almost midnight. I'm dead tired. I'm emotionally spent, but I feel like the world just handed me a gift.

"That's her, isn't it?"

I glance at my grandfather for a split second.

He pats my cheek with his hand. "No words. That tells me that beautiful brunette in the killer blue dress is Emma."

I brush past him, drop my bag, and race to her. I don't fucking care that tears are streaming down my face. I run, full speed until she's in my arms.

I kiss her as I twirl her in a full circle.

Her hands land in my hair. A small moan escapes her when the kiss breaks.

"I love you," I whisper against her mouth. "I love you, Emma."

"Me too, Rush. I love you so much."

***

I finally turn the lock on the deadbolt of the hotel room door. After seeing Emma at the airport, I thought we'd skip the hotel and head back to my apartment.

It turns out Drake and Jane picked today to fly to Manhattan.

They can have the apartment to themselves tonight. I got my grandfather settled in his room after sending Emma to the suite we're in now.

"I have so much to say." Emma jumps to her feet from where she's been sitting on the corner of the bed.

I tug my T-shirt over my head. "Just let me look at you, Freckles."

Her gaze falls to my bare chest. "Let me look at you. I've missed this view."

I huff out a laugh. "I couldn't believe my eyes when I saw you at the airport."

She shakes her head slightly. "I had to come. I need to tell you something."

I take two steps toward her before I fall on both knees. Wrapping my arms around her, I beg for forgiveness. "I'm so sorry, Emma. I was an asshole to you. I should never have left, but something happened. I saw someone."

Her fingers sift through my hair. She gently tugs it so I'll look up and into her face. "You saw Delaney."

I stare at her. "What did you say?"

That brings her down to her knees too. "You saw Delaney at Sweet Bluebells."

Nodding, I can't find words.

"I need to show you something, Case." Her hands tug on my biceps. "Sit on the bed."

I do as I'm told. I'd do anything for her.

I help her up before I settle on the bed. Kicking my shoes off, I watch as she crosses the room to grab her purse.

Before I can say a word, she's dumped it on the bed.

Her hands grab for a large envelope. I recognize the logo on it immediately. It's from Printe.

"You're going to show me a picture?" I sigh. "Can this wait, Emma? I want to hold you. I need to make love to you."

"She bends to brush her lips over mine. "I want that too, but you need to see this."

The envelope's contents flutter to the bed when she turns it upside down. Prints spill out. She spreads them out with a jerk of her palm over them.

I reach out to grab a photo of her with what looks like a mark on her forehead left by a pink-lipstick kiss. "What's this?"

She glances at it. "Bella's grandma gave me a kiss."

I grab another picture, and then another. It's me. I'm on the bed. She took them the morning she sang to me.

"I'm putting those in my scrapbook." She plucks them out of my hand with a pinch of her fingertips.

"I want one for my scrapbook," I tease.

Her eyes hunt for something on the bed. "You don't have a scrapbook."

"I want the one of you with the lipstick mark on your head." I grab it again. "You're beautiful, Emma."

She picks up a print from the bed and hugs it to her chest. "Case. I need to…I want to… I know Delaney."

I nod. "That makes sense. You love that bakery. She works there."

Her teeth bite into her bottom lip. "I took a picture of her."

I don't need a picture to tell me what she looks like. I'll never forget her face again. Sorrow consumed it both times I've seen her. That's rooted in my memory forever.

"Can I show you?" she asks with so much tenderness in her voice that it bears down on my heart.

I feel it stall in my chest.

"You can show me anything," I answer.

"This is Delaney, but you know that," she says as she turns the picture to face me. "And this is her son, Mickey Easton Wilts."

Chapter 68

Emma

Case can't take his eyes off the picture.

He keeps running his fingertip tenderly over the face of little Mickey Wilts.

"He's the spitting image of Apollo." He pulls in a deep breath. "Right down to the blond curls on his head."

I watch as he reaches behind him to tug his wallet out of the back pocket of his jeans. He opens it and carefully removes a photograph. It's taped down the center, and as he hands it to me, he hesitates for a split second. "That's the last picture I have of the two of us."

I take it and cradle it in my palm. I know it's a treasure.

I gasp when I see the young man next to Case in the photo. There's no mistaking that Mickey is this man's son. They share the same hair color. The shape and color of their eyes are identical, and their smiles are carbon copies of one another.

"Mickey looks so much like him."

Case nods. "He looks just like my brother."

I settle next to him on the bed. I hold the picture in my hand next to the one in his hand.

"Look at that, Emma." Case's gaze volleys between the pictures. "I wish to fuck Apollo was here."

I bite back a rush of raw emotion. "He would have been proud. Mickey is so bright, Case. He's the sweetest little gentleman."

"He's a great kid, isn't he?" He smiles. "I can tell just by looking at him."

"You're going to love him."

"I already do." He swallows. "I can't wait to tell my grandpa that he has a great-grandson. Is Delaney all right with us meeting him? She'll let us see him, won't she?"

I took a second to text Delaney in the car on the way to the hotel. I told her that I was about to tell Case the good news, and she insisted that I bring both him and his grandfather to the bakery in the morning to meet Mickey.

"You're going to see him in the morning."

His eyes track a path over my face. "Hours from now?"

I glance at the watch on my wrist. "Just a few hours from now."

He darts to his feet. "What the hell am I going to say to him? Does he wonder why we haven't been around?"

"We'll talk about all of that." I carefully slide the picture of him and his brother back into his wallet. "You should get some sleep before you meet your nephew."

"You're staying with me."

I nod. "I'm not going anywhere."

Before I know what's happening, he's sliding his hands over the bed, searching through everything I dumped out of my bag.

"What are you doing?" I laugh. "Let me clean that up."

"Tell me you threw at least one condom in here before you came to the airport."

I swat his hands out of the way so I can take on the search myself. "I brought two because with you, one is never enough."

"You knew we'd end up in bed?"

"Hoped," I correct him. "I crossed my fingers and hoped."

"It worked." He unbuttons his jeans. "Get naked, Freckles. I've missed you."

***

Crawling up the bed, I take in the sight of Case on his back. It's almost too much. He's gorgeous. I settle between his legs, sliding my hand up his thighs. I stop just short of his erection.

"You love this, don't you?" He glances down with heavy-lidded eyes. "Driving me mad with desire turns you on."

I inch my fingertip over the plush head of his cock. "This right here turns me on. Is it bigger than the last time we were…?"

A deep laugh escapes him. "Get on it."

"Get on what?" I lean down to flick my tongue over the tip.

His hands fist the blanket. "Jesus, Emma. Please."

"Please do this?" I take him in my mouth, inch-by-glorious-inch.

"Goddammit," he bites out between clenched teeth. "I. Want. To. Fuck. You."

I nod as I take him even deeper.

"Please," he hisses out as his hands dive into my hair. "Wrap my dick up so I can feel you, Emma. I'll beg if need be."

I slide my mouth along him, slowly savoring the taste of him.

With an audible pop, I release him.

"That was fucking hot." He points at one of the condom packages next to him. "I need that on me now."

"That will be my pleasure." I reach for it, ripping it open with my teeth.

He watches every movement, spellbound.

As I sheath him, he takes in a heavy breath. "I'm going to lose it."

"You won't rush," I tease as I crawl up his body. "You always take your time."

His hands shake as he yanks me over him, positioning his cock at my opening.

With a single drive up, he's inside of me.

I moan because it's too good. It's so good. "Case."

Before I can find my rhythm, he flips us over. He starts on a thrust, and then another, each deeper than the last.

I wrap my legs around him, stare into his eyes, and let his powerful body take me to the edge as I watch his lips silently chant my name over and over again.

Chapter 69

Case

The day I found my brother in bed cold and alone, I lost it.

I crawled under the covers with him and held him against me. I thought in my fucked up mind that I could breathe life into him through my embrace.

I knew he was gone.

His body was stiff. His lips were blue.

His eyes were closed. He looked as peaceful as he would have been if he were lost in a dream about being out on the ocean with his favorite surfboard.

When I called 911, I told the woman who answered that he was gone, but she did her job. She got everyone who needed to be there to rush over.

I watched as firemen, an ambulance crew, and two police officers burst into that small apartment to try and save my brother's life.

One-by-one they left the room. Some were in tears because who wants to see a young life taken before its time?

Today, my grandfather and I are getting another chance.

Mickey's not Apollo, but he's a part of him.

He's the best part of the best man I've ever known.

It was my decision when to tell Cadby about his great-grandson. I didn't want to put the picture in his hand and make him wait, so I got Delaney's number from Emma.

I called her at daybreak, and we spoke for an hour.

We sorted through some of the pain and talked about what matters more than anything. Mickey.

The kid was named after Apollo's favorite baseball player. Mickey Mantle.

We're two steps away from walking into Sweet Bluebells and a future that looks a hell of a lot better than the past we're leaving outside the door.

I turn to my grandfather.

He's got the tan suit on that he always wears for special occasions. I had it pressed at the hotel this morning when I told him that we were meeting someone special.

He joked if it was Emma's grandmother because he's in the market for a sweetheart.

That brought a smile to Emma's face. My grandpa loved the sight of that.

He'll bring a lot more happiness to her life when she moves in with me back in California.

I haven't asked her about it yet, but I know she wants it as much as I do.

"Do they have red velvet cupcakes in there?"

Emma jumps in to answer that. "They do, Cadby. They have cream cheese frosting and small candies sprinkled on top."

"Be still my heart." He grabs for the center of his chest. "Did I tell you that you're prettier than the sun in the sky today?"

It's the yellow dress she's wearing. She ducked out of the hotel early to shower and change back at my apartment.

I'm wearing a pair of jeans, a blue button-down shirt, and a navy blue suit jacket. I want my nephew to see the best in me.

I don't have a road map to follow, so I'm taking a chance that when my grandpa sees Mickey that he'll put two-and-two together.

I tug on the handle to open the door. Emma steps in first with Cadby on her heel. I take the rear because I need an extra second to catch my breath.

"Emma." Delaney stretches her arms out in a greeting. "I'm so happy you came."

Emma steps into her embrace. I watch in awe as the woman I love hugs the woman that loved my brother.

Apollo may have only known Delaney for a brief time but they made a child together. She created a living, breathing human being with the boy I grew up taking care of.

"Delaney, this is Cadby Easton." Emma steps aside to let my grandpa have his moment.

"Dear?" His voice quivers as he approaches her. "I'm sorry. I'm so sorry we weren't there for you."

Her arms reach for him too. She cradles his head next to hers. "You're here now. That's what matters."

I search the bakery for any sign of blond curls, but I come up empty.

"Hey, Rush... I mean Case." Delaney shakes her head. "I'm sorry about last week."

I move to embrace both her and my grandfather together. "Last week is the past. It's time we all started living in the present, and you can call me whatever the hell you want."

She chuckles. "I'll call you Case."

When I step back, my grandfather does the same.

Delaney takes a breath. "There's something I need to tell you, Mr. Easton."

"Cadby," My grandpa smiles. "You'll call me Cadby."

"Or great-grandpa," I say quietly.

His head turns slowly. "What are you saying? Emma is knocked up?"

Emma bursts out laughing. "No. There is no way."

I shake my head as Delaney giggles. "I didn't think that one through."

"Think what through?" His eyes narrow as he stares at me. "What's going on, Rush?"

"Let's try this again," I say.

We both catch sight of a little boy with blonde hair as he rounds the counter and heads toward us.

"Rush." My grandfather reaches for me. "Do you see him?"

"That's Mickey," I whisper as I hold tightly to his hand. "That's our Pol's little boy."

Mickey marches right past his mom until he's standing in front of the two of us. "I'm Mickey Wilts, sirs. My mom told me you're here to meet me. She said you loved my daddy very much."

My grandfather brushes his hand on Mickey's shoulder. "He was my grandson."

"My daddy was your grandson?"

"Yes."

"Are you my Papa?" Mickey takes a step closer. "I always wanted a Papa."

"I'm your Papa." My grandfather takes Mickey into an embrace. "And this is your uncle Case."

The smile I get when the kid's eyes meet mine chases every ounce of pain I've felt away. "It's good to meet you, Mickey."

His gaze darts back to his mom. "Is this real? I get an uncle and a Papa in the same day?"

"It's real," she says through a sob. "This is your family."

Mickey reaches an arm out to pull me into a hug with my grandpa. "This is the best day of my whole life."

I look over at Emma. "It's the best day of mine too."

Epilogue

Three months later

Emma

"It's a girl," I announce to anyone within shouting distance. "Sandy is going to have a girl."

"That makes two little princesses on the way to add more beauty to this world." Cadby wanders into the kitchen of our beach house wearing his three-piece tan colored suit.

Sandy is as thrilled to learn that she's having a girl as Bella was.

I text out a quick reply to Sandy asking if she's still planning on meeting us in New York two weeks from now to celebrate Case's thirtieth birthday.

That includes the entire Abbott, Owens, Easton, and Wilts crew.

I moved in with Case after he crossed New York off my contract and wrote in San Francisco. I signed the contract immediately and started working at Cabbott Mobile a few weeks after.

Delaney and Mickey were eager to come to California. Case has been taking Mickey out into the ocean with a life jacket and a tight grip on his hand.

The first day we were all here together, we had a remembrance service for Apollo.

There weren't any tears. We played music and laughed, and Mickey tossed a baseball on the beach with his Papa.

Delaney enrolled Mickey in school for the fall semester, and it's going well. I tutor him a couple of times a week when I stop by the condo that Case rented for them. It's not on the beach, but it does have a view of the ocean.

Case held on to the Manhattan apartment. It's where we stay whenever we head east. He bought the apartment for Apollo, so he said that it only seemed fitting that his brother's son has a chance to stay there and experience Lester and the view. That will happen when Delaney takes her son back to see his family in Manhattan.

Case rejected the offer from Pam and Rod, but they didn't seem to mind. They purchased another unit in the building.

We shared an elevator ride with them when we were in Manhattan a few weeks ago for the Letter Leap launch party. Once we got off on the twelfth floor, Case joked about how I thought he had slept with them right after we met.

We laughed until we fell into bed together. The laughter stopped when he crawled between my legs.

"How's your brother?" Cadby asks with a wink. "I heard that he's got a couple of babies on the way himself."

Jane's pregnant with twins and Drake is terrified.

Case and I have worked things out with him. Our relationship may never be the same, but it's all out on the table now.

Drake has a life to live in London, and I have one next to the man I adore.

Speaking of him…

"Where's Rush?" I ask his grandfather.

"He's on the water." He points to the beachfront that sits right outside our door. "Why don't you go and find him?"

It's near dusk now.

I put in a full day at the office, before I came home to a perfect dinner of pizza, a bottle of red wine and a box of cupcakes baked by Delaney.

She found a job at a bakery only a mile from here. Cadby watches over Mickey after school. It gives them time together that they both treasure. A Sweet Bluebells location in San Francisco is in the works, but it'll take time to sort through everything to make that a reality.

I smooth my hands over the lapel of Cadby's suit jacket. "You're dressed to the nines tonight. Do you have a date?"

"You do." He motions to the door. "Go see my grandson."

"I'm on my way." I reach over to plant a kiss on his cheek. "I love you."

"I love you, sweet girl." He tousles my hair. "I'm going to steal one of those Bright Bagels to toast for breakfast and then I'm going home. You go find that boy of yours."

I laugh as I watch him dip his hand inside one of the bag of bagels that were delivered this morning. "That bag is for you."

"All for me?" He winks.

Nodding, I start toward the door. "Your grandson knows how much you love them."

"I know how much he loves you," he calls after me.

***

"Rush?"

I expected him to be out on the ocean on his surfboard, but he's gazing at the water. He's dressed in jeans and a white button-down shirt.

When he turns to face me, I smile.

"You shaved?"

He runs a hand over his smooth chin. "Do you like it?"

I race toward him, my bare feet kissing the sand with each step I take. "I love it. I love you."

"I love you, Emma. Do you know how much?"

I stretch my arms out to my sides. "This much?"

"No." He shakes his head before he drops to one knee. "This much."

I grip the skirt of the white sundress I'm wearing to keep my hands from shaking. "Oh my God."

A ring box sits in the palm of his hand. "Marry me, Emma. Let's make it official. We'll have kids. I want us to love each as much as we can forever."

I gasp when he pops open the box. The beautiful ring is set with an emerald in the center with small diamonds surrounding it. "This was my grandma's ring. Cadby gave it to me the day after we came home from New York."

"Really?"

"He said it belonged to you, and it was my job to get it on your finger."

I hold out my left hand. "It's beautiful."

"You're saying yes to marrying me?" He inches the gold band up my ring finger. "Tell me you'll marry me, Emma."

"I'm saying yes." I gaze down at the ring. "It's perfect."

He moves to stand. Taking me in his arms, he presses his lips to mine for a deep, lush kiss. "I'm the luckiest man ever."

"Did she say yes?"

We both laugh as we hear Cadby call out the question.

"She said yes," Case yells back.

"I knew she would. Goodnight," Cadby responds before we hear his whistling fading into the distance.

Case's voice lowers to an almost whisper. "You gave me my life back. I'll do whatever I can to bring you happiness every day."

"Let's start now, Rush." I grab his hand and point to our beautiful home on the beach. "I'll race you to the bedroom."

"I'll do you one better." He laughs before he scoops me up into his arms like a bride. "I want you to save your energy for when we get inside."

I kiss him softly. "You're my everything, Cason Abbott."

"You're my dream come true." He presses his lips to my neck. "I'll make every day better than the last."

I know he will. He already has.

THANK YOU

Thank you for purchasing my book. I can't even begin to put to words what it means to me. If you enjoyed it, please remember to write a review for it. Let me know your thoughts! I want to keep my readers happy.

For more information on new series and standalones, please visit my website, www.deborahbladon.com. There are book trailers and other goodies to check out.

If you want to chat with me personally, please LIKE my page on Facebook. I love connecting with all of my readers because without you, none of this would be possible.

www.facebook.com/authordeborahbladon

Thank you, for everything.

Preview of CATCH

I found something that belongs to Keats Morgan, the notorious bad boy sports agent. So I do the right thing.

I return it.

You'd think the man would be happy to have it back.

He's not.

Instead, he proceeds to fire his assistant right in front of me.

He looks to me to step in as a replacement, but I want nothing to do with the jerk.

Keats is gorgeous and charming as hell. It's his arrogant attitude that makes me turn around and almost walk out the door.

The problem? I desperately need a job. Any job.

And Keats is offering me an incredible one.

I agree to his terms before I realize there's a catch, and it's a big one.

Chapter 1

Maren

"Dudley's daddy can't keep it in his pants." I flick a wrist toward my laptop screen. "I have another five DMs from women this morning."

"You have even more responses to your post on the Manhattan Lost and Found Dog group?" My roommate, Arietta Voss, comes marching into the dining room to get a better look.

I glance up and take in her outfit for the day. For a twenty-two-year-old petite blonde with gray eyes, Arietta looks nothing like you would expect her to.

The frumpy navy blue skirt wrapped around her waist hits her legs mid-calf. It's not half as bad as the lime green blouse she's buttoned up to her neck.

"You must still be beating the men off with a stick, Arietta."

She lets out a laugh. "I am trying to be professional, Maren."

"You're never going to get that sexy beast of a boss of yours in bed if you keep dressing like that."

Her eyes widen behind her dark-colored, rectangular eyeglasses. "Mr. Calvetti is still in Italy, and besides, I would never sleep with someone I hate."

"You hate him as much as I hate my vibrator," I quip.

With a shake of her head, she crosses our apartment to pull a bottle of orange juice from the fridge.

Technically, it's my apartment. If we're getting down to actual specifics, it belongs to my father. He bought this three thousand foot dream on the twentieth floor of a high rise in Tribeca as a gift for me.

It's not a standard gift, though. There are terms, and I'm already in violation of one of them.

I lost my job yesterday.

I need to stay gainfully employed to keep this lavish roof over my head.

Keeping it over Arietta's head is important to me too. We met at a vintage jewelry store a year ago. Arietta mentioned that she was looking for a place to live, and even though she's six years younger than I am, I invited her to move in.

We're as close as sisters now.

After pouring herself a glass of juice, she bends down to stroke her hand over Dudley's head. "How are you today, sweetheart?"

Arietta has been calling him that since I found him wandering the street last night without a collar.

A whole host of responses to my posting on the Manhattan Lost and Found Dog group have clued me into his name.

They also directed me toward his irresponsible owner.

Keats Morgan.

Mr. Morgan is a twenty-nine-year-old sports agent. His client list is impressive, but that's not why he's so popular in Manhattan.

Every reply to my posting about the lost dog has come from a woman.

Twenty-three women have messaged me to say that they met Dudley when they spent the night with Keats.

I push my curly red hair back behind my ears. "I sent Keats a DM on Instagram, but I got nothing back. When I called his office just now, the woman who answered the phone put me on hold and then hung up on me."

"I'd get fired if I tried that trick." Arietta bites her bottom lip. "I'm sorry. That was insensitive. I can ask at work if there are any available positions."

Arietta works as an assistant at a wealth management firm. My background is in public relations. "You're an angel, Arietta, but I'm going to put out some feelers today."

I'll do that very quietly, so my dad doesn't get wind of my employment status.

"If you know the address to Mr. Morgan's office, I can drop the dog off on my way to work."

Keats Morgan is all kinds of gorgeous, and I haven't been on a date in two months. I could use a glimpse of something tall, green-eyed, and handsome today.

"I'll get dressed and head over to his office." I point at the cute dog sitting on the floor watching us. "Say your goodbyes to Dudley because he's about to be reunited with the man who can't keep him on a leash."

Coming soon!

ABOUT THE AUTHOR

Deborah Bladon has never read a romance hero she didn't like. Her love for romance novels began when she was old enough to board the bus, library card in hand to check out the newest Harlequin paperbacks. She's a Canadian by heart, and by passport, but you can often spot her in New York City sipping a latte and looking for inspiration for her next story. Manhattan is definitely her second home.

She cherishes her family and believes that each day is a gift for writing, for reading, and for loving.